THE TELEPHONE RANG

Sarah's throat tightened with panic. The telephone was still unconnected. It was not even plugged in.

It rang again.

Finally, she lifted the receiver and held it to her ear. She did not speak. A distant, windy, rushing sound met her ear. And then a voice.

"Sarah." It was a deep voice, without emotion, yet not mechanical. "I am so glad you have come back, Sarah."

"Who are you?"

"You know who I am. You have felt me inside you. You have come back for me, to give yourself up to me."

"I have not," Sarah said loudly. "You can't have me."

"I can."

FAMILIAR SPIRIT

LISA TUTTLE

BERKLEY BOOKS, NEW YORK

FAMILIAR SPIRIT

A Berkley Book / published by arrangement with
the author

PRINTING HISTORY
Berkley edition / February 1983

ISBN: 0-425-05854-9

DEDICATION

For Bill and Sally Wallace and the rest of my
ghost-hunting, spirit-raising, table-rapping friends,
and
for Harlan Ellison, a few years late, but still with
gratitude and affection. Forget the one about Texas
under water; it was a dumb idea.

Prologue

After a long while Valerie rose from her slumped, broken position like a puppet whose dangling strings have at last been gathered and pulled. She looked down at herself, running hands over arms, legs, breasts, stomach, and a triumphant smile stretched across her face. Without haste, she walked down the short hallway from the bedroom to the bathroom, and stared into the soap-spotted mirror above the sink.

The smile grew harder and brighter. But although the triumph in it doubled, shining out of the mirror, the odd golden gleam in Valerie's eyes, almost like a glimpse of flame, had no reflection.

"Yes," she said, testing her voice. "Yes, you'll do. You'll do for now. A temporary home." She leaned closer to the mirror, intent upon the reflection, studying her face. "I'll make some changes, of course. I'll take better care of you, Valerie, than you ever took of yourself." She laughed, a rich, satisfied chuckle, all the while watching the face in the mirror to see how she looked when she laughed.

Her hands had been resting lightly on the porcelain rim of the sink, unneeded and unnoticed as she concentrated on face and voice. Now, still unnoticed, they moved. The right arm lifted and reached in an old, familiar gesture, and the right hand took hold of the drinking glass that hung on the wall. That hand then brought the glass down, cracking it against the side of the sink with a deft flick of the wrist. Half the glass sheared away and fell to the floor, leaving behind a curved glass dagger in a heavy base.

Hardly more than a second had passed; the tinkling crunch of breaking glass had not yet registered on the mind of the woman who spoke to herself as to a stranger.

Left hand turned over, presenting the pale, veined throat of a wrist to the sacrificial knife. Right hand brought the glass blade jabbing down hard, then ripped inwards, towards the body, tearing the skin and letting a blood-river halfway to the elbow. Only then did Valerie look away from the mirror, down to see what her hands were doing.

"No!" she roared in someone else's voice, and flung the broken glass away. It smashed to fragments against the hard side of the bathtub and flung out tiny jewels of crimson against the flesh-colored floor.

She clutched her left arm with her right hand—they were hers again—and tried to push the edges of skin back together. Her lips drew back from her teeth and she hissed in frustration as she fumbled about in the tiny bathroom, unable to find tape, gauze or bandages of any kind.

Blood continued to run in rivulets down her arms, dyeing her clothes and spattering walls and floor. She lurched into the bedroom and began jerking open bureau drawers. She found only heavy jeans, sweaters, nothing that would do, nothing she could tear easily.

"Tell me!" she roared in that other voice. "Find something! I won't let you die, damn you, not yet!"

The next drawer yielded T-shirts. Valerie snatched up one and tore it down the seams. She managed to make a rough bandage of it, wrapping it tightly around the wounded arm. It was blood-soaked already, as she knotted it, but that didn't matter; she had stopped the worst of the bleeding and Valerie would not die just yet.

But the moment she relaxed her vigilance the right hand was busy again, plucking at the knotted fabric, trying to let loose the blood.

Furious, Valerie slapped the left hand, then the right. Then her eyes rolled up in her head, her eyelids fluttered, and she collapsed on the floor.

Painfully, Valerie opened her eyes and saw the dirty floorboards. Her head hurt and she ached all over. Why was she on the floor? When she tried to move she felt as if someone had stabbed her. She gasped with pain, sitting up, then saw that her arm was wrapped in a blood-soaked cloth.

Quite suddenly the pain and dizziness turned to nausea. Valerie managed to move just enough to be sick on the floor rather than into her own lap, but afterwards she had not the strength to move away and remained staring dully into a pool of vomit, retching dryly every now and then.

Later—how much later? She only knew that the room had filled with shadows—Valerie managed to stand, the puppet miraculously moving without strings, and stumble into the bathroom to rinse her mouth. A sharp new pain made her look down, and she saw that she had gashed her bare foot on a piece of broken glass. Broken glass, and blood, littered the floor. She stared dully, unable to make any sense of it.

Then a voice told her what to do. It was a relief to be spared thought, a relief to obey. Under direction, Valerie washed her wounded arm with antiseptic and bandaged it cleanly, cutting up two of her favorite T-shirts to make the dressing. She also tended her foot, picked the glass off the bathroom floor, and cleaned up her vomit. Finally the voice told her to go to bed and sleep and, a grateful automaton, she did.

Hours later she woke screaming.

She fumbled for the light and, blessedly, it came on. Valerie looked around, the sound of her own breathing harsh in her ears. She saw her clothes in untidy heaps on the floor; she saw the dirty, cream-colored walls; she saw the magic circle she had painted on the floor. From the corner of her eye she saw the awkward lump of bandage binding her aching arm, and began to tremble again. It hadn't been a nightmare, after all. What had happened to her was real.

It was true. Using spells learned from books, she had summoned up a spirit. Only it hadn't gone as the books had promised. Something had gone wrong, despite all her care, despite the magic circle. The spirit—Valerie remembered suffocating, remembered drowning—the spirit had not obeyed her commands—the spirit had—

"Possessed you," said a voice so close it might have come from a man in bed beside her.

A little wildly Valerie turned, but she was somehow unsurprised to find herself still apparently alone.

"You tried to kill me!" she cried to the air.

"No. You tried to kill yourself."

Valerie remembered the curving glass dagger she had made, and how she had plunged it into her own flesh and dragged it down, watching the blood bloom, feeling no pain.

"I was trying to kill *you*," she said.

"You cannot kill me," said the voice. "And how ungrateful of you to try. Did you not summon me?"

"But you were supposed to obey me, not—"

"Do you imagine you are worthy of being obeyed?" said the voice with awful contempt. "But there is much I can do for you, many benefits to be gained by accepting my presence in your body."

"No," said Valerie dully. It was unthinkable. She had only the dimmest memories of what it had been like, but she could remember the sense of suffocation, the utter darkness, the helplessness, and that was enough, more than enough. "I'd rather die," she said.

"Little fool. Yes, you made that clear. Don't worry—I need not stay where I am unwanted; not when I have so many options."

"Why do you want a body at all?" Valerie asked. "Why not just be—free, like you are now?"

The sound of laughter in the empty air made her skin crawl.

"I need a body for the same reason you do, little Valerie. In order to live. When I left you, I found myself another temporary shelter."

There was a soft thump against the window screen. Valerie sat up and looked across the room. Twin yellow flames glowed out of the darkness beyond the window. She caught her breath, and then heard a cat's soft, inquisitive cry, and relaxed.

"Let me in," said the voice in the air.

Valerie looked at the ceiling. "You're . . . the cat?"

"We are one."

"Poor little thing."

"Not at all. It is a mutually agreeable relationship. A fine, healthy cat which I shall keep fine and healthy for as long as I use its body."

"It would be better off dead," Valerie muttered.

"Let me in," the voice said, more sharply. "I shall not ask again."

Valerie got off the bed and crossed the room, not knowing if her body obeyed her own will or another's. She decided it really didn't matter. She unlatched the screen and the cat leaped in lightly past her, and onto the bed. There it sat and purred and regarded her with gleaming eyes.

"A witch and her cat," said the voice. "How appropriate."

She tried to shut out the voice and think. There had to be some way out, some way of escape if only she could figure it out. She was smart—everyone had always said so. Too smart for her own good. But this should not have happened. She had been so very careful to follow the rules as they were set out in the books she had studied, to say the right words, never to step outside the boundaries of the consecrated circle . . . All that care should have kept her safe, according to the books she had read.

"Maybe you read the wrong books," said the voice, as silken-smooth as a cat's fur.

Her stomach clenched, and she felt sick. It was reading her mind. That awful sense of invasion. Would she never be whole and alone again?

"Remember why you summoned me?" said the voice. "You can still have what you want. I can give you what you want."

"I just want you to go away and leave me alone."

"Oh, no, you don't want that. I remember what you want, ah, yes. Money, and all the good things it can buy. A nice car, nice clothes, and lots of drugs. That's what you want. That's what was important to you, so important that you summoned me."

Was that true? Valerie supposed that it was, but she could

not remember what it had felt like, to want things, to think that money was important or even necessary. There was only one thing she wanted now, and it was a negative kind of want, the desire to be left alone.

"You can have that too, in time. I'll leave you in peace —let you kill yourself, if you like. But first you must do something for me."

It *was* reading her mind. It could read her thoughts, and there was no way out. Revulsion made her convulse, and she bent over, coughing and heaving, but there was nothing left to bring up. She staggered back to the bed and sat down, wiping tears from her eyes and shivering uncontrollably. Why couldn't she just die? She had to escape.

The cat was purring, making the bed vibrate softly. Think, think, she had to think, but she didn't dare, not when the demon could read every thought.

Valerie stretched out her hand. "Here, kitty," she said absently, and the cat came and fitted its sleek head into the palm of her hand just like any ordinary cat. She stroked it, feeling the delicate, fragile skull beneath the fur. She looked across the room at the magic circle, where she should have been safe.

Numbly, she rose and began to dress herself, trying to keep her mind a blank, trying to think of nothing. A plan, the barest image of a means of escape, had presented itself to her, but to think of it was to risk warning her enemy, and to be lost forever.

She slung her heavy leather purse over one shoulder and wondered if he would let her leave the house. She felt rather than heard the cat bound lightly off the bed behind her, and, not thinking but simply doing, Valerie turned and bent as if to pet it. But instead of stroking, her fingers closed on the back of the cat's neck and gathered up a wad of loose skin. The cat let out a hiss of surprise as it was hauled firmly into the air, and claws shot out and legs flailed wildly.

Valerie held the cat away from her, not looking at it, clutching the scruff so tightly that the animal would have had to shed its skin to escape, and she carried it into the dubious protection of the magic circle. It was the only hope she had.

The cat was howling now and struggling furiously, body

whipping around with a strength and agility that seemed supernatural. Valerie was aware of the burning pain as claws once, twice connected with the flesh of her arms, but that did not matter. Her wounded arm was bleeding freely again, too, but nothing mattered so long as she could still move. The pain, because she could feel it, was almost a relief after her earlier numbness.

She rummaged one-handed and with difficulty inside her purse, fingers trembling until they closed upon the solid handle of the knife. Terror and triumph rose in her like a sickness, and she withdrew the knife and looked down at the cat. At that moment it went limp in her grasp. But although it was not struggling physically, fury blazed out of the golden eyes, and Valerie felt his power like a hand which grabbed her heart and squeezed. But she would not give in; she would die first. This time, *her* will would be done.

It was shockingly easy. Valerie had expected a queasy struggle of hacking and sawing, but the knife bit easily into the cat's furred throat. Fur and skin parted before the sharp blade as if they were water. Warm blood ran over her hands and spattered everywhere. The cat jerked once and was still.

Valerie stared at the dead animal, hardly daring to believe. The golden eyes were blank and empty now. The demon was gone. A silvery-grey line moved through the fur, and Valerie realized she was watching the fleas abandon the body. Already they knew their host was dead.

Her voice trembling, Valerie recited the prayers and exhortations she had memorized for this moment, the formulae designed to lay evil spirits. Now he would show himself, she thought, and her body was tensed anticipating an attack. Now he would make a mockery of her attempt to escape.

But nothing happened. The cat stayed dead in her hand and the room was empty and still, filling gradually with the thin, grey light of early morning.

Valerie dropped the knife back into her purse, careless of the blood. Her arms and hands were sticky with it—some of it the cat's, some her own—and her wounded arm throbbed with pain, but she did not care. She had won. The demon had needed a body to live, and she had killed that body. She was free.

As she stepped out of the circle, he struck.

She felt his return as a body-blow which knocked the breath out of her. She fell forward onto the floor, unable to cry out, or even to try to break her fall. The limp, warm body of the cat was crushed beneath her. Her body vibrated with agony. For a moment she knew she was dying, and she was grateful.

Then the pain subsided, and she knew he would not let her go so easily. Tears started to her eyes, and she gasped for air. The hated, familiar voice was in her ear.

"When will you learn it is useless to fight me? When will you learn that you are mine, to use as I will?"

She could not speak. If she could have made a sound it would have been an anguished scream. She would never have another chance. She had failed.

"You will obey me. You will bring me what I require."

With one blow, he had knocked all the hope, all the will to fight out of her. Now she wished only to avoid his presence and to wait for oblivion. Of course she would obey him. She had no choice, no resistance left. Perhaps, if she served him well, he would let her die before too much longer.

The crushing weight lifted, and Valerie sat up, feeling like a mechanical doll. She didn't mind the feeling. She would do what she was told. Nothing mattered.

"You learn slowly, but you learn," said the voice. "You will bring someone to the house, someone young and physically healthy, but someone pliant. A woman, I think. An attractive young woman who is alone and unhappy. Someone who will be more receptive to me than you. After you have found her and brought her to me, I will let you go. Oh, and I will give you what you need for your new life. I will give you what you wanted. You will have the money, and the car, and the drugs . . . and there will be someone to look after you, to make sure you don't take too many of those drugs, until I have done with you."

She felt a pain as if a knife were cutting through her brain, but that didn't matter. The dead cat, her painful, bleeding arm, her failure, the numbness inside—none of it mattered. Valerie nodded her acceptance.

"And to help you in your search—"

An invisible hand seemed to push her head to one side. Valerie looked towards the doorway that led into the kitchen and saw something out of place on the mottled pink and brown linoleum. Something about the size of her fist, something like a clod of earth—but it moved.

It hopped forward, over the threshold into the bedroom, and Valerie saw that it was a toad, grey-brown and hideous, glistening slightly as if it were wet.

At one time Valerie would have recoiled, scrambled to her feet and backed away, face twisted in disgust. Snakes, lizards, toads—whether harmless or not they were all the same, all horrible. The idea of touching one would make her skin crawl. But she didn't move now as the toad came towards her. She felt as if she were very far away, watching this happen to someone utterly unimportant. And so she did not flinch when the toad came closer still and hopped onto her leg. She bent down to take a closer look. They stared at each other, eye to eye. The toad's eyes were yellow. She knew them well.

Chapter One

The house was out of the way, on the west side of town, and much too large for one person, but Sarah wanted it.

It stood well back from the road on a huge corner lot, a weathered green frame house surrounded by trees. Even now, in mid-October, with the leaves beginning to fall, the house was nearly invisible from the street. Only the grey cement steps, a glimpse of the black tarpaper roof, and the bright red splotch of a crookedly leaning mailbox revealed the house to a passing observer.

The first sight of it made Sarah's heart beat more quickly. She could live there, yes, she could. She responded to this solitary, unkempt house almost with recognition, a feeling more positive than any she'd had in a week of examining sterile apartments and dreary, refurbished duplexes. To have a whole house, all to herself . . . She followed the gleaming black Ferrari off the street and up a short concrete ramp, the merest fragment of a driveway, and parked behind the house.

Valerie, a thin, young redhead dressed in blue jeans, high leather boots and a dirty yellow sweater, climbed out of the Ferrari. Sarah switched off her engine, but didn't get out of her car. Something about the other woman, something she couldn't quite define, made her nervous. She wondered if she had made a mistake in coming here.

The house had been built on a slope, so that while the back door was only three wooden steps from the ground, an imposing flight of cement stairs rose more than ten feet to the sagging wooden porch and the front door. The lawn—if anything so wild and weedy could be called a lawn—rolled out before the house, down to the street below and vanished on either side into a little wilderness of bushes, trees and creeper vines. Behind the house there was only a small patch of bare ground, lightly sprinkled with gravel broken up by the occasional hardy plant, which provided space for cars to be parked. The back boundary was defined by a high wire fence.

Curious, nerves forgotten, Sarah got out of her car and nodded towards the fence. "What's that?"

"Camp Mabry, National Guard," the other woman said in a dull, uninflected voice. She gestured along the fence, westward. "All that down there is wilderness, government owned, no trespassing. You'll hear them sometimes, on weekends, playing war games. Other than that, it's very quiet here. Very quiet."

Sarah nodded. The isolation pleased her. There were no near neighbors, the nearest house being on the other side of the four lanes of West 35th Street. Living here, she would never be bothered by the sound of neighbors quarrelling, never have to worry about keeping quiet herself, or suffer another's fondness for high-volume disco. Here, she would have plenty of room, plenty of peace, plenty of the solitude she had always lacked.

I'll be alone, she thought, and in that moment the idea of solitude became not a longed-for treat but a punishment. Why was she doing this, sentencing herself to loneliness? Did she have to look for the biggest, most isolated house she could find?

"Let's go inside; you have to go inside." Valerie had made another of her disturbing transfers from dullness into a feverish liveliness. Her voice had become shrill, and she was jigging slightly with impatience, or some other ill-repressed emotion. Sarah moved away, back towards her car, reluctant to follow this woman anywhere, fearful of some trap.

She looked back up at the house and felt it again, that basic attraction, the desire to live here. It was an old, worn house, old-fashioned and somehow rural in appearance. It reminded her of an old farmhouse near Bellville, where she had spent many happy weekends as a child. Well, why not? Why shouldn't she be happy here?

She looked at Valerie's tense, miserable face and wondered if it was pills, or an incipient nervous breakdown. Whatever it was, surely she didn't have to be afraid of this poor thing, younger and frailer than she was herself. Sarah prided herself on her ability to cope.

"Yes," she said. "Let's go inside. I'd like to see it."

Valerie moved away and bounded up the three wooden steps to the back door.

Sarah blinked, startled, and followed more slowly. Valerie's movements had reminded her of some animal running free, and that type of grace was completely at odds with the neuroses she sensed in Valerie's behavior.

The back door led onto an enclosed porch; there, a heavy wooden door with a window opened into the kitchen. Sarah realized that Valerie had opened both doors without using a key.

"Don't you lock your house?"

Valerie shook her head. "Why bother? If anyone wants to get in, he'll get in. Locks don't work, they just fool you into thinking you're safe. There's a lock here, see, but it's just a button—anyone could pick it. And there's a skeleton key for the front door, if you want to use it."

The bitter fatalism in Valerie's voice made Sarah faintly queasy. She would have bolt locks put in, she decided, and a screen or burglar bars to protect the pane of glass in the center of the inner door.

"Did you get broken into, while you lived here?" she asked Valerie.

She was startled by Valerie's laugh, which had more of pain than amusement in it. "Oh, God," she said. "Don't ask me that, don't ask me! Just go—no, stay. Stay." She shut her eyes and stood, swaying slightly, in the middle of the floor. Her messy hair was an aureole of pinkish light around her thin, bleached face. "I don't care," she muttered, scarcely moving her lips.

Sarah wished herself elsewhere. Seeking an escape from the embarrassment of Valerie, she looked around the kitchen. It was huge and dirty, with horrible splotchy linoleum which Sarah suspected had never looked clean. There was an old gas range, the burners encrusted with black accretions of grease, and a mammoth white refrigerator.

"The stove and the fridge both work O.K.," Valerie said in a normal voice. She had opened her eyes. "The freezer door's off, so you have to keep defrosting it, that's all. Come on, I'll show you the rest."

Not wanting a repeat performance, Sarah resolved she would say nothing more to Valerie beyond what was strictly necessary. She followed her into the next room, which was long and bare with scratched, cream-colored walls, a wooden floor, and four or five windows which let in the leaf-dappled sunlight.

"This is the living room and dining room," Valerie said flatly. She walked on, her boots clopping loudly and echoing in the empty house. Sarah lingered, looking around and envisioning her posters and prints on the walls, her own odds and ends of furniture filling the bareness and making it a home. One wall jutted out oddly, an unexpected corner breaking the room's smooth geometry.

"There are two bedrooms," Valerie said from another doorway, and Sarah joined her, glancing curiously at the front door as she passed. It had been painted a hideous burnt orange.

"You could use this as an office or a guest room," Valerie said. "Or as your own bedroom, I guess. I never did anything with it, myself."

Sarah looked around the large, square room, imagining bookshelves hiding the dirty walls, all her books neatly arrayed with her desk at the cosy center. There were four windows, the two on the east side latticed with leaves, the two in the south wall offering a view, only slightly obscured by branches, of the long, weedy front lawn and the street below. Sarah stood looking out, long enough to see several cars glide past. The street was far enough from the house that the sounds from it could be heard, but were not a noisy distraction. Living here, she thought, she would get to know this view well. She imagined herself waiting here, watching for some visitor to arrive, and when she turned away she felt a sense of dislocation at the sight of the bare room, shocked by the disappearance of the furniture she had felt behind her.

Valerie, too, had vanished, along with the imagined books and desk. Sarah walked through the far door into a short hallway. She glanced into the tiny bathroom. The floor was tiled in pink and brown, the fixtures and the wooden walls were white. It was no cleaner than the rest of the house—there were some spots and smears which looked unpleasantly like bloodstains. Sarah wrinkled her nose and moved on hastily. She'd give it a good cleaning. It was never a good idea to speculate on how or why something had gotten dirty.

The back bedroom was also empty, with the same cream-colored walls as the rest of the house, but the floor was covered by a stretch of hideous carpet. Whatever color it might have been originally had been altered by age and dirt to an extremely unpleasant pinkish-brown, and it gave off a faint but definite odor of mildew and ancient dust. The windows on the east wall must be invisible from the street, covered as they were by a tangle of bushes. Walking closer, Sarah saw that an accumulation of primal cobwebs filled the narrow space between the screens and the glass. The back windows were cleaner, and the view from them was unobstructed. Sarah looked out at the two parked cars, the fence, and the wilderness beyond before turning back into the room. First thing, she decided, she would get rid of that horrible carpet. Then she'd paint the walls pale blue, and the ceiling white. She wouldn't need much furniture, just a bed and a chest of drawers. Then she smiled, amused at the way her imagination had taken over and was already settling her into this place.

Some small sound distracted her from her pleasant musings and she turned to see Valerie standing in the doorway staring at her with a ferocious intensity that made the hairs on the back of her neck prickle.

Valerie blinked, and seemed to return from some other place. "All right, you're O.K.," she said. "When do you want to move in?"

"I'm not sure," Sarah said, lying cooly. "I'm not sure it's right for me. I'd like some time to think about it. Can I call you?"

"No, you can't." The edge of hysteria was back in Valerie's manner; in a moment, Sarah thought uneasily,

Valerie would go white and rigid, her eyes would close, and she would sway in the breeze of her own madness. "Tell me now, you have to. Do you want it or not? Will you live here?"

She had known from the moment she set eyes on the house that she wanted to live here, but something, perhaps just her visceral response to Valerie, made Sarah hesitate and even doubt her own feelings. Why did she want this house, why should she? She could list the drawbacks of it as easily as she could list the positive aspects—perhaps they were the same. The size, the isolation . . . Was she about to rush into something she would later regret? Was it just her angry pride which made her want this house, to show the world—and Brian in particular—how happy she was to live all alone?

"Why are you moving?" Sarah asked, staring hard at Valerie. "If it's such a good house, and the rent is so low, why are you moving now, six weeks into the semester?"

Valerie's mouth quirked into a tight, unhappy smile. "Why are *you*?"

Of course. She'd walked right into that one, despite her best intentions. Sarah crushed the paranoid suspicion that Valerie somehow knew the answer already and was laughing at her. She drew a deep breath, determined not to reveal her distress, and said calmly, "I broke up with the man I was living with."

It burned her throat like a lie. But it wasn't a lie, not wholly. She made it sound like a matter of choice, her choice, and only that part was untrue. But she wouldn't think about it now.

Valerie made a sound that might have been laughter. "All right. I don't care. I . . . didn't want to live here anymore. I'm living somewhere else now, somewhere much nicer. With someone who is very rich. He gives me lots of nice things." She sounded anything but happy about it, and Sarah felt a twinge of pity for this stranger and her problems.

"Now tell me," said Valerie. "If you won't live here, then I have to find anyone else. I . . . I don't want to waste any more time. You can see I've already moved out, and . . . the house shouldn't be empty."

It would be silly to say no to a perfect house just because the former tenant was a little crazy. And it would be cowardly to say no because she was afraid of the isolation and solitude—isolation and solitude were just what she wanted.

"I want the house," Sarah said firmly.

Valerie smiled, and the feral, self-satisfied nature of the smile gave Sarah goosebumps, made her for one wild moment want to retract her agreement and run like hell.

"I've given Mrs. Owens your name," Valerie said. "She's the owner. There's no lease, no deposit. She was grateful to me for finding someone to take my place. She's very old, and she doesn't like the bother of showing the house. She trusted me to find someone who wouldn't be any trouble, someone who would pay the rent on time. You won't be any trouble, will you?"

Now Sarah had a reason for her unease. How could Valerie have presumed to give Sarah's name to the owner before Sarah agreed, before she had even seen the house? She could still back out—

Valerie dug into a pocket of her tight jeans and withdrew a scrap of paper. "This is Mrs. Owens' address, where you'll send the rent. Don't go bothering her; she doesn't like to be bothered. That's one reason the rent's so low. You'll have to keep the lawn mowed and do any minor repairs yourself." When Sarah did not move to take it, Valerie pushed the scrap of paper closer and flapped it impatiently in Sarah's face. "Rent's due the twenty-second of each month. Eighty-five dollars. Remember that."

And when had Valerie had time to call Mrs. Owens?

Valerie cocked her head and smiled slowly, mockingly. "Of course . . . if you want to change your mind . . . if you think you'd be scared, living out here all by yourself . . ."

But Valerie was lying, of course. She was crazy. And what she said didn't matter. This was Sarah's house now, and she could just send Valerie away. Sarah plucked the piece of paper from Valerie's hand, accepting the house, committing herself. "I'll send Mrs. Owens the first month's rent next week."

"Good. Move in whenever you want, the sooner the better. He . . . Mrs. Owens doesn't want the house standing empty for long." Again Valerie dug into her jeans. "Here's the key to the back door since you were worried about it." She tossed a bit of light metal at Sarah, who managed to catch it in midair.

Halfway to the door, Valerie paused and looked back. The mad, sly smile was on her face again, and it still gave Sarah goosebumps. "Do you have a cat?"

Sarah frowned and shook her head. "No. Why?"

"You might want to get one. I think there's a rat in the cellar."

"Cellar?"

Valerie turned without answering and hurried away, almost running. She slammed the door so hard behind her that the house shook. Bemused, Sarah stood still in the empty house, listening for the sound of Valerie's car. When she heard the Ferrari roar away, she moved again, walking into the kitchen and then making the same circle of the house that she had made first by following Valerie.

My house, she thought. My own. *Home*.

But the word *home* conjured another image. Against her will, she saw again the small, upstairs apartment she had shared with Brian for the past year and a half. One bedroom, one bathroom, a living room, and a kitchen barely large enough to turn around in, all made even smaller by the bulk of furniture, books and records, and a *laissez-faire* attitude towards housekeeping. It might have been comfortable for one, but it was not really large enough for two. Sarah and Brian had been forever bumping into each other. At first, they had found it romantic.

Although romantic wasn't really the word for their relationship, Sarah thought. Necessary—that was more like it. Their constant companionship had been a necessity of life, like food or drink or sleep. They had been addicted to each other.

The realization of that had frightened Sarah. Sarah, who wasn't afraid of flying, or of insects, or of going to the dentist, was afraid of what she felt for Brian. She'd had boyfriends before, but never had she felt this obsessive need which—it now appeared—was what everyone had meant all along by the word "love."

And although this new life, this sense of being half of a greater whole, was nearly always pleasant and could be exhilarating, Sarah feared being trapped by it, becoming lost. When Brian proposed marriage, Sarah felt as if she'd been pushed out of an airplane: a giddy surge of pleasure, and then terror. She had seen herself taking the path she'd always sworn she would avoid, and turning into her mother, a hollow creature who hardly seemed to exist apart from her husband and children.

So she had put Brian off with excuses about being too young, and wanting to finish her degree, and how they should wait until they had both settled into careers. She had tried to tell him the truth—that she was frightened—but Brian, who seemed to know everything else important about her without the need for words, had not understood.

"But what's wrong with being happy?" he had asked.

"Nothing. It's not the being happy . . . it's being dependent on you in order to be happy."

"But, my love, I'm every bit as dependent on *you*."

She had given up trying to explain. The difference between them, she thought, was not that he was less dependent or less vulnerable, but that he didn't find those states of being threatening, and she did. From that moment, she began to work at keeping her separate identity. She made plans that didn't include Brian, she met old friends for lunch, she spent long hours in the library instead of studying at home, she briefly took up a political cause, and she stopped rushing home to share every meal with Brian. She imagined she could win back her old independence without losing Brian. She should have known better.

Brian had seen Sarah's campaign to save herself as a sign of loss of interest in him, as a lack of love, as a threat, and, finally, as a betrayal. And so, in the end, he had betrayed her: he had found someone else.

All along, Sarah admitted, she had been pulling away from him, seeking her own freedom, but she had imagined that they were engaged in a balancing act. When she pulled away, she expected him to pull back. The one thing she had not counted on was that he might stop pulling—that he would let her go.

It's over, Sarah told herself. It doesn't matter how it happened, or who was right or who wrong—it's over, and time to stop brooding. But she could not get Brian out of her mind.

Sarah leaned back against the living room wall and closed her eyes. She might as well have a good old wallow while she was alone, she thought. Get it out of her system, for a time, at least, and maybe she wouldn't break down in front of her friends again. She didn't try to stop the tears as she remembered that terrible evening when Brian had told her he loved someone else.

"I didn't mean for it to happen, Sarah," he said. He sounded sincere; his broad, handsome face was more miserable than she had ever seen it. "But she needs me. Melanie needs me."

"What about me? Don't I count anymore? I need you, too."

He almost smiled. "It's funny that you've never said that before."

"Did I have to? Is that what *you* need? Someone to feed your ego? Someone to go all helpless and cling to you, and worship you?"

Her fear of loss had come spilling out, sounding like anger, and Brian had turned her own bitter words against her: proof that she didn't really need him, didn't need anyone.

Oh, yes, Sarah thought. She had dug her own grave. She had opened the door and shown him the way out. It had been her own insistence on independence, her fear of showing any weakness that had led to this. If she had been able to give more, to let go a little—but, no, that wasn't right, either. Did she really want a man who needed constant reassurance, who could only see his strength reflected in someone else's weakness? If Brian couldn't love her without pretense, for who she really was—

But Brian did love her—Sarah felt certain of that. Melanie was just a distraction. In time, Brian was bound to recognize his true feelings and come back to her. He had to. He couldn't have loved her for so long, so intensely and then simply stopped. He had to come back to her, because she needed him. Despite all her precautions and her carefully developed other interests—she needed him. She couldn't go on forever with this emptiness inside, this aching, lonely feeling as if some vital piece of her had been amputated. Sometimes she imagined that, when she thought about it hard enough, her need must be tugging at Brian physically, reminding him that they were still in some way attached, pulling him inexorably back to her . . .

Sarah tensed and her eyes snapped open, her wishful thoughts vanished like spray. She was not alone.

What had alerted her? What small sound? Sarah held very still and strained her ears to hear the echo of a footstep, the creak of a hinge, the heavy wooden slide of a window being opened, but there was nothing. Her imagination offered her the image of Valerie, returned for some insane, unknowable purpose, sneaking around outside the house, peering in at the windows. Sarah pushed herself away from the wall and went through the house, room by room, but found it as empty as ever.

She looked through each window as she passed, seeking some sign of a visitor, but saw nothing unusual. Her car still waited for her in the sunlight, parked alone on the flat, sandy ground. The doors were all still shut. Still Sarah could not relax. She could not shake off the feeling that someone was nearby, spying on her.

Back in the dining room, Sarah's attention was drawn to the built-in cabinet in the east wall. Above were three shelves behind glass-fronted doors; below, two drawers and a second cabinet with plain wooden doors. Sarah opened one of the glass doors and looked inside at the deep shelves, wondering what they had been used for. A display of the best china? Idly curious, she pulled at one of the drawers. It moved sluggishly, and she pulled more firmly until it came open. Inside she found a few playing cards: Three of Spades, Queen of Hearts, Jack of Diamonds, Two of Clubs . . . and something, probably just another playing card, was stuck at the back of the drawer. Sarah could see a protruding white corner. Her fingers scrabbled at it uselessly until she realized that even if she did manage to catch hold and pull, it would probably tear. Finally she took the drawer out, struggling fiercely with it, shifting and tugging until it came free. The fragment she had been curious about proved to belong to a photograph stuck to the back of the drawer.

Carefully, Sarah peeled it away from the wood and examined it. It was an old snapshot, torn jaggedly in half. One figure remained: a dark, suited, unsmiling man in a hat.

His features were shaded by the hat brim, and the photograph was not very clear, but Sarah had the impression of an extremely attractive man. That impression might have come from the figure's stance, or the symmetry of his features, or merely the mystery and romance of an old photograph.

The blacks and whites of the snapshot were fading towards shades of brown. Sarah had no idea how old it might be—forty years, fifty, sixty? The man's suit told her little—to her unpracticed eye it might have been fashionable in almost any decade before the Sixties. The stiff, high, white collar he wore suggested an era long past. She turned the photograph over, looking for some clue, but there was nothing written on the back, and so she turned it back again, looking at the picture. In the background was a tree, and the edge of a building. A hand—a woman's?—rested on the man's arm, but the rest of the person belonging to that hand had been ripped away. The man was alone now, paying no attention to the hand, staring into the camera, his face impassive and self-assured, giving away nothing.

Sarah stared back, wanting to question him, wondering who had torn the picture and why. A woman hopelessly in love with him? He would accept that as his due, she thought: he would be a man used to inspiring passion and devotion, always remaining aloof himself, always in control. As she stared at the small image it seemed to her that she could see his eyes gleaming in shadow, and that the thin, straight line of his lips was on the verge of moving; that he looked into her eyes and in a moment would smile at her.

Sarah looked up, frowning, blinking, feeling odd. The hand holding the photograph dropped to her side. How long had she been standing there, lost in featureless daydream? It was late in the day—the light from the leaf-shrouded windows seemed different, thinner, than it had when she had last noticed. She saw by her watch that it was nearly five o'clock.

She tucked the photograph away in her purse. Time to get moving: Pete and Beverly were expecting her for dinner.

She walked slowly towards the back door, feeling as slow and confused as if she had been asleep all afternoon. On the back porch she paused, frowning. What was she forgetting? Was there something else she had to do? The house, around her, was silent, yet Sarah had the uncanny feeling that she was not alone. Someone was waiting for her, waiting for her to speak. She shrugged off the feeling as best she could, annoyed with herself for her befuddlement, and went out to her car.

Chapter Two

After the break-up, Sarah had gone to stay with Peter and Beverly Marchant, her closest friends. They were supportive and undemanding, and it was a comfortable place to stay, but nevertheless Sarah was anxious to find a place of her own. Until she did, she knew she would feel displaced and uneasy, in limbo. Once she was settled, she could start to work out the details of her new life. Maybe she would find she didn't miss Brian quite so desperately, in a room of her own.

Going back to the Marchants' apartment, Sarah drove down Speedway—and swore at her subconscious for being so predictable. There were other routes, just as simple and just as fast, for getting to 45th Street, but every day Sarah found herself making the same turn and driving down Speedway as if the route were pre-programmed and she could not deviate from it. In her mind it was "the way home." Even though it was not her home anymore.

Driving down Speedway, Sarah had only to glance to the right as she passed East 33rd Street, to catch a glimpse of the building at the corner of Helms and 33rd and the driveway there. One look was enough to tell her if Brian's beat-up old blue pickup truck was parked there—and if it was parked alone or with Melanie's brown Datsun.

No matter what she saw—if the truck was there alone, or with the car, or absent altogether—Sarah felt the same dull despair, followed by a flush of shame. Why did she put herself through this silly ordeal, day after day? It was better not to know if Brian was in or out, with Melanie or alone. It was nothing to do with her.

Her hands tightened on the wheel and her foot pressed harder on the gas as she glimpsed the blue and the brown together in the driveway. "I hope they drive each other crazy in that little rat-hole," she muttered, a hot, murderous wave of jealousy passing through her.

A few minutes later she had parked her car in the large parking lot of the complex where the Marchants lived. Engine off, Sarah remained seated in the car for a few minutes, her head against the steering wheel. She breathed slowly and deeply, consciously relaxing herself, flushing the jealousy and anger out of her system. She had cried and raged and cursed and confessed all sorts of secrets within the comfortable confessional of the Marchants' home, but it was time for a change. It was time to stop talking and thinking so incessantly about Brian and the relationship that had not worked out, time to embark on something new.

And today was a good day to begin, she reminded herself as she got out of the car. She forced up feelings of pleasure in herself like an adult coaxing a sulky child. A house! A whole, wonderful, cheap house all for her very own! Pete and Beverly would be pleased for her. Walking along the concrete path that wound between the apartment blocks, Sarah imagined Beverly's enthusiasm, and managed a smile herself. Sweet Beverly could always be counted on.

Beverly and Sarah had met as freshmen, thrown together by the whim of the computer as dormitory roommates. They had quickly become the closest of friends, and had continued to room together until Beverly's marriage to Pete Marchant, an assistant teacher who was working on his doctorate in psychology. Sarah and Beverly were now graduate students in the American Studies division at the university, uncertain what they would ultimately do with their degrees, but both reluctant to leave the familiar comforts of Austin and academia. Sarah and Pete had liked each other from the start, and when Sarah began dating Brian, the two couples had spent a lot of time together. Since the break-up, though, Pete and Beverly had sided wholeheartedly with Sarah, effectively declaring war on Brian. Their response cheered her, although she was ashamed to admit it. Except in the depths of tearful misery, Sarah liked to voice the civilized sentiments of the modern lover, and told all her friends that they mustn't take sides. But, in honesty, Sarah was pleased to hear Pete and Beverly express their anger against Brian, although sometimes it seemed but a dim reflection of her own.

As she opened the door to the Marchants' apartment, Sarah felt herself at once enveloped by the comforts of their world. The air was filled with the warm fragrance of roasting chicken, and soft, eerie music which Sarah recognized as the soundtrack from a German film called *Heart of Glass*—modern German cinema being one of Pete's enthusiasms.

"Hello," called Sarah, closing the door behind her. Pete's hollow-cheeked, pale face appeared above the bar separating kitchen from living room. "Hello, with you in a second. I'm just basting the chicken. Want some wine?"

"Sure," said Sarah, tossing her books onto the big brown couch. "We can celebrate. Where's Bev?"

"She ran out to the store. What are we celebrating?" He popped out of sight again, and Sarah heard the oven door close and the refrigerator door open.

She sank down onto the gold shag rug, leaning her back against the couch, and waited until Pete appeared, bearing two large glasses filled with white wine.

"I found a house," she said, reaching up for her glass and smiling.

Pete grinned back, his normally melancholy face transformed. "Great! Where is it?"

"You know West 35th Street? The other side of the expressway, the way we drive to Mount Bonnell?"

He nodded.

"There's a house by the back gate of the National Guard camp. An old green house, set way back from the road. We must have passed it a hundred times. I remember wondering who lived there. It never occurred to me it might be for rent."

He frowned, obviously trying to visualize it.

"Maybe you never noticed it. It is pretty far back from the road, and it blends in with the trees around it. I noticed it because I thought it was cosy and mysterious at the same time."

"You've got the whole house?"

"The whole house, all to myself. And—you won't believe this—only eighty-five dollars a month!" She laughed at his expression.

"Oh, I get it. A dollhouse, right? Two feet by two feet."

Sarah shook her head, still laughing. "It's huge! Two bedrooms. And so much land around it I could grow my own vegetables and keep chickens in a pen in the back—"

Now Pete laughed. "You're dreaming! Is this place for real?"

"Absolutely. It's a real, down-to-earth, old-fashioned farmhouse with a rent fixed sometime in the past. The windows are all covered with leaves so it's like a treehouse, or a house in the middle of a forest. It's magical."

Pete leaned forward and touched her face with the back of one hand. "Hmmm, no fever. You didn't eat some funny mushrooms today, did you?"

She made a face. "I'm not high, I'm just happy. I found a house—a perfect house—and I'm looking forward to living there. That's the whole story."

The door opened then and Beverly came in clasping a bag of groceries. Pete leaped up and took the bag from her. "Sarah's found her dream-house," he said. "We're celebrating."

Beverly rushed across the room and dropped to the floor beside Sarah, embracing her.

"Sarah, that's marvelous! Where is it, and what's it like? Cheap and two blocks from here, I hope."

"Cheap, but on the other side of Lamar. The other side of MoPac, in fact," Sarah said. She began to recite a litany of the new house's marvels, enjoying the dramatics of Beverly's reactions as her pretty, expressive face mimed first astonishment and then delight.

Pete soon joined them on the floor with the bottle of wine

and a glass for his wife. "How did you happen to find this prodigy of cheapness and space?" he asked.

"Well, that's a sort of a strange story," Sarah said. She leaned back against the couch and extended her glass to be refilled. "I was sitting in the commons, reading, when I had the feeling I was being watched. So I looked up and, what do you know, I *was* being watched. There was this skinny, red-haired girl standing and staring at me. I caught her eye and smiled but she didn't smile back. She started to give me the creeps. Then she came over to me with a piece of paper in her hand. I thought she was going to try to convert me to something—those types are always coming up to me—but she just asked me if there was a bulletin board around, for advertising. I told her I thought there was, but she should ask at the information desk. But she didn't move, she just stood there, kind of flapping the paper at me, and giving me this *look*.

"Well, you know me," Sarah said. She paused to sip her wine. "I had to ask. And, for a wonder, it wasn't krishna consciousness or scientology, but something I really was interested in. A house. She told me she was moving, and trying to find somebody who could move in now, in the middle of the month. When she mentioned the rent, I thought I'd heard wrong. I knew I had to see it."

"The hand of fate," Beverly said. "Did she tell you that in order to qualify for the special low rent you'd have to join the Universal Life Church or take up TM?"

"Nothing like that. Although it wouldn't have surprised me, coming from her. I almost expected something even weirder from her. She gave off such a strange aura—Pete, quit smirking! If you'd met her, you'd have to agree. There was something about her that made me uneasy from the start, and it wasn't just the way she stared at me. I'd be willing to bet she's mixed up in something weird."

"I wasn't smirking," Pete said, striving to look blameless. "I certainly wouldn't want to argue about your response to her. I've experienced the same thing myself with certain people. It seems instinctual, but later you usually find that there were plenty of rational reasons for disliking that person. It may be a matter of body language, or their choice of words, or even body odor. On a subconscious level, all sorts of—"

"My love," said Beverly hastily, catching hold of Pete's arm, "is dinner going to be ready anytime soon?"

Her question threw him, and for a moment he looked confused. Then he said, "I need to steam the broccoli; once that's done, the chicken and potatoes will be ready. Probably in about ten minutes?"

Beverly nodded and nudged Sarah. "Go on. About how strange she was."

"Oh. Yeah." She had been interested in Pete's diversion —she was looking for reasons to substantiate her feelings about Valerie. But that could wait—the kind of meandering, theoretical, philosophical/psychological discussions Pete and Sarah loved to get into usually bored Beverly. "The whole thing was strange," Sarah went on. "Not the house. I mean, the house is great. I think. So far. At least . . ."

Beverly laughed. "I don't believe it! You're talking yourself out of it!"

"I'm not!"

"But something upset you," Pete said.

"The girl?" said Beverly.

Sarah nodded. "It was the way it happened. It was as if she was looking for me, as if she knew—the way she stared at me, like she was reading my mind. How could she have known I was looking for a house? What made her pick me, out of all the people sitting around the commons this afternoon?"

"It's called luck," Beverly said. "Or maybe she was attracted to you, because you looked so nice." She rubbed her shoulder against Sarah's and gave her a kittenish look.

"Maybe you don't really want the house," Pete said. "Maybe you're just not ready for making the commitment to a house of your own."

Was he right? The image of the house resurfaced in her mind, and with it a pang of longing. She wanted to live there. The house might have been made especially for her. "Of course I want the house," she said. "It's perfect. I knew the moment I saw it. And if I'm not ready to live by myself, I should be. Brian and I are finished. I can't hang around here as if I expected him to call me back. The only thing that upsets me is Valerie."

"Perhaps she's an excuse," Pete said. "A focus for all your doubts."

Sarah grimaced and shook her head hard. "No. There's a reason for my feeling this way. There's something very odd about how this happened—something very odd about *her.* When we were at the house and I decided to take it, she informed me that she'd already told the landlady my name. She was that sure of me. Before I'd even seen the place. How could she have done that? How could she have been that certain?"

Pete shrugged. "She was lying. Maybe it was all a part of her game, to tell you that. All a part of her own strange reality. You sensed something disturbing about her—maybe she's whacko, a nut-case."

"To use the scientific terminology," Beverly said wryly. "You didn't give her any money, did you?"

Sarah shook her head quickly. "No. She gave me the landlady's name and address. The rent is due the twenty-second."

"Maybe you should call her," Pete suggested. "Just to make sure everything is fair and square, and to let her know about you. That might make you feel better about it, too." He stood up. "I have to attend to dinner. Would one of you ladies set the table?"

"When did you plan to move in?" Beverly asked as she and Sarah distributed the flatware on the round, glass-topped table in a recess of the large living room.

"I thought maybe this weekend."

Pete looked in from the kitchen. "I have a student with a van," he said. "I'm sure I could talk him into helping us on Saturday morning. It shouldn't take more than a trip or two to get all your things moved."

"The things his students do for extra credit," said Beverly.

Sarah concentrated on the pepper grinder she was holding, placing it precisely in the center of the table as she replied. "Brian has a truck, you know. And he could move the heavy things for me."

"Sarah," said Beverly, sounding dismayed.

"You don't have to ask him," Pete said.

Sarah turned away from the table. She had to look at one of them, so she chose Pete. "Brian might as well do it," she said. "All my stuff is at his place, after all. And he said he'd do it."

Pete was silent. Sarah saw him look at Beverly, cautioning. Then he said gently, "We could easily take care of it, Sarah. You don't have to worry about it. You don't even have to see him."

Sarah shook her head. "That's silly. Of course I have to see him. It's his apartment, and we have to sort out our things, decide what belongs to him and what to me. We bought a lot of things together during—"

"I could do it, Sarah," Beverly said. "You could just tell me—I remember your things from when we lived together."

Sarah half-turned so she did not have to face either of her friends directly. She tried a laugh. "Look. Brian exists. My things are in his apartment. It's not going to kill me to see him, and it's the most sensible way to handle this. I have to get used to it, and so do you. I can't have a nervous breakdown every time I run into him on campus. This is a small town, and we know the same people and we go to the same school—I can't avoid him forever. I have to see him sometime, and it might as well be this weekend."

Pete went back into the kitchen. Beverly moved closer to Sarah, touching her arm. *"You* look. You don't have to be sensible, you know. We won't think any less of you. I know you're tough and all that; I know you're capable of going over there and packing up all your stuff and being cool and perfectly friendly to that jerk, but you don't have to do it. There's no point, if it might upset you. You don't have to put on a front for anyone; you don't have to prove anything. Don't rush it. Just wait until you happen to run into him . . . wait until you're well and truly over him before you try to see him."

"But I *am* over him," Sarah lied. "Mostly, anyway, I think. How can I know for sure unless I see him, to test myself? I've gotten used to being alone . . . but then, you know, we were drifting apart even before he met this Melanie. It was just a matter of time, really." She looked cautiously at Beverly to see how her story was being accepted.

"I always thought you could do better," Beverly said. "Honestly, Sarah. I mean, O.K., I'll admit Brian's a hunk, and he's very nice—at least, I always *thought* he was nice until this business—but . . . I could never see you spending the rest of your life with him. He's so lazy. You know, in five years you'll be a professor somewhere, and Brian will still be living in that same little apartment with all his books and records and games, and he'll be taking classes in Zen and the art of basket-weaving, or something equally useful, and he'll be no closer to getting a degree than he is now. And he'll be perfectly content."

Sarah had to smile and admit the accuracy of Beverly's prediction. "All right, he's not ambitious . . . but he'll find himself eventually. Is it better to be ambitious than to be happy? You know he's intelligent, and talented, and good-natured. A much nicer person than I am, really. And he did so much for me—he was so good to me—all the time, little things and big ones. He'd—" She faltered and broke off, trapped again by memories. Brian's warmth, his smile, the way he said her name when he had one of his surprises for her.

"Oh, Sarah," Beverly said softly, sadly

Pete came back into the room with the platter of roast chicken. "Let's talk about something else," he said.

"I'm all right."

"Of course you are," Beverly said softly as they all sat down to dinner.

Brian was not mentioned again that evening, but Sarah was so aware of the unspoken name that she sometimes felt he was physically in the room with them, Pete and Beverly ignoring him out of loyalty to her. It gave her an odd feeling, but she did not mention Brian again, either, observing the unspoken rules—and then wondered who the rules were for, who was being protected. They talked about Sarah's new house, and the oddity of Valerie, and an experiment Pete had been observing in the psychology department. They talked about books, and watched a well-meaning but extremely dull local arts program on television, and played a game of Scrabble. By the time she went to bed, Sarah felt ready to burst with self-restraint and self-denial. In bed at last, alone and free, her thoughts flew greedily to Brian.

He had been so good to her, and always there; she had basked in his love, or blinked and moved away, annoyed by its intensity, but it had seemed a constant, like the sun. It had never really occurred to Sarah that someday Brian would leave her, that the bright, nourishing beams of his affection would be directed at someone else.

Before the final surprise of Melanie, Brian had specialized in good surprises. He would send her flowers, or mysterious telegrams signed "Alexei" or "Nikolai"; he set up a midnight treasure-hunt across a nearby golf course which ended in a cache of champagne and fried chicken for a moonlit picnic; he hired a local band to serenade her on her birthday.

And he had been just as thoughtful, just as clever, just as determined to please her in bed. Once, Sarah remembered, she had discovered a vibrator under her pillow, and looked around to find Brian watching her with his wickedest grin. Another time it had been a can of whipped cream and a jar of chocolate syrup; another, massage oils. He had been an inventive and seemingly tireless lover, quick to learn what she liked, and so eager to provide it that she believed him when he said that his pleasure came from giving her pleasure.

So much love, so much attention—Sarah dreamed of a man beside the bed who brought a pillow down on her face while she slept, and woke, thrashing and panting for air, hot, breathless and disoriented, thinking frantically of escape when Brian put his arms around her and tried to comfort her.

Escape! Fully awake, the thought seemed traitorous and absurd. Sarah's dreams made her feel guilty, and she winced away from Brian's smile and tried to find ways around his generosity. He tried to give her more, and she asked for less.

Finally, it seemed, he had taken her at her word, and given her less, so that now she had nothing. She was free now, freer than she had ever wanted to be. Tears came to her eyes, but she fought them off. She didn't want another miserable, wakeful night spent going over that dreadful litany of mistakes, quarrels, misunderstandings and lost hopes. They'd had more good times together than bad, she and Brian, but the memories that clung now were the ones with burrs, the prickly, uncomfortable ones. Sarah wanted to remember the good times, the long, safe, sexy nights, the lazy mornings; she wanted a sweet memory with which to lull herself to sleep, hand between her thighs.

She commanded a memory: Brian's lips on hers, the two of them together in bed. But that was too vague. She had to pick out a moment in time, some time when he had been hers.

She remembered coming in from class one afternoon, trudging up the stairs, her head down. She hadn't seen Brian waiting for her, hadn't even known he was there until he pounced, grabbing her tightly from behind.

Sarah had squealed, and then giggled as he pawed her and breathed heavily in her ear, but the books in her arms were uncomfortable, slipping. "Brian, could I put my books down?"

"Ha! 'oo ees thees Brian? 'E cannot 'elp you now!"

One book fell. Wincing with annoyance, Sarah let the rest of them go. Why did she worry about such trivial details? Why couldn't she just forget everything else and play, as Brian did?

But he had done a good job of distracting her. His hands caressing her breasts through the silky material of her blouse, his breath hot in her ear, became the only important things. He tumbled her to the ground, and tugged her jeans partway down, and touched her until her panties were wet and she was wriggling with impatience, but he held her down, held her hands down, not letting her touch him or undress herself, laughing at her, murmuring, "Ah, no, you naughty girl, we'll keep our clothes on and stay out of trouble." And he'd gone on teasing her, sucking her breasts through her blouse, until—

She knew what happened next; it was what always happened next. But she was helpless to visualize it. Instead she saw Brian's face change, saw him melancholy, no longer loving or lustful. And she heard him say, "Melanie needs me. I'm sorry; I didn't mean for this to happen."

Brian wasn't hers anymore, not even in her fantasies.

Chapter Three

On Saturday morning Sarah left the Marchants' early, while Pete and Beverly were getting breakfast ready.

"I'm not hungry," she said. "I may as well go now. I told Brian I'd be there first thing. We'll get started—don't hurry."

Their silence was sympathetic and said more than words. Sarah hurried away before they could suspect her mood. The prospect of seeing Brian again had lifted her spirits higher than they had been in the past two weeks. She had tried to bury the fantasy of winning him back, but it would keep poking up its seductive face.

As she drove the few blocks to Brian's house, Sarah hoped she wasn't *too* early. She wouldn't mind catching Brian still in bed—she would have loved such a psychological advantage—but not if Melanie was there with him. It was a relief to see only the blue truck parked in the driveway. But, Sarah reflected, Melanie probably wasn't any more eager than she was to meet her.

Sarah still had her key, so, heart thudding, she opened the door without knocking, and entered the tiny foyer which rose almost immediately into a flight of steps. Suddenly aware of herself as an intruder, she made herself stop at the bottom of the stairs, and called out Brian's name.

His head appeared at once, looking down over the railing, the slightly shaggy fair hair falling forward in a soft aura around his face. "Hi," he said. "Come on up."

Something in her chest seemed to tighten at the sight of him, and she was already short of breath before she had mounted the first of the steep stairs. Brian took a step backwards when she reached the top, and Sarah felt that slight, flinching movement like a slap. All right, so she wasn't allowed to touch him. She bit back a nasty retort and just looked at him.

"Pete and Bev will be here soon. Pete can help you carry my couch down. I thought I'd get started sorting out my books and records from yours."

Brian turned and gestured at boxes stacked against the far wall. "I already went through and separated your books and your records, and most of them are in those boxes. The rest of your books are still in your black bookcase."

Your, your, yours. Each time he said it it was like another little cut. *Ours* was dead now. *Ours* meant something else. She wondered if it was Melanie who had put him up to the sorting job—it wasn't like him to be so organized. She wondered what he had thought, what he had felt, as he went through their mingled possessions and divided them up.

"You'll probably want to look through and make sure I didn't miss anything," Brian said. "And there're some records I wasn't sure about . . . things we bought together. If I kept any you especially wanted, just say."

"That's all right. You're the one who mostly listens to records." Didn't he know she didn't care? Had he stopped understanding her so completely, so abruptly? She wanted to weep. His careful, distant politeness and steady refusal to meet her eyes hurt her more than she had expected. The fantasy that had sent her over here in high spirits had dissolved, and she had no anger to protect her. Here in this familiar room, where they had lived together, the distance he maintained—Brian, who had always been so ready to please her—seemed especially unnatural, almost a sacrilege.

"Shall I start loading some of these boxes onto the truck?"

She was sure he spoke only to break the silence, which might have seemed too close to intimacy. She shrugged hopelessly. "Put them in my car. It's not locked." She watched as he bent and lifted a heavy box, seeing the fabric of his blue shirt stretch taut across his broad back. She had to look away quickly, to keep from crying. When she heard him walking slowly, heavily down the stairs, she roused herself and looked around the tiny apartment for things which were hers.

Some were easy. The dishes were hers, and most of the flatware. The glasses with super-heroes on them belonged to Brian. One skillet and one saucepan were hers, the other two were his. The beanbag chair and floor lamp had been with her since dormitory days. The good stereo system and color television were Brian's; the old black and white set, two speakers, a radio and the blender were hers.

Other things could not be so easily categorized. They were gifts, or had been bought together, and the sight of them brought back vivid memories of other times. The onyx bookends and ashtray from Mexico—the Rackham print —the armchair they had clumsily attempted to reupholster —the "Risk" and "Diplomacy" games—the hideous table lamp made to look like an orange cowboy boot—

They belonged to the apartment, to a time and a place, not to either Brian or Sarah but to something intangible now vanished, the relationship between them. Sarah could not imagine the ugly table lamp in another house, even her own house, but she did not want to leave it to Brian knowing that it would then become a part of Melanie's life, a part of her personal mythology. She chewed her lip, feeling like Solomon about to divide a baby. This for Brian, this for me, this to go, this to stay . . .

She found the photograph beneath the Art Deco cigarette case Brian had bought once on impulse. For just a moment, lulled by the familiar surroundings, Sarah simply looked at it, trying to remember the dark-haired, thin girl with the strained smile. One of her friends? One of Brian's? And then she knew. It must be Melanie.

Brian came back into the room at that moment, slightly

out of breath, and she glared at him, and waved the photograph in the air.

"What's she so scared of?"

Brian gave her a wary look and came no closer, although Sarah could see by the way his hands moved that he was longing to snatch the precious picture away. "She doesn't like being photographed."

"Is that all? My God, she looks terrified, not just uncomfortable. All huge eyes, and that grimace, and the way she's standing, kind of clutching herself—"

"All right, Sarah, that's enough."

"Is that what you like? Scared little girls? Is that what you need to feed your ego? Didn't I shiver enough when you turned out the light?"

"Stop it. You don't even know her."

"I don't need to. I'm talking about *you*." She dropped the photograph onto the table. "Let's have a little truth session here. I don't want any more about how you didn't mean it to happen, or how much she needs you, I want—"

"Yes, it's always what *you* want, isn't it?" he said bitterly.

Their eyes met, and Sarah felt a shock. He was not distant now; the old current was in the air between them again.

"What do you mean?"

"Everything was always on your terms—I could adapt or get out. I felt like I was always running after you, trying to please you, trying to tempt you to stay a little longer."

"You could have told me how you felt."

"Yeah, sure. And had another lecture about my possessiveness and your need for independence, and how you were *afraid* to be dependent on anyone, especially me. Yeah, afraid," he said, his tone heavily ironic.

Sarah's skin was prickling all over with shame, and with hope. "I'm sorry," she said in a small voice. She moved a step closer to him, saw he noticed, saw that he didn't back away. "You did make me happy, Brian. I'm sorry if I didn't tell you that enough. I thought you'd realize . . ."

"It's all right," he said wearily. "It's all over now."

No. She wanted to shout, but restrained herself. "It isn't. It doesn't have to be." He *must* feel the attraction that charged the air, she thought. He *must*. If they could both let go at the same moment, their bodies would take over, come together, never to be parted again.

"We just didn't understand each other well enough," Sarah said. "I know now—I'm not afraid to admit I need you." She rejoiced to see the pain flicker in his eyes.

He shook his head hard. "Don't say that."

"It's true."

"It's too late for that. I don't . . . Things have changed."

She realized he didn't want to bring up Melanie's name, and she felt another surge of hope. "Things haven't changed that much. Not between us." She took another step closer and laid her hand on his arm. She felt him jump, but he didn't pull away. They looked into each other's eyes. Distantly, Sarah was aware of the sound of a car pulling into the driveway outside, but she was preoccupied by more immediate sensations, and willing Brian to kiss her.

There was a knock on the open door below, and Pete's voice: "Hello . . . Marchants Movers at your service!"

Brian jerked away as if he'd been shot.

Sarah reached for him. "I'll tell them to go away," she whispered. "I'll say we don't need them . . ."

But Brian moved away, not letting her touch him, and showed himself at the top of the stairs. "Come on in, Pete," he said in a voice that was nearly normal.

Sarah made herself move, although it was like managing a clumsy robot. She crouched on the floor and began fumbling in a box of books, to appear to be busy when Pete and Beverly came up.

After that, Brian kept his distance. Their eyes met only once, by chance, and Brian broke that brief contact as swiftly as if it had burned him.

It was odd to see Brian in her new house—odd because it was wrong. He didn't belong here in her refuge. Seeing him move through the rooms of the house she had rented, his boots loud on the bare wooden floors, his familiar voice echoing as he asked where she wanted the couch, Sarah found it too easy to fall into old patterns of thought, to forget what had just happened between them, to imagine all was right with the world and he was moving into this house with her. She had to stop herself from asking his advice on the placement of furniture. His opinion didn't matter; he wasn't going to live here, or even visit her here. She told herself that again and again, hurting herself, trying to get used to the pain. He would go away, and these walls would not know him again. Only she would—and as she gazed at Brian, unable to stop herself, Sarah imagined that he was leaving behind an image on the air which would remain to haunt her in the lonely nights to come. She would turn a corner, she thought, and catch a sudden glimpse of him; hear the distant echoes of his voice; and listen, heart pounding, as she waited for his return. Already, Brian was a ghost in her house.

The tears were too near the surface. Abruptly Sarah left her supervisory position and went outside. She walked around the house to the front, eyes on the ground, breathing slowly and deeply. She looked away from the weedy ground to the trees, and then up at the overcast sky. The day was cloudy and warm; the air moist and soft against her bare arms and face. A rainstorm, and colder weather, were expected that night. Sarah walked across the open expanse of ground, leaving the house and sheltering trees behind. A single tree, a low, spreading mesquite, stood at the far southwestern corner of the lot. She approached it, and then turned and looked up at her house.

Two red-brick chimneys thrust out of the black roof. Sarah frowned in surprise. She hadn't noticed them before. Two chimneys, but no fireplaces. Then she remembered that odd, jutting corner in the living room, and the surprising shallowness of the kitchen pantry. The old fireplaces must have been covered up. A pity, but probably for the best, she thought. An old wooden house like this one would be a fire-trap.

As she began to walk back towards the house, Sarah noticed something else. There were windows at ground level, two of them on the front of the house, the glass grimed and revealing nothing, half-hidden by the bushes which crowded around the house below the high porch. She paused at the foot of the steps, remembering Valerie's parting comment about a cellar. Perhaps she should have a look at it, but the idea of exploring a dark, damp, dirty space beneath her house was not immediately appealing.

While she considered it, the front door opened and Pete came out onto the porch and looked down at her.

She mounted the steps to meet him, seeing the concern on his face. "Just surveying my domain," she said lightly. "I just noticed there are chimneys, so there must have been a fireplace or two here back in the good old days."

"The good old days," Pete echoed. "Do you suppose this was a farmhouse? It was probably still outside the city limits in the Thirties, or whenever it was built. By the way, I noticed that your back steps aren't too sturdy—the wood is pretty old, and one of the steps looks like it's about to go. You should probably replace it."

"I suspect the number of things wrong with this place will mount up as I get to know it better," Sarah said. But her voice was cheerful. The thought of getting to know the house, finding out what repairs had to be made and then dealing with them was somehow appealing. It would give her something new to think about, something to keep herself occupied.

It didn't take long to move, and by the time Sarah had made her last trip from Brian's apartment it was still early in the day. Brian hurried away with obvious relief, eager for a friendlier environment, but Beverly and Pete stayed on, helping Sarah clean the house and put things away. They worked until after dark, papering drawers, unpacking dishes, nailing up bookshelves and filling them with books, helping Sarah plan and believe in her future in this house. When they finally rested, too hungry and tired to go on, the house was beginning to look lived-in. Only the bedroom was untouched, since Sarah had no furniture for it.

"You might as well come back and sleep at our place," Beverly said, rubbing her face and leaving dirty marks on it.

Sarah shook her head. "I want to stay here, now that I'm moved in."

"But you don't have a bed!"

"I can sleep on the couch." Sarah began to prowl the living room, assessing the look of her things in this new place. "I'll check the newspaper ads tomorrow and find some sort of cheap bed, and I might be able to find a chest of drawers and other things at a garage sale."

"But until you do, you stay with us," Beverly said firmly.

Sarah shook her head, equally firmly.

"Let's get some dinner," Pete said. His voice was brisk, on the edge of impatience.

"Food!" Beverly said triumphantly, wagging a finger at Sarah. "You don't have any food! What are you going to do about breakfast?"

"There's a twenty-four-hour Safeway a few blocks up Thirty-fifth. I can get whatever I need there."

"It would be so much easier . . ."

Pete grasped his wife by one arm and pulled her to her feet. "It would be so much easier to argue this over dinner," he said. "How does Mexican food sound?"

But even after a stupefyingly large meal at El Rancho, Beverly did not give up. As they stood in the parking lot between their two cars, saying goodnight, Beverly launched her final attack.

"Sarah, just follow us home and we'll have a few more beers and watch *Saturday Night Live*."

"Thanks," Sarah said. "But all I want to do is go to sleep." Although she had left the heavy work to the men, her muscles ached slightly from the exertions of the day; she was full of food and pleasantly weary.

"But you can sleep at our place."

"Honey, Sarah knows what she wants to do," Pete said. He put one arm around Beverly. "We just spent the day helping her move in—and now you won't let her move in."

"I have to make the move some time, and it might as well be tonight," Sarah said. "I've slept on the couch before —it's comfortable enough. And all my *things* are there—I'd worry about them if I left them. I'll be very cosy there, surrounded by all my things, in my own house—really." She smiled.

Pete looked at Sarah intently, his face seeming even more gaunt in the harsh streetlights. "Just as long as you know," he said quietly. "That you're always welcome. Always. Even if that means you come knocking on our door in the middle of the night."

Once again Sarah felt close to tears, but this time for a different reason. She felt their concern, their affection, like a net she could fall into, fearlessly letting go. She struggled a moment and then said lightly, "God forbid I should ever have to. I'll be all right."

"I know you will," said Pete. For a moment Sarah thought he would step forward to embrace her, but the moment passed, and his arm only tightened around his wife. Pete and Sarah had always been awkward with each other physically, touching only through words. Beverly was the conducter between them, able to hug and kiss and freely express her emotions.

Driving home, pleasantly stuffed and a little high on Mexican beer, Sarah felt no regrets. But by the time she had bought a few things at the supermarket, and reached her dark, empty house, she was sober, tired, and feeling the first brush of unease as she remembered that she had no telephone.

Well, I won't need one, she thought. She was tired enough to sleep soundly through the night, even on the couch and in a new place. She wished, as she walked slowly towards the black house, that she had thought to leave the porch light on. Lightning flickered in the western sky, and Sarah's spirits rose again at the prospect of a thunderstorm. Nothing could make her feel at home more quickly than to spend a night, cosy and sheltered, while the rain pounded down outside.

Inside with the lights on, reflections in the windows startled her. Curtains, of course. How could she have forgotten about curtains? With the windows set so high, and the house so far from the street, Sarah knew she was safe from any spying eyes, but she didn't like the flat blackness of the glass; and the dim reflections of herself, moving, which the windows cast back at her, kept tricking her into whirling around in the expectation of discovering she was no longer alone.

Sarah unrolled her sleeping bag across the couch, slipped into the flannel nightgown she usually wore only when she was sick or very cold, and settled down for the night. With the inside lights off, the windows were no longer evil mirrors, but only windows again. There was a streetlight on the corner which faintly illuminated parts of the front room, and every few minutes the lightning flashed. Sarah lay with eyes open for a while, looking at the shapes of leaves and branches outside the window, noticing how the occasional lightning altered them, and waiting for the rain. Sleep arrived before the storm.

Suddenly she woke, feeling that something was wrong. She could hear the gentle sound of rain, but it was not that which had woken her. She had heard something else; a sound from inside the house.

She heard it again: a scuffling, scurrying sound from the floor. Sarah turned her head and saw it.

It was an enormous rat, moving across the floor with a terrible purpose, making straight for her. The small amount of light in the room was enough to show her its large sharp teeth, and the unholy gleam of its tiny eyes.

Sarah struggled to sit up, but she could not move. It was as if she were utterly paralyzed. She realized she could not even feel her body. Only the muscles of her face seemed responsive, and she could turn her head. She had the choice to look at the rat or not to look at it, but no more than that.

The rat had reached the couch now and she heard it scrabbling at the base. In a moment she would feel it on her, and those horrible teeth would close on her flesh. Sarah opened her mouth to scream, knowing how useless a scream would be, in this house where no one could hear—

And she woke, heart thumping wildly and breath sounding harshly in her ears. And she could move. Relief flooded through her, relief beyond words that she was not paralyzed. And there was no rat. It had been a dream.

But as her breathing slowed Sarah could hear another sound. The sound came from within the room, just as in her dream. It was the very same sound she had heard in her dream, in fact—a scuffling, scratching noise. The sort of noise a rat might make.

The breath caught in her throat, and Sarah sat up and grabbed for the lamp beside the couch. Squinting against the sudden brightness, she looked around the room for the source of the noise. She saw nothing and gradually, as the sound continued, realized that it did not come from within the room, but from the far wall. The noises came from that odd, protruding corner which covered the old fireplace. That made sense, Sarah thought, relaxing slightly at the understanding that there was nothing actually in the room with her. Something—a rat, a bird, a bat—could be trapped in the old chimney.

The noise stopped.

Sarah continued to stare at the wall as she waited for it to begin again, but she was no longer frightened. It would not be a rat like the one in her nightmare, and she was not paralyzed. Real rats could be dealt with easily enough. On Monday she would buy poison and traps. If it became a major problem, she would call an exterminator. Still she hesitated to turn out the light and go back to sleep. She waited to hear the rat again. It was ridiculous, of course, but she had the unnerving feeling that it was waiting her out, holding still and keeping silent until she went back to sleep.

Sarah shivered, realizing that the room was much colder than it had been when she had gone to bed. The cold front must have come in with the rain. She closed the window behind the couch, which she had left partially open, and then turned out the light and burrowed back into the warmth of her sleeping bag.

After the nightmare, sleep was a long time coming, and, when it came, was fragmentary. Nightmare images of rats kept jarring her awake. She heard sounds—or thought she did—and felt tiny claws scraping at the fabric of her sleeping bag. Something was hunting her—the rat was coming to get her. She had to be alert, on her guard. Half-asleep, Sarah moaned and twisted about within the confines of the sleeping bag, trying to escape the rat, trying to order her dreams. Dawn came and filled the room with cold, early light before Sarah finally sank into untroubled sleep.

—

Chapter Four

Sarah stood in the doorway between kitchen and bedroom and gazed at the ugly carpet. It had to go; it was beyond cleaning. Getting it out was the next task of the day, a job which had to be done before she could move any furniture into the room. She had gone to a discount bedding house that morning, amid the clutter of surplus, furniture and discount stores that lined Burnet Road, and arranged for a new mattress and box springs to be delivered on Monday.

Pushing her sweatshirt sleeves above her elbows, Sarah squatted on the floor to take a closer look. She wrinkled her nose at the musty smell. There were no nails or tacks, and when she tugged at the edge, she was surprised to find it came up easily. Although old and bulky, the carpet was not difficult to move, and Sarah soon had it pushed into a lumpish roll against the far wall. Then she stood back and stared at what she had uncovered.

There was a design painted on the wooden boards in greenish-white paint: three rings encircling a five-pointed star. There were words within the rings which she could not read, and symbols at each point of the star. Although she couldn't translate it precisely, Sarah knew very well what it meant.

Magic.

Was it Valerie's? Sarah's mouth twitched, and then a smile broke through at the picture she imagined: Valerie, standing in the center of the pentacle, candles flickering around her, her face tense with concentration, her arms raised in supplication, her voice shrill and high as she spoke to imaginary demons. The idea pleased her, somehow. It labeled Valerie, and explained the aura of strangeness Sarah had sensed about her. So Valerie was a witch—or thought she was, which amounted to the same thing in the end. Perhaps she even thought she had cast a spell on Sarah and made her rent this house.

So I live in a witch's house, thought Sarah. It was an interesting thought, and already she was shaping events into a story to amuse her friends, recasting her encounter with Valerie in a new light and choosing her words. *And there, underneath the bedroom carpet* . . .

A sudden rapping sound made Sarah turn, her smile fading. "Who is it?"

But when she went to look, she found no one at the back door. As she hesitated, wondering, the sound came again. This time it seemed not a knocking, but a muffled thumping. Following the sound, holding her breath in order to hear it better, Sarah came to the bathroom. The noise had a focus now: something was moving beneath the bathtub. She listened a moment, then reached out and pounded sharply on the wall. The sounds of movement became more frantic, scurrying and scrabbling.

Valerie's voice came to mind, and her sly smile: "I think there's a rat in the cellar."

Sarah nodded grimly and went for her flashlight. It was time to take a look at that cellar. At the back door she paused a moment, then turned back and exchanged her tennis shoes for a pair of sturdy boots. Outside she shivered at the unexpected chill in the air and glanced up at the overcast sky, but didn't bother going back for her jacket. She didn't plan to be outside long.

The door to the cellar was on the west side near the front of the house. Old, unpainted, warped, it had no handle, and Sarah had to grasp the splintering edge and struggle to wrest it open. Inside it was dark, the windows too dirty and hidden by leaves to let in much light. Sarah thumbed the button on her flashlight and slipped through the doorway, ducking her head to avoid a spiderweb and looking around cautiously.

The space below the house was cold and damp and filled with a rotten, penetrating odor. Generations of rats might have lived and died and disintegrated here to judge from that smell, and Sarah wondered that it hadn't seeped up into the house yet. The floor was earth, soft and dusty. Sarah stepped carefully, crouching to avoid the overhanging pipes, and breathing shallowly through her mouth. She swept the space ahead of her with the beam of light, alert for any motion, any unexpected mass or movement that might give form to the noises she had heard. And as she looked, she prayed she would find nothing. Later, she would put out poison and traps, but for now she hoped the rat would have the sense to stay out of sight. She began to regret her impulsive rush down here, armed with nothing but a flashlight, and a sudden internal chill made her grind her teeth together as she remembered her dream.

Her boot struck something soft.

With a cry, she leaped back. Heart pounding, Sarah forced herself to stand still, and she turned the light in the direction of the thing she had so nearly stepped on.

It was a dead cat. Coming closer, Sarah saw that its throat had been cut, so ferociously that the head was nearly off. The fur seemed to shimmer and move in the light—the small corpse was crawling with maggots.

Shivering, her stomach twisting unpleasantly, Sarah backed away from the butchered animal. All heart for further exploration was gone, and the previous tenant's excursions in sorcery no longer seemed amusing. Whoever had killed this cat was senselessly vicious, possibly dangerous. Sarah felt a perhaps groundless but still powerful conviction that Valerie had killed the animal, probably as one of her witch-spells, a blood offering to some evil spirit.

Do you have a cat? I think there's a rat in the cellar."

Sarah remembered the gloating madness that had twisted the woman's face. Crazy. She was crazy.

And her throat tightened in sudden fear. Valerie had wanted her here, living in this house. Why? She thought of the nearly useless locks on the doors upstairs and decided to have them changed the next day. She would have bolt locks installed on both the inner and the outer doors. Just in case.

Hating it, but knowing it had to be done, Sarah used some old newspapers to transport the cat's body to the garbage can, and fastened the lid down with a shudder. She could almost feel the maggots squirming on her hands as she hurried inside to wash.

When she came out of the bathroom she paused in the doorway, staring at the floor. The green-white pentacle seemed to mock her. Had there been blood spilled on this floor? Sarah wondered. Had Valerie raised the knife here in this room and brought it down on her unsuspecting cat, later discarding the body in the cellar? Had she meant for Sarah to find it, pointing the way with her hints of cats and rats and cellars? Stop thinking. *Do* something. She squared her shoulders.

But soap and water, ammonia, and a scrub brush had no effect on the paint. Looking at her watch Sarah guessed that it was too late, on a Sunday, to find anyplace open that would sell paint remover, and added that item to her list of things to buy. She closed off the bedroom and went into her office.

She couldn't settle down. She couldn't concentrate. Sarah laid aside the letters of Flannery O'Connor and prowled restlessly through the house. Her nerves were strung tight, and every small noise made her heart beat faster. She looked sharply at the windows time and again, expecting, beyond all reason, to find Valerie's mad, grinning face looking in at her, expecting to see a thin figure lurking in the bushes. The doors were locked every time she checked; the windows undisturbed. Still there were sounds —scrabblings behind walls, beneath the floors, overhead. Sometimes aggressively loud, sometimes so quietly that it might have been someone whispering in another room. Sarah had the irrational feeling that the rat, having seen her fearful departure from the cellar, was taunting her now, daring her to do something.

Twice Sarah grabbed her purse and jacket and headed for the back door only to stop herself. She wasn't going to leave. She wouldn't let her own silly fears drive her out.

Where would she go? Beverly and Pete deserved some respite from her company, and she had to get used to living alone.

The house began to feel cold as evening came on. Sarah plugged the electric heater in the living room and closed the door to her office to conserve the heat. She busied herself making dinner: a large plate of macaroni and cheese with a few strips of bacon on the side, and then settled with the food and a glass of wine on the living room couch. She wrapped a soft blue blanket around herself and turned the television on to a movie about a husband and wife detective team.

The show was mindless and relaxing and Sarah was grateful for the opportunity not to think. The sound of pleasant, California voices and bland background music covered any other sounds she might have heard, and Sarah felt herself drifting, the food and wine and pleasant warmth all comforting her. The movie ended and Sarah meant to rise and turn off the television, but it was too much trouble. Just too much trouble to move. She was stretched out on the couch, the blanket enveloping her, and the thought of sitting up, unwrapping the blanket, and walking across the room to the television set was exhausting. It was too much work. It was much easier to stay where she was, with the light and the television on, and make no effort. Easier to relax. To let go. To give in.

It took her a little while to realize that these were not her own thoughts. Giving in, letting go—that was what the rat wanted her to do.

The rat's eyes were like flames. It sat up on its haunches and glared at her, and burned its will into her mind.

Give up. Let go.

She had to look away, Sarah thought, confused. It was hard to think, but she could feel the urgency of that. If she kept looking into those eyes it would become harder and harder to resist. The rat was hypnotizing her, compelling her, and, in time, those flaming eyes would burn her mind away. Already the flames were singeing the edges of her will, and once it was gone, she knew, once her will had been burned up like a piece of paper, the rat could do whatever it wanted. She would not be able to oppose it. She knew that, and yet it was so hard to look away. She had to, to save her own life, and yet it was hard to think of anything beside those golden, glowing eyes. But if she did not turn away, she would die. The rat would leap upon her with its cold, sharp claws, and scrabble up her motionless, will-less body, and bite out her throat.

In a moment she would turn her head, and save herself from those twin flames. In a moment.

Sarah woke, shuddering, to darkness and cold. For one horrible moment she thought she was lying in the cellar, but then she felt the solid, rather hard cushions of the couch beneath her, and the softness of the blanket, and knew where she was. She had been dreaming.

But why was it so cold? And why so dark? She missed the hum and glow of the electric heater, and the light, and the television. She didn't remember turning any of them off. Her last memory was of falling asleep amid babble and glow.

Who had turned out the light?

Sarah's heart pounded and she held her breath, listening. She was afraid to sit up, afraid to reach out to the lamp beside the couch, afraid that someone was waiting for her to move, waiting to grab.

Perhaps a fuse had blown. Perhaps she herself had turned off the light and forgotten about it. It was ridiculous to lie here terrifying herself with fantasies. Sarah sat up and made herself reach out, her skin prickling with fear, anticipating sudden, tearing pain from the jaws of a rat.

But the rat existed only in her nightmare. Her hand found the lamp just where it should have been. The switch clicked back and forth between her fingers with a loud, empty sound. There was no light.

It had been many years since Sarah had been afraid of the dark, but that long-buried, nameless fear rose up to assail her now. The dark closed around her, menacing, suffocating. She tried not to imagine what dangers it might hide. She forced herself to stand up and walk away from the couch, towards the kitchen. The flashlight was there. She realized she had no idea what to do if a fuse had blown, but she was far too tense, now, to go back to sleep and wait to deal with it in the morning.

Sarah made her way slowly and carefully towards the kitchen, her whole body rigid with dread. At every step she expected to encounter something horrible—to run into a waiting human figure, or to step on something warm and alive. She scarcely knew which would be worse. The darkness was oppressive. Sarah stretched her arms out, trembling, and pushed her way through it.

At the doorway to the kitchen there was a light switch, and she groped for it eagerly. Her spirits fell again when it clicked emptily. It must be a fuse, then, and not merely a dead bulb. In the kitchen she experienced a few long, horrible seconds of running her hands over the clammy tiles beside the kitchen sink before she finally felt the comforting metal roundness of the flashlight. She held it close to her chest and switched it on.

Feeling safer already with the light in her hands, Sarah turned towards the back door. The yellow beam carved a path out of the darkness before her, illuminating a segment of linoleum and wall, and threw back the gleam of two eyes.

Two evil, golden eyes, set in a narrow head. Crouching before the door, barring her escape, was a huge, grey rat.

It wasn't the monstrous creature of her nightmare—it was no larger than a rat might be. And Sarah knew that she was awake. So the rat had to be real.

But real rats didn't have eyes like that, huge, glowing golden flames which dwarfed the small, pointed head. Rats didn't stare and compel attention with eyes that hypnotized. Sarah tried to look away and could not. She was trapped by those eyes—and the will behind them—just as in her dream. But this was far more horrible than her nightmare. This time, she could not wake up.

Sarah tried, tried desperately, to move. Any physical motion at all, however small, would be a release from this numbing paralysis. At last she managed to flutter her eyelids and then, with a feeling of triumph, to close her eyes. Saved, she thought. If she couldn't see the rat, she couldn't be trapped into staring into those dangerous eyes.

It was like cold, dirty water moving into her head. Sarah realized she couldn't breathe. She had to keep blowing air out through her nose, to expel the water, to keep from being suffocated. Her chest labored, and each breath required more energy, more struggle, more strength. She was weakening rapidly, feeling the filthy water catch at her lungs, and she wondered how long she could continue to fight for air.

Easier, much easier to stop. Had someone said that? The words seemed to ring in her ears, like kindly advice. Give in. Relax. Easier to give up. Easier to let go.

She continued to struggle, but she did not quite understand why. It was a dream, after all; only a dream. What happened in dreams didn't matter. She couldn't really drown in a dream—if she let go, let the water fill her lungs and bear her under, she would wake up. And her waking life would be so much easier. No more struggle. She didn't need air; she didn't need to breathe. Someone else would do it for her, while she slept undisturbed and peaceful. She had only to stop, to let go.

And still Sarah fought, breathing in and out, accomplishing each breath with greater struggle. She wasn't sure why she continued to fight—she supposed it was because the habit of breathing was so strong that she didn't want to give it up, even in a dream. Even though it would be so much easier, and she thought, more and more, of letting go.

But there was something else that bothered her. A small, distant pain. She couldn't isolate the feeling—to do so would have required too much effort, too much concentration, and she could not spare anything from her struggle for air. Like small, sharp teeth worrying at her flesh—something she was forgetting—something important—

The rat!

Sarah opened her eyes and saw the rat, still fixed in the beam of her flashlight. Had it moved closer? She couldn't be sure. Bitterness welled up inside her, a pain in her chest. She could breathe—she was in no danger of suffocation—that had all been a trick. The rat had made her think she could not breathe in order to distract her, to keep her from recognizing the real danger. And the real danger was in the rat itself. She felt its evil, its almost overpowering will, burning out of those eyes. It had nearly tricked her into giving in. It meant to destroy her. Sarah stared back at it, briefly free of the power of those hypnotic eyes, and she recognized her enemy. Self-preservation rose up inside her, strengthening her, and a feeling of hatred stronger than any she had ever known. She would not let herself be destroyed or used—she would kill the thing that had tried to kill her —she would smash it, burn it, crush it, cut its throat—

Crying out incoherently, Sarah hurled the flashlight at the rat, and heard the sound of metal striking the floor.

Darkness swallowed them both.

Chapter Five

"I won't!" Sarah mumbled.

The childish protest rang in her ears, as if she had been repeating it for hours. She looked around groggily, trying to understand where she was and what had happened. She was slumped on the kitchen linoleum. Her bare feet were so cold they ached. The grey light of very early morning filled the room.

Sarah squinted against the pounding in her head and struggled to her feet. She managed to reach the bathroom before she vomited. Then, bewildered and shivering uncontrollably, Sarah leaned against the side of the door and tried to think. She couldn't remember anything, not even what day it was. All she could cling to, through the painful fog that filled her head, was a knowledge of her own identity. And she clutched that as if even that last certainty might be snatched from her.

"Sarah," she whispered. "Me."

Who had tried to take that away from her?

A dim memory of struggle and pain surfaced and then sank again. Sank into cold, dirty water. Her stomach heaved and Sarah grabbed the doorframe and swallowed hard. She remembered drowning. Almost drowning.

She broke out into a light sweat, no longer cold, although she still shivered. She remembered the fires that had burned on the other side of the water. The eyes that had burned like fire, burned into her brain, almost consuming her.

Sarah moaned softly and closed her eyes, pressing a hand against her head. Pain pulsed through her body. She ached as if she had been beaten. But she had not been beaten. She had survived. She still lived. And now she had to rest. It was safe to rest now; she had fought long enough for now. That knowledge came from within her, and Sarah trusted it.

Safe now, she thought, staggering back to the couch. Safe to sleep. She wasn't ready yet to remember what she was safe from.

Knocking woke her, long hours later.

Sarah opened her eyes on daylight. The knocking persisted, and the sound made her shudder. The rat! It was the rat, she thought, within the walls, mocking her. She struggled to sit up, panting with terror, the blanket trapping her legs and slowing her.

"Sarah? Sarah, are you there?"

She heard the faint, faraway voice and recognized it as Beverly's. She relaxed, then, and unwound herself from the blanket. "Coming," she called. Her voice sounded cracked and strange in her ears. Despite the sleep, her body still ached and she felt weak and feverish.

"I was worried about you," Beverly said when Sarah opened the back door. "When you weren't in class—" She frowned, stepped forward and put her hands on Sarah's shoulders. "Are you all right? You look . . ."

Sarah shrugged Beverly's hands away, stepping back. "I was asleep."

"A nap?"

Sarah frowned. "What time is it?"

"Nearly three."

Sarah stared blankly, trying to comprehend. Why had she been asleep in the middle of the day? What had happened the night before? Something dreadful, which had weakened her and made her sick, but she couldn't exactly remember . . .

"Poor thing," Beverly said, smiling ruefully. "I woke you up. You go sit down and rest, and I'll make you some tea."

"Coffee," Sarah said. She had to clear her head; she had to remember.

"All right, coffee."

The sound of a truck in the yard behind her made Beverly turn around. "Looks like your bed has arrived," she said to Sarah.

"Oh," said Sarah. Her mind was a blank. The words made sense, but she didn't know how they related, how she was to respond.

"You poor baby," Beverly said. She laughed, but her laughter was a caress, not a mockery. She took Sarah by the shoulders again and walked her backwards. "You just lie back down and I'll take care of everything. I'll get you your coffee, and I'll show the men where to put your bed."

It was wonderful to give in, to relax, to let someone else take over. Like an obedient child, Sarah let Beverly sit her down on the couch. She sat there, her mind like an empty room, and listened to the sounds of activity from the back of the house.

But images pushed in at the edges of her mind, dimly recalled. Suffocation. Burning. Twin fires. Golden eyes. A rat—

Sarah opened her eyes and saw Beverly before her. "What *is* that," said Beverly. "On the bedroom floor?"

Sarah shook her head.

"Something painted on the floor," Beverly said.

Now she saw it; now she remembered.

"A rat," Sarah said, wondering. "I was up all night fighting a rat. It wasn't a dream. But I don't know *how*—"

Beverly's expression turned to one of alarm. With the palm of her hand she touched Sarah's cheeks and forehead. "You're coming home with me," she said.

Sarah tensed and drew back. "No."

"Come on, Sarah. You're sick. You need someone to look after you."

"I can't leave."

"Of course you can! Why not?"

Sarah shook her head, groping for the reason. She had to stay, she knew that much. Unfinished business. Someone waiting for her. She remembered something else. "The rat," she said. "It wasn't *just* a rat. It was something else, something much more powerful. And it was trying to kill me. Not kill me physically"—she tried to think of the right word, remembering the feeling of being suffocated—"but push me out, destroy my soul. But I hung on. I woke up this morning, I was lying on the kitchen floor, and I was sick."

"That's why you're coming home with me," Beverly said gently. "Because you're sick, and I can take care of you. I'll just get your shoes and we'll go."

Sarah shook her head, staring after her friend. She couldn't leave; she had to stay here. But then, through her confusion, she wondered why—and wondered if the reluctance to leave was even her own. Was it another trick, another trap? Her head ached so she could hardly think.

"Put these on," Beverly said. Obediently, Sarah accepted a pair of socks and her boots and began to pull them on. She would leave with Beverly, she decided. She had to think, to figure things out. But first she needed to rest—and she could not rest safely here, because the rat might come back for her. She yawned suddenly, hugely, and then smiled wanly at her friend. "I'm glad you came by," she said. "I guess I do need somebody to take care of me today."

Beverly helped Sarah to her feet and kept one arm around her as they walked to the door. "Nurse Beverly to the rescue," she said.

The next morning Sarah was herself again. The fever, confusion, pain and fear had all vanished in the night, and she ate breakfast ravenously, eager to get on with the day. She had lost Monday, and the thought of that made her feel anxious and pressed for time.

"Maybe you should take it easy today," Beverly said. "Just lie around the house and relax."

"I don't have time for that," Sarah said, spreading jam on an English muffin. "I have to pick up my telephone, go to the bank, do some grocery shopping, decide on my research topic for the Faulkner seminar, finish my paper on sexist language—"

"You're not going to do yourself any good if you just get sick again," Beverly said.

"I'm not going to get sick again," Sarah said. "I'm perfectly fine."

"No more nightmares?"

"Not a one. I dreamed it was summer, and you and Pete and I had a house on an island in the middle of Lake Travis. We got there by swimming through an underwater tunnel that no one else knew about."

Beverly smiled, and Sarah smiled back, swallowing the last of her eggs. She didn't want to talk about nightmares —she wanted to forget them. When Beverly had questioned her earlier about her experiences Sunday night, Sarah had pretended not to remember, and had quickly turned the subject. In fact, she remembered strange, unpleasant snatches of a nightmare about a rat with glowing eyes, a supernaturally powerful rat which she had struggled against for her very existence. She wanted to forget it. She remembered how seriously—probably the effect of the fever —she had taken that nightmare, and it embarrassed her to think of the things she had said to Beverly about it, her mad babblings about fighting a rat. But it was excusable—she had not been herself—she had been ill.

"I know what I wanted to ask you," Beverly said. Sarah met her eyes across the table. "That design painted on your bedroom floor—remember?"

Sarah nodded slowly. "Something else I need to do today. Buy some paint remover and clean it off."

"What *is* it?"

Sarah rose and began clearing away the dirty dishes. "It's called a pentacle. Magicians and witches use them in magic rituals."

"Ah," said Beverly. "So old weirdo, the one who used to rent the place, was a witch?"

"I suppose so."

"And used that pentacle—what? To talk to the devil?"

Sarah shrugged. "To conjure up spirits, I suppose."

"Leave those," Beverly said. "I'll wash them all later. I've got to get to class—come on, I'll drop you off. Do you suppose she was part of a coven?"

They went out the door together. "I doubt it," Sarah said. "She struck me as a more solitary type of loon."

Outside it was beautiful. The sky was a hard, bright blue and despite the heat of the sun there was a welcome crispness in the air, the faintest smell of autumn. Sarah breathed in deeply, feeling revived. She thought with pleasure of the trees around her house—soon the leaves would be turning brown and falling, and she could rake them into big piles and set them alight.

"I just hope she sent back whatever she conjured up," Beverly said as they walked across the parking lot together. "Let's hope there aren't any leftover spirits hanging around your house."

Her stomach lurched; fragments of nearly forgotten nightmare scratched at the back of her throat. Sarah opened her mouth, meaning to tell Beverly that she had changed her mind, that she couldn't, mustn't, go back to that house.

But Beverly, unaware, had already changed the subject. "That wasn't much of a norther we had the other night, but I guess summer's gone for good. I guess we won't get out to the lake again this year."

The moment passed, leaving Sarah feeling slightly disoriented. She grasped at Beverly's words to anchor herself. "The lake . . . yes . . . I told you about my dream?"

They had reached the car. Pausing before unlocking the door, Beverly turned to Sarah with a slightly puzzled smile. "Yes, you did—about an underwater tunnel at Lake Travis? You'd better not tell Pete—I'm sure there's probably something embarrassingly Freudian in that."

Sarah nodded and smiled mechanically. There was some other dream, she thought, confused. Some other dream she should be remembering . . . She was silent as Beverly drove, but after a few moments she stopped trying to puzzle out the lost memory and simply enjoyed the familiar sights of this east-west drive through Austin: the students and street-people and corner flower-sellers; the rows of ugly, functional apartment complexes alternating with gracefully aging, tree-shaded frame houses; the rolling green lawn behind chain-link fence of the state hospital.

And then, her favorite sight, the one she never tired of, as they rose up the overpass over the expressway: the hills. Just a glimpse, the gentle curve of green on the horizon, but it never failed to make her heart lift. The hills to the west of town where the Colorado River wound. They were a symbol of freedom to her. Sarah would never forget her first astonished, joyful discovery of them her first day in Austin six years before. After a lifetime spent on the flat Texas coast the hills of Austin were like a sight of heaven, as exciting and important to her as the facts of being away from home, on her own and enrolled at the university.

"This is it, isn't it?" Beverly asked.

"Yes, turn off here. It's not much of a driveway, I know . . ."

"Oh, this old car doesn't mind." Beverly steered skillfully off the street and behind Sarah's car. She shifted into park and turned to give Sarah a long, measuring look. "Promise me," she said. "If you start feeling the least bit sick, or tired, or even doubtful, you will either call me or come over."

"I'll be fine. I've got a bed now, and I'll pick up a phone today."

"But it won't be connected right away. Maybe you'd better stay with us until—"

"Bev, I'm *fine*. I've got tons of stuff to do, and I don't feel sick at all, really."

Beverly looked doubtful. "You're so isolated out here—"

"Okay," Sarah said hastily, feeling the morning slipping away from her. "If anything happens, if I get sick or have a bad dream, I'll come to you to make it better. You'd better go now, or you'll be late for class." She got out of the car as she was speaking, and closed the door firmly.

Beverly hesitated, as if she still had more advice to give, or another promise she wanted to extract, but finally she mimed a kiss and drove away.

Sarah turned towards the house and stopped short in surprise at the sight of a cat on the back steps. It was a nice-looking animal, a sleek calico, body curved gracefully as it washed one white paw. Sarah smiled at the picture it made: cat on wooden steps. It looked very much at home. She wondered if it planned to stay. She had never had a pet before. She continued to watch it as she approached the house, but it was utterly self-absorbed and did not look up from its grooming.

At the foot of the steps Sarah stopped again, and her breath caught in her throat with surprise. A small body lay on the ground a few inches from the bottom step: a dead rat.

The fur at the throat was matted with dried blood, and the small, nasty teeth were revealed in a final snarl.

She let out her breath in a long, slow sigh. It was dead. No more knockings within the walls, or beneath the bathtub; no more mocking scurrying sounds. She looked from the tiny corpse to the cat. "Good work!" she said, pleased. "Maybe I should keep you around, if you're looking for a new home."

At the sound of her voice, the cat finally stopped washing and turned its head to look at her.

Sarah went cold as she met that steady, malevolent gaze. Those hard, yellow eyes. She knew them. She remembered the rat's glowing eyes, and how they had locked with hers.

The cat leaped down from the step and stalked towards Sarah, tail switching back and forth. Sarah jumped back.

"Miaou?"

A plaintive cat-sound. It looked up at her with bright, inscrutable eyes. A cat's eyes. Yellow was a common color for cat's eyes.

Sarah managed a shaky laugh. She was being silly, letting her dream affect her so. She knew it was only a cat.

"Good cat," she said, looking down at the animal. She couldn't quite bring herself to touch it. "You killed that nasty old rat, didn't you? Now, how did you know that's just what I'd like? If you're looking for a job as rat-catcher, you've got it. But probably you already have a home—you look well-fed to me." As she spoke, she climbed the steps and fumbled with her keys, very aware that the cat was watching her intently. But, then, cats often stared. She knew that.

As she opened the door, the cat was suddenly right beside her, slipping inside the porch with rapid skill.

"Hey," Sarah said. "I didn't invite you in! If you want to stay in the cellar and catch rats, that's fine, but I don't need a house cat, thank you very much."

She looked down, and the animal looked up, and their eyes met. Golden, burning—they are like flames, Sarah thought. She broke the gaze by turning her head aside. She was breathing rapidly. I must not look, she thought. I must not let it trap me. Those flames will burn into my mind and consume me.

Her own thoughts appalled her. Was it the return of the fever? Was she crazy, to imagine some horrible connection between this cat and the demonic rat of her nightmare? No matter how she argued with herself, she could not reason away the visceral fear she felt, the fear that strung her nerves taut and made her keep her eyes averted. It was crazy, but she could not shake her conviction that the cat —standing very still now, head cocked to one side to gaze unblinkingly up at her—was dangerous.

Moving slowly and carefully, Sarah opened the door to the kitchen and slipped inside. The cat did not move, as if it understood any attempt would be foiled. Sarah had left the back door open, and she hoped the cat would soon leave the porch.

Inside, Sarah leaned against the solid kitchen door, feeling weak. Her sudden perspiration dried on her skin, and she shivered, chilled. Dazed, hardly knowing if she were awake or dreaming, Sarah wandered back to the living room and slumped onto the couch.

It was just a cat, she told herself. Cats often had yellow eyes. It was just the likeness of those eyes to the eyes of the rat in her dream which had disturbed her, stirring up scenes she didn't want to relive. Her own explanation did not convince her.

A low moaning interrupted her thoughts. Skin prickling, Sarah turned towards the front window. Through it she could see the cat, crouched on the porch railing on a level with the window, glaring balefully in at her.

Sarah stared back, waiting for it to move. But nothing happened. The cat went on moaning and staring. Its eyes seemed to expand, and she thought, distractedly, of the story of the tin soldier and the dog with eyes as big as saucers.

She must not look into them; it wasn't safe.

Making a great effort, Sarah managed to turn away from the window. She dropped back against the couch, breathing hard, feeling dizzy, as if she had done something far more strenuous than simply turn her head.

The cat had killed the rat, she thought.

But the rat wasn't dead.

The rat—or something which had been inside the rat

—lived on, now within the cat. Sarah had seen it staring out of those golden eyes. She knew, beyond possibility of doubt, because she had felt it clawing at the edges of her mind.

She remembered, now, what she had blocked out of her memory.

After the suffocation, after the drowning, after the pain, the rat had leaped at her in the darkness. Throwing her hands up to protect her face, Sarah had encountered two other hands which had seized her and thrown her to the floor. Someone or something—she had thought, in what little time she had to think, that it was a giant rat with human hands—had ridden astride her, legs in a painful vise around her hips, hands throttling her neck. Blood-red light had blazed before her eyes, but Sarah had not passed out. She had managed to pull the hands away, and wrestled to keep them away although she could not dislodge her assailant entirely. It was like wrestling with her own shadow: the attacker made no sound, and seemed to match her exactly in size and strength. Despite the sensation of the legs and hands which gripped her, Sarah could not feel any head or body. Perhaps her attacker had no body? Perhaps her attacker existed only in her mind, and she was wearing herself out by fighting herself?

At that thought, because she was exhausted already, Sarah stopped fighting abruptly and let herself go limp.

Her attacker vanished.

And then all Sarah's fears and exhaustion had been extinguished by a feeling of bliss.

It was a feeling she had experienced before, although not often, when she was with Brian, just after making love. A sense of being enhanced, of being joined. A dream of swimming slowly through a vast, sentient ocean. Not knowing or caring where her body ended and Brian's began, because they were both the same.

Sarah knew she was not alone, and she was glad. It was wonderful not to be alone. She could feel another presence close to her—more than close. It was with her, a part of her, beneath her skin.

At first, it was wonderful. A kind of ecstasy.

Then Sarah realized that she was standing, without any

memory of having done so. And she was walking across the room, feeling her legs move without willing them to. Sarah's hand, without Sarah's will, turned on the light, and then she could see. She felt as if she had been detached from her body and was floating slightly above and to the right of it. She watched herself walk through the rooms of the house and knew she was only a passenger—a passenger who could not even feel the seats, or the motions of travel. Only an observer.

The bliss was gone. Sarah felt nothing. Nothing but fear.

No, she said, but no mouth opened to pronounce the word. No. No voice spoke. No, no, no.

Her body moved back and forth erratically, jerkily. Arms swung back and forth. Head twitched on shoulders. Legs lost their strength, and let the body fall heavily to the floor.

Sarah, somewhere deep inside, could feel none of this, although she knew it was happening. She could still think, and she still had hope of regaining her body. If only she knew how to fight. How could she fight when she could not move?

Think.

As she had learned to do in the nightmares she had as a child, Sarah struggled to close her eyes. If she could close her eyes, she would know she was dreaming. Sarah concentrated all her strength on closing her eyes. Such a little thing to do; she had been doing it all her life. Suddenly everything went black. Did that mean her eyes were closed? Had she done that, or was it the other? Sarah opened her mouth. She felt the roaring darkness rush in. She couldn't breathe. She was choking on darkness, but she couldn't close her mouth even if it filled her—she had to breathe. She choked but went on trying to scream. If she could scream, she could expel the darkness. She screamed. And heard herself scream. And knew that she was herself, alone in her body again.

Sarah shuddered under the force of the memory. All night she had fought against that thing, her invisible assailant, the rat who wanted to kill her and take her body.

She had thought, by morning, that she had won because she was still alive, still alone in her body. But all she had won was a resting-spell. She had only survived. But so had her enemy, the thing that changed bodies like suits of clothes.

The rat was dead, but the spirit had survived and was inhabiting the body of a cat. Sarah was certain that it would attack her again—and she was not at all certain she could survive another round.

In a panic, she leaped to her feet. She had to get out, get far away from the house and the cat.

The cat was waiting on the back porch.

Sarah stopped just in time, her fingers curling around the big, old metal doorknob, and stared through the window in the door at the evil-eyed creature. Her panicked breathing rasped in her ears. How had it known what she would do? Could it read her mind? She knew that if she turned and ran to the front door, the cat could make it around the house and meet her there, attack her there.

Sarah whimpered softly to herself, closing her eyes and leaning against the door. She had to get out, somehow. She had to get away. Why had she come back at all? What sort of spell had the thing put on her, that she forgot about it as soon as she was away from the house?

This time she swore that she would remember, if only she could get away. She'd run and run and never look back . . . if only it would let her. But it was guarding her, a cat before a mousehole. Last time it had been a rat, but now she was the timid rodent.

Sarah struggled to conquer her fear and think. There had to be a way out, a way past the cat. There had to be a way of tricking it, or overpowering it. She opened her eyes and looked through the glass at the cat. It stared back quietly, unmoving, yellow eyes huge.

Sarah's skin crawled, and she could imagine the burning pain of raking claws, the piercing bite of sharp teeth as the cat leaped on her. She felt faint. She needed air, fresh air. She had to get out . . . her hand grasped the doorknob and began to turn it.

Her breath came out in a sudden hiss and she dropped her hold on the doorknob at the same moment as she tore her gaze away from the animal. She had forgotten the most dangerous thing about it—those eyes, and the power they had when she looked into them. It would hypnotize her if she wasn't careful; it would leap through her eyes into her brain.

Because it was her mind, far more than her body, that was in danger. Physically, the thing was only a cat, and Sarah knew that she was much bigger and stronger than a cat. Unless it had rabies, it couldn't do her much harm—not if she was quick and careful, and ran like hell for the safety of her car.

The idea of going outside, past the cat that waited for her, was still frightening, but it was far preferable to the idea of staying here, trapped in the house, waiting for whatever new horrors the darkness would bring.

She drew a long, deep breath. Then, slipping her purse over one shoulder, she took the broom from the corner and gripped it firmly. Then she opened the door.

At the first click of the knob the cat sprang forward. Sarah slammed the door immediately, and the cat backed away, shaking its head as if its whiskers had been pinched. Giving it no time to recover, Sarah opened the door again, and this time she slipped through and pulled it firmly shut behind her. She took the broom in both hands and held it warningly as the cat glared. The animal did not move, and it blocked her way to the outer door. Sarah shifted uneasily from one foot to the other, finding it a struggle to keep the cat in sight without being trapped into looking into those glaring yellow eyes. But although she kept expecting the cat to spring at her physically, it did not. It was not attacking, it was playing with her, daring her to make the first move. That idea annoyed Sarah, and stirred her to action. She lifted the broom up and brought it down in an arc, swatting the cat flatly against one side.

The cat let out a screech that set Sarah's teeth on edge, but the force of the blow swept the animal through the doorway and out onto the steps. Before it could regain its footing, Sarah had rushed through the door herself, slamming it behind her.

She stared down at the cat, only inches away from her now. Its back was arched and the tail swollen up like a balloon. It hissed, revealing dagger-sharp teeth and a pink-white tongue, and for one paralyzing moment Sarah was certain it would leap for her face. She closed her eyes, hands tightening on the broom, and said a mental prayer.

Nothing happened.

Sarah opened her eyes just in time to see the cat leap off the steps and bound around the side of the house, out of sight.

Setting the broom crossways against the door, Sarah walked to her car, feeling the fear and tension leave her body, swirling away like water down a drain.

Now, what was all *that* about, she wondered. It was only a cat, and she'd never been afraid of cats before. What sort of nightmare was it that had upset her so much? She touched her face and found it hot. Maybe she did have a fever. People with fevers often had strange dreams.

She looked back at the house and found that she still felt a strong aversion to going inside, although she couldn't remember exactly why. Bad dreams? An evil spirit? A cat? Images flickered through her mind but would not be pinned down for examination.

Finally, with an effort, Sarah pushed the whole problem out of her mind. She would think about it later—right now, she had things to do. She felt weak and shaky, and decided that a touch of flu might explain everything.

Sarah drove first to Dobie Mall, a shopping center in the base of a high-rise dormitory on the southwest edge of campus. There was a telephone office there, and she could save money by picking up a telephone and installing it herself.

Once she had done that—holding fast to her request for a standard telephone, refusing the charms of telephones hidden inside boxes or shaped like Mickey Mouse—Sarah crossed the street and wandered down that part of Guadalupe Street known as The Drag.

It was filled, as always in term time, with crowds of students. Sarah knew it might have been cheaper to do her shopping in one of the malls, or among the strips of discount stores in North Austin, but going to The Drag was a treat she gave herself. She felt comfortable there, at home wandering among the colorful crowds, her senses tickled by smells from the eggroll and barbecue stands, the music of street musicians, the vivid displays in shop windows and on the temporary stalls of vendors selling pottery, cheap clothing, wooden toys, jewelry and leather belts and bags. Sarah let herself be seduced by her favorite bookstore, emerging after half an hour's browsing with a package under her arm; she tried on rings she knew she couldn't buy; she ate lunch in a vegetarian cafe, one of the vantage points for people-watching; she paused to talk with a couple of acquaintances; and she even managed to buy a few of the things on her shopping list.

Sarah felt calm and relaxed as she drove home. Her mind was on her Faulkner seminar, and she was trying to think of something new to say about Southern Gothic as she parked the car behind her house. It wasn't until she had walked up the steps and into the kitchen that the horrible memories came back to her in a rush.

She knew despair, and impatience with her own foolishness, as she realized that she had walked right back into the trap.

Sarah turned, dropping the shopping bags she carried, and ran, not even closing the doors behind her, stumbling down the short flight of steps and just managing not to fall. She clutched the door handle on her car and stopped, heart racing. She swallowed hard, feeling the sweat of fear drying on her skin, and turned slowly and looked back at the house, feeling the fear dying away.

The old wooden door hung on its hinges, still swaying slightly in the breeze of her passing. Nothing waited for her there, Sarah told herself. No cat with glowing eyes, no evil, supernatural rat, no diabolical spirit. Because such things didn't exist.

She could remember, now, what she had been afraid of —she could recall quite clearly the thoughts and fears that had led to her earlier flight from the house. But she didn't believe in evil spirits, nor in witchcraft. She had always been certain that people who believed that demons possessed them were simply crazy. So did that mean she was crazy?

Two unsavory alternatives. Either she was crazy, or there was a demon in the house. Either way, Sarah knew she didn't want to go back in the house and risk a repetition of what had happened to her before. She was afraid to go into the house.

'Fraidy cat.

There had been a time when Sarah was the only kid in her neighborhood who dared to walk through the cemetery after dark. Who dared go up and look in the window of the witch house. But Sarah hadn't been afraid, then, because she didn't believe in ghosts or witches.

Did she now, a grown woman in broad daylight?

Depressed, frightened, and self-doubting, Sarah got back in the car. She could always spend the night with the Marchants again. But she knew neither of them would be home now, so she decided to go to the library where, if she could manage to concentrate, she might get some work done.

On campus she was lucky enough to find a parking space within a few blocks of the library. She had just switched off the engine when she caught a glimpse of a familiar figure, and her heart played yo-yo. Yes, it was Brian, and that slight figure by his side must be Melanie. She had dark hair nearly to her waist, and a little pointed face that gazed adoringly up at Brian. Not wanting to have to speak to them, Sarah stayed in the car.

As Sarah watched, a big black bird—one of the grackles which infested the campus—suddenly left its perch on a parking meter. Giving its characteristic, water-gurgling cry, it flapped heavily and clumsily away, about on a level with Melanie's head, although nowhere near her. But too near, obviously, for Melanie, who let out a wild cry, dropped her books, and threw her arms protectively over her head.

Brian responded immediately, pulling Melanie into the shelter of his arms. Sarah could see his lips moving and knew he must be speaking to her soothingly.

I could scream all night and you'd never come rescue me, Sarah thought. Her stomach churned bitterly, and then the misery she felt turned to self-loathing. Was that it? A trick played by her subconscious? This sudden fear of evil spirits a ploy to make her weak and trembling . . . and in desperate need of Brian? If her problems were even bigger than Melanie's, would he come rushing back to save her from herself?

No.

Anger rose in her, anger at herself and at Brian, and at the demonic nightmares which had been tormenting her.

She wouldn't give in. She wouldn't crack up, and she wouldn't run away. If Brian didn't want her as she was, she would learn to live without him. She didn't *need* him, and she was proud of it. She refused to cringe and crawl and cry for anyone. She was going home.

Anger was a fine thing, invigorating, powerful, more intoxicating than drink. It fueled her all the way back to the house and kept her from stopping to think about it. Sarah didn't see the cat anywhere as she stomped up the steps and into the kitchen, slamming the door behind her.

"All right," she said loudly. "I'm back. I'm not scared of you."

Behind her, the telephone rang.

Sarah's throat tightened with panic, although she didn't understand why, and she whirled around. Then she realized: the telephone was still unconnected. Not only that, but it was not even plugged in. It was still inside the bright orange and brown plastic bag where she had dropped it on the kitchen floor.

It rang again.

As she stared at it, she saw the bag vibrate slightly with the sound. Sarah moistened her lips and looked around. Then she bent down and took the telephone out of the bag. She stared at the bright red plastic, feeling the vibrations shake her hand, hearing the bell ring. How could this be a delusion, when it felt so real? Finally, she lifted the receiver and held it to her ear. She did not speak. A distant, windy, rushing sound met her ear. And then a voice.

"Sarah."

The hairs stood up on the back of her neck. It was a deep, dead voice, without emotion, yet not mechanical.

"Sarah."

Sarah could not reply. She could scarcely breathe.

"I am so glad you have come back, Sarah. I have been waiting for you."

"Who are you?"

"You know who I am. You have felt me inside you. You have come back for me, to give yourself up to me."

"I have not," Sarah said loudly. "You can't have me."

"I can. I shall. I will. One way or another, Sarah, I will have you."

The intimacy of that inhuman voice, buzzing in her ear, was unbearable. Sarah slammed the receiver back into the cradle, shuddering violently. Then she put the telephone down on the floor and stared at it, waiting, almost daring it to ring again. But nothing happened.

She couldn't stop shaking. The sound of that dreadful voice in her ear . . . She wanted to run away. But although she was more frightened than she had ever been in her life, she was also as angry as she had ever been. She was damned if she would let that thing, whatever it was, drive her out of her house. She had managed to hold on to her self throughout its monstrous attacks, and she would go on doing so until it gave up.

Suddenly she swooped down and picked up the receiver again.

"*You're* scared," she said loudly into it. "You know you've met your match . . . so you're just trying to scare me off. Well, I'm not leaving. I'll make you leave instead!"

The telephone was dead plastic in her hand: there was nothing there at all. A little embarrassed by her outburst, Sarah put the receiver gently back. Then she found the jack in the wall by the bedroom door, and plugged the telephone in. If it rang now, she thought, it would seem more normal.

Sarah wondered what she should do. She was primed and ready for battle, the adrenaline pumping away, and she didn't know what to do with so much energy in the suddenly still and empty house.

Then, through the door, Sarah caught sight of the figure painted on the bedroom floor, and remembered that she had bought a jar of paint remover. A good first step towards exorcising the house might be to erase this mocking reminder. She settled down on the floor and began to scrub at the paint fiercely.

It took nearly two hours, but Sarah finally erased the design. When she stood to appraise her work, she became aware of the ache at the back of her neck, the soreness in her arms, the stiffness of her legs. She switched on the overhead light, realizing for the first time that the room had grown dark with the onset of evening. It was time for dinner, time to go out . . .

Sarah felt a rush of loneliness that almost overwhelmed her. She was not going out; she had no one to spend her evening with. The thought of cooking for herself and eating a meal alone took away her appetite. She missed Brian acutely. She didn't want to go out, she didn't want conversation, or sex, or comfort, or encouragement—all she wanted was his physical presence. She wanted the comfort of habit and routine, another presence in the house from whom she could draw wordless, emotional support. It was that very aspect of living with Brian that she had never appreciated, that she had struggled to pull away from.

Sarah felt heavy and slow, hardly capable of moving at all. She went to the new, still unmade bed, and stretched out on it. Her thoughts marched leadenly down a familiar trail. Brian, she had lost Brian, and it had been her own fault. She had driven him away. She had been afraid of needing him, afraid of admitting her need for him, afraid of letting him get too close. She had been utterly preoccupied by her own needs and had not considered Brian's. If she could have forgotten herself, and given instead of always taken, maybe she wouldn't have lost Brian. She should have lost herself, instead. Maybe it wasn't too late. She could still give up, let go . . . It was so nice to drift and forget, so nice to stop thinking and simply give in . . .

Then she felt the touch of the claw beneath the velvety fur, and the shock brought her sharply out of the trance she had nearly fallen into. She sat up on the edge of the bed, trembling convulsively. She knew that mental touch, she knew she wasn't alone. Most horrible: those thoughts had not been her own.

Feeling hunted, Sarah looked nervously around the room. The bare floorboards gleamed slightly under the harsh glare of the overhead light. The windows were black mirrors, throwing her dim reflection back at her so that her own movements made her flinch in terror. The night had crept up and trapped her unaware.

Sarah leaped to her feet and looked around wildly for her purse and keys. Her blood pounded with the imperative to get out, to escape. She hurried into the kitchen and saw two blazing yellow eyes in the black window-glass above the sink.

She screamed, jumping back. Through her terror she made out the shape of a cat around the yellow eyes, and realized that the animal was clinging to a tree outside the kitchen window.

Then she was angry. It was playing with her, she realized. Patting a sheathed paw against her mind, teasing, testing for weak spots. Trying to lull her, then trying to scare her, ready to pounce when she made the wrong move.

"I'm not leaving," Sarah said loudly, staring back at the cat. "Damn you, do you think you can scare me out of my own house? I'm staying."

She looked directly into the animal's eyes as she spoke, and as she did so she became aware of the presence she had earlier sensed in her mind. The recognition was like a faint electric shock. She tried to turn her eyes away and could not. She realized that she was caught by the creature's gaze, that some force as real as an electric current linked them together along the line of sight. A greedy, powerful presence pushed at her, entering through her eyes. Give in, it commanded, give in and let me in. Just try to get away from me now. She felt it crowding her like some horrible, aggressive stranger. Frightened, she tried to pull away, and her fear grew when she realized that she could not, she could not detach her gaze or move to escape.

So she pushed back. It was the only thing to do, aside from giving in. She forced her own will, her own strong sense of herself as an individual, back at the usurping spirit. Get out, she thought furiously. Get away from me; get back; get away. And she *pushed*.

She felt it squirm. The cat blinked, then ducked below the window. Sarah could hear it scrabbling down the tree. She laughed out loud, momentarily giddy with the sense of victory, and relief. No, she wouldn't leave. She would stay here, and fight, and win.

As she made a cup of coffee and a sandwich for her revived appetite, Sarah remained wary, listening to the small sounds of the night outside. She didn't dare relax.

A few minutes later, seated on the couch in the living room, the electric heater plugged in and pulled close, Sarah recognized a pattern in the sounds she was hearing: the crackling in the leaves, the tread on the rooftop, the light bump against the window. There was never anything there when she looked, but she knew it was the cat, stalking the house, looking for weaknesses, seeking a point of entry. Its persistence kept her on edge.

But despite her nerves, Sarah realized she was tired. Her eyes were hot and weary, and whenever she tried to read, the words blurred in front of her. She was yawning. She had to sleep. If she didn't lie down, she would pass out sitting up, she thought dazedly, setting aside her cup and book and pulling off her boots. She couldn't think why she was so tired . . . she couldn't think anything at all . . . she could hardly keep her eyes open. Sarah stretched out on the couch, telling herself it was only for a minute, and it was like falling backwards into a pool of black water. Sarah was asleep before she had time to think about it.

There was a loud, rumbling sound somewhere nearby —so close and so loud that her whole body vibrated with it. Not an alarming sound, but distracting. She couldn't sleep with it going on. Sarah opened her eyes and saw the cat. It was sitting heavily on her chest, purring loudly.

She tried to sit up, but the cat was much too big. It had not been nearly so large when it was outside, she thought confusedly. She hadn't realized what an enormous animal it was. And heavy. She could hardly breathe with the weight of it.

She tried to move her arms, to knock the cat aside, but her arms seemed paralyzed, as did her legs. She tried to arch her back and dislodge the cat that way, but she simply was not strong enough. She could only move up and down slightly, ineffectually, until she was drenched with sweat and heaving with effort, and the cat purred on, undisturbed. It seemed to grow heavier by the minute, or perhaps her exertions made it harder for her to breathe. The pressure in her chest was becoming painful.

The cat looked down at her complacently. A demonic intelligence stared out of those disturbingly brilliant eyes. The eyes—of course, the eyes! She remembered now that it was the eyes she had to beware of—the pressure on her chest was unimportant, perhaps even an illusion. But it might kill her with its eyes if she wasn't careful.

Making a tremendous effort, Sarah turned her head to one side.

Instantly, there was only darkness.

The weight had vanished from her chest, and the sound of purring lingered only in echo. She felt weak and sore when she breathed in, but she could move again.

Slowly, Sarah sat up. She heard a noise on the roof and knew the cat was out there, still prowling.

She sighed, enjoying the relief of breathing freely. Only a dream. She put her hand out for the lamp on the end table. But instead of cool metal, her groping fingers met warm fur.

Sarah cried out, snatching her hand back, and jumped to her feet. Her heart pounded furiously and she could not think, but she forced herself to move through the blackness to the front door, where her fingers found the light switch. When the ceiling light came on she saw, sitting on the couch in the precise spot where she had just been, the calico cat with huge yellow eyes. It stared at her, unblinking.

Sarah stared back. This was no dream. She was awake this time, and the cat was in the house.

Well, she would make it go out again. She looked around for something useful, wishing for heavy gloves, a net, a weapon. But all she saw was the television set, pillows, her shoes, books. She took up a heavy volume—*The Poetry of the Victorian Period*—and hefted it warningly, watching the cat for some sign that it might attack.

The cat began to clean itself, one leg cocked and tongue lapping neatly at its nether parts, for all the world like any ordinary cat.

But it was now, while the cat appeared to be so ordinary and self-absorbed, that Sarah felt it stalking her. She felt as if it were patting gently around the edges of her mind, seeking her weaknesses, pawing through her thoughts. The sense of invasion was so powerful that for a moment Sarah thought she would be ill.

Sarah shook with the effort of controlling herself, but managed to hold her ground. She thought hatred and refusal, hurling her thoughts like weapons at the cat-thing.

She was determined, this time, to do more than merely hold out against the invader. She would not merely survive; she would triumph. She wanted to defeat this thing that threatened her, to destroy it, to send it back to whatever hell had let it loose.

It left her mind so suddenly that Sarah gasped, feeling as if a cold wind had swept through her. Then she became aware of a new danger. There was someone else in the house.

She caught just a glimpse of him, a man standing in the next room. Almost before she had time to be afraid, Sarah had recognized him. Brian stepped towards her, out of darkness into the light. He was smiling diffidently and gazing at her with a look she recognized, intense, direct, and loving.

"Brian," she said, amazed. She felt happiness like a slow, steady warmth, filling her. Everything was going to be all right.

But Brian was no longer there.

Startled, Sarah jerked her head around, facing the couch again. The cat, too, had vanished. Was she dreaming?

The light went out. But there was something wrong with the darkness, Sarah realized. It was absolute. The window glass might have turned to rock, letting no light pass through—there should have been at least a yellow glow from the streetlamp on the corner, not this muffling, all-embracing dark. Then, in front of her, Sarah saw two small yellow lights flash and begin to glow. They might have been eyes, she thought: two glowing cat eyes without the face.

At that thought, she turned her eyes aside, afraid to look directly into the light. She backed away, but not far, crippled by the terrible fear that the darkness would swallow her like a gigantic mouth. She wrapped her arms around herself and held on tight, hoping she would be safe if she kept still.

From out of the darkness a deep, empty voice spoke. "I could keep you here forever, playing with you. Let us have an end to games. Let us reach an agreement. I will give you what *you* want, and you must give me what *I* want."

"And what's that?" Sarah asked harshly. "My body? My soul?"

It laughed.

Sarah clenched her teeth and shut her eyes, wishing she could shut her ears against the horrible, scraping sound.

"You have put up a respectable fight," it said. "You are braver than most, and with a strong will. I admire your spirit, and I would like to reward you."

"Then go away," Sarah said. "Vanish. That's how to reward me. Go back to hell."

Again that awful laughter.

"I prefer this earth to any hell, thank you. And I need a body to enjoy it. Animal forms are plentiful, and easy to take, but they are limited. I need a human body. All you must do, on your side of the bargain, is to supply me with one. Just bring someone here, and I will do the rest."

"Forget it," Sarah said. "No way will I help you."

"But I can give you whatever you want, whatever you most desire. Your lover. I can tell you how to win him back."

Rage bubbled up, almost burning away Sarah's fear. "NO!" she shouted furiously. "I don't believe you. I won't help you, go away!"

"I will go when you have brought me my body."

"I'll never help you."

The temperature of the room dropped several degrees, and Sarah shivered.

"Then I shall have *you*, Sarah. I will have a human form, with or without your consent. If you want to save yourself, bring me another victim."

"You can't," Sarah cried, although there was no conviction, only bravado in her words. "You've already tried, and you couldn't. I'm too strong for you—you know that's true, so you're trying to bribe me now."

There was a terrible stench in the air. Sarah gagged and tried not to breathe through her nose. Then she realized she could not breathe at all, for the air had turned as thick as mud. It was filling her mouth, and she was blind, she was dying . . .

She was lying on the floor, still blind, but breathing. She sucked in the sweet, clean air greedily.

"You have not tested my limits yet," said the voice. "You do not know how powerful I am, nor how long I have been waiting, how long I *will* wait to have what I want. You cannot hope to fight me off forever. I grow stronger while you grow weaker. It is only a matter of time. If you would save yourself, get out. But remember that you can have whatever you want if only you help me. Think about it. I will be waiting."

Then there was silence. The darkness lifted, and became normal night. The oppressive atmosphere was gone. A faint beam from the corner streetlamp filtered into the room, and Sarah could hear the distant rush of the highway and the sound of the wind in the dry leaves.

Chapter Six

"She's a witch," Sarah said. "She conjured up a demon, asked him something, and in return gave him *me*. I was supposed to be the payment in blood, only I turned out to be stronger than they had expected." She stifled a yawn and leaned back, sinking a little more deeply into the Marchants' large, overstuffed couch. Earlier, she had been half-wild, pounding on the door, waking Pete and Beverly and insisting that they listen to her story. But now, having told it all, Sarah felt relaxed, even ready to sleep. Sharing was such a relief.

She looked from Beverly's face—pale, wide-eyed, and framed by sleep-mussed hair—to Pete's faintly sad, serious one. She laughed softly, not amused but touched.

"All right," she said. "I'm crazy. I've gone around the bend. Thwarted love has driven me mad."

"Is that what *you* think?" Pete asked quietly.

Sarah made a face at him, but before she could answer, Beverly spoke.

"I saw that pentagram-thing on the floor. Whoever went to the trouble of painting it didn't do it just for decoration. And Sarah said before that there was something very strange about what's-her-name—Valerie."

Pete nodded acceptingly. "It's possible that Valerie *is* a practicing witch. Austin is full of people like that."

"Nuts," said Sarah. "That's what you mean. The people exist, but not the things they believe in. It isn't *Valerie* who has been bothering me, but this demon of hers. Do you believe in demons, and demonic possession?"

"I believe that something happened to you," Pete replied. "I don't know how to define it, but I'm not denying the validity of your experience."

"Thanks a lot. I don't need you humoring me . . . what I need to know is, am I crazy? I'm hearing things, seeing things, talking to a demon . . . I don't even believe in demons! But this one . . . it's too real to deny. I need someone else to tell me what's real and what isn't—am I crazy or not—and what should I *do*?"

Beverly moved closer to Sarah on the couch and took her hand. Pete sighed and looked directly into her eyes. "Move out of the house," he said flatly.

"Then you believe it *is* haunted?"

"Is that important? I don't know. I don't believe in demons, but what I believe isn't important. Magic works whether you believe in it or not. People do die of curses, even today. People are possessed by demons, or think they are, which amounts to the same thing. The results are the same, whether demons exist or not. I've read plenty of case histories, and I don't think there's any question but that these experiences are real."

Sarah frowned. "But you're talking about religious people, or primitives. I've read studies of witches and sorcerers in believing societies, too. But why should that affect me? Valerie, okay, she wanted to believe. She called up her demon. But I just stumbled onto this; I was her random choice for victim. I wasn't expecting anything like this; I wasn't raised to believe in demons."

"Not consciously," Pete said. He reached for his tea cup and found it empty.

"I'll make some more tea," Beverly said softly, leaping up. "Go on."

Pete nodded. "Subconsciously is another story. The clues were all there for you. You noticed Valerie's strangeness, how eager she was that you rent the house. She impressed you in a strongly negative way. Then, when you found the pentacle on the bedroom floor and a dead cat in the cellar, a picture formed in your mind of Valerie as a witch. You imagined her performing violent, magical rituals. Expectations were planted."

"So you're saying that my subconscious took a few clues and wove me this whole fantasy experience?"

"No, not at all. I'm just pointing out that if magic works because of shared expectations, because of small clues not immediately obvious to the outsider, then you had those clues to prepare you—and that perhaps on a subconscious level you *do* believe, despite all your intellectual rationalizations."

Sarah thought of things she had read: an Australian aborigine dying because a bone was pointed at him; a woman feeling pains because her enemy poked pins in an image; Aleister Crowley making people respond to him by an act of will; high school covens claiming credit for accidents and illnesses. She thought of all the books she had read, all the movies she had seen. Her mind was well-stocked with detail. Whether or not she wanted to believe in them, the images were there in her mind, and perhaps that very fact made her susceptible. She looked at Pete. "But what does it mean? Is there a real demon, or is it just my imagination?"

Pete shook his head. "It won't go away because you decide it's imaginary. Whatever it is, it's serious, and you have to deal with it seriously."

Beverly came back into the room with a pot of tea and refilled the cups on the coffee table. She sat down next to Sarah again and looked at her husband.

Pete stared into his steaming cup and then looked up at Sarah, a tentative expression on his face.

"What if I . . . why not let me stay a night in the house and see what happens?"

Beverly let out a small cry.

Sarah tensed. "Pete, no!" She bit her lip. "Don't you see? That's what it wants. That's what it asked me for—a new victim."

"You don't think I could fight it off as you did?"

Sarah shrugged, then shook her head. "Look, don't get

offended. Maybe you could, maybe you couldn't. I don't know. Maybe being warned would help you, or it might make you more vulnerable. But even if you survived —Pete, you don't know what it's like, or you'd never suggest such a thing. It's horrible, feeling that thing inside . . . feeling it clawing at your mind . . . I've never been so sick, so terrified, in so much pain . . . Believe me, you don't want to go through that."

"It wouldn't prove anything, you know," Pete said, in a too-casual voice. "Even if nothing happened to me. That wouldn't mean that you were wrong, or crazy."

Sarah expelled her breath in a sharp burst. "Do you think I'm afraid of *that*? Do you think it's selfishness? Pete, I'd love for you to prove me wrong. I'd be happy to know I was hallucinating. But that's *not* what I'm afraid of. I'm afraid that something would happen to you. I'm afraid . . ."

"He's not going," Beverly said flatly. "I won't let him."

Pete shrugged, the corners of his mouth twisting slightly down.

In a moment he'll be pouting, Sarah thought, half amused and half dismayed. "Pete," she said gently. "What good would it do?"

She saw him relax; the moment of childishness past, he looked at her openly and said, "None, I guess. I'm just jealous of your experience. After reading about these things, I'd love to have an experience of my own. I'd like to talk to your demon myself. But I don't suppose I could. I'm too interested, and for the wrong reasons. I'm too skeptical."

Sarah looked at her watch and winced at the time. Four a.m., and she'd had hardly any sleep. No wonder she was exhausted, and ready to snap at Pete for his selfishness.

"It's not a game, Peter," Beverly said low-voiced. "Sarah needs help."

Pete nodded. He, too, looked weary. He picked up his cup and sipped the hot, black tea. "You want my advice? Get out of that house. Don't go back. Find another place to live."

Sarah frowned. "Just . . . run away from it?"

"Why not?"

"But what if . . . what if that doesn't work? What if it *is* only in my mind? What if I take it with me wherever I go?"

"There's no reason to think you will. It's the obvious thing to do—at least, the first thing. You've only had trouble when you were in the house. So stay away from the house."

"You can stay with us," Beverly said. "I'll help you look for a new place."

"I don't want to move again," Sarah said.

"Of course you don't," Pete said gently. "But you don't want to stay there."

Sarah nodded her head hard. "Yes I do. I *do* want to stay."

"Why?"

She sighed and held up her fingers to enumerate. "It's incredibly cheap. I've just moved in and gotten settled. I like having so much room to myself."

He cut her off. "That's not the point. None of that has anything to do with what has happened."

She glared at him. "All right, you tell me why I should move."

"Sarah. Come on. What have we been talking about? Why did you come banging on our door in the middle of the night?" He met her glare with a steady, reproachful look. Sarah sank back on the couch, feeling a little ashamed.

"I guess I want you to talk me out of it," she said quietly. "I want you to tell me I'm letting my imagination run away with me, and that if I go home believing that, everything will be all right." She plucked idly at the cushion beside her. "But you can't, and it won't be. But there has to be something I can do, and I have to find it. I *can't* move out."

"Why not?" Beverly demanded. "You're safe here, you know you are. If you stay away from there—"

"Listen. Either that thing that attacked me is real, or it's not. Either it has some objective reality, or it's all in my mind. If it is just a creation of my mind, some sort of . . . schizophrenic manifestation, say . . . then leaving the house will make no difference to it or to me. It will still be with me—my problems will still be with me, in my mind. And I'll still have to deal with it, somehow, sooner or later.

It won't matter where I move to, because you can't run away from your own mind.

"But if this thing is real—and that's the assumption I'm going on now—then I *can* run away from it. I can leave it behind in the house, just as I did tonight. If there is a demon in that house, it is still there. And when someone new comes through the door, when someone new moves in, it will attack. And I can't be responsible for that. I can't run away and let some innocent person be destroyed without even warning them—"

"Warning them would probably be the wrong thing to do," Pete said. "You might just make trouble, by planting the suggestion. Someone else might be totally unaffected as long as they had no reason to expect anything unusual. There are haunted houses, you know—supposedly haunted houses, anyway—where nothing happens for years, but where certain people, certain families, will stir up the forces that had been sleeping before. I'm not saying that you imagined the demon, but you might have been more receptive to it—in a way, Valerie prepared you for it. You had a strong, negative response to her, and then when you found the pentacle, you were receptive to thoughts of demons and magic."

"In other words, it's all in my mind," Sarah said wearily.

"No. I'm not saying that. But I thought we agreed that when magic works it's because of shared expectations. Your demon is *real*, but it doesn't have an objective, physical reality. Someone else could probably coexist in the same house with it, never suspecting anything other-worldly."

"We don't know that," Sarah said.

"No, but it's logical . . . And you can't hold yourself responsible for anything that *might* happen to anyone who moves in after you're gone. You've got to look out for yourself. It's not your house—you can't know what will happen—you can't take on that responsibility—"

"But I *am* responsible," Sarah said. "I have to be. There's no one else who can be. Valerie may have let it loose on the world, but I'm responsible for what happens next, because I know about it, and I know what might happen. It's not just the life of the next person to move in there I have to worry about, because if the demon manages to get a human form, who knows what it might do, what horrors—I can't wash my hands of it. I can't run away. That's what it's counting on. It wants someone else to live in that house so it can try again, and succeed where it failed with me. If I went away, knowing that, I'd be just as responsible for the results as I would be if I saw a rabid dog and didn't tell anyone, but left it to bite the next unsuspecting person who came along."

"Do you think telling people would help?" Pete asked. "What do you plan to do, call your landlord about it?"

"I don't expect anyone would believe me," Sarah said. "You two, maybe, because you're my friends and you're receptive to bizarre ideas . . . I can imagine what my landlady would say if I went to her with some crazy story about an evil spirit. I don't imagine she would leave the house empty at my request. Anyway, that's not enough. This thing has got to be destroyed. There must be some way of destroying it."

"You could call an exorcist," Beverly suggested.

Sarah shrugged. "Well, maybe, but the idea gives me shivers. I can just imagine some poor innocent priest getting savaged by that thing—maybe if I was religious myself I'd believe in the power of prayer, but as it is—"

"We just don't know what the rules are," Pete said. "Still, there must be things we could try, old spells in ancient books or something."

"We?"

He grinned. "As if I'd let you fight it alone! You need reinforcements. Maybe we could recruit some more friends . . ."

"Pete, it isn't a game," Beverly said again.

"I'm serious," Pete said, looking steadily at Sarah. "I want to help. Many hands make light work, and all that. I can help you research, if nothing else. I once took a course on magic and religion from Dr. Fischer—you know, the head of the anthro department? He's something of an expert on magic rituals, so it might make sense to talk to him. I don't know how much he believes in them, but he can certainly rattle off some spells. And while we're doing all this, I think you should stay away from the house. Stay with us, just until you have a plan of action."

Sarah nodded. "Yes, I . . . don't really like the idea of going back there just yet. But I'm sure we'll come up with something. There has to be a way to send it back, or destroy it. There have to be rules in magic like everything else. And if Valerie—who frankly didn't strike me as being all there —could figure out the way to call up a demon, I'm sure we can figure out the way to vanquish it."

"Why not ask Valerie what she did?" Beverly suggested.

Sarah stared at her. A grin dawned on her face, and she slowly nodded. "That's it," she said. "That's exactly what I'll do. I'll find Valerie and make her tell me."

Chapter Seven

But how to find Valerie?

Sarah didn't know how to begin. She didn't even know Valerie's last name.

Waking Thursday, still at the Marchants' apartment, Sarah thought of her landlady, Mrs. Owens, and the scrap of paper Valerie had given her. She retrieved it from the blue-jean pocket where it had been since she took it from Valerie's fingers. She recognized the name of the street; it wasn't far from her own house. She might as well stop by, since she would be in the neighborhood.

A cold wind was blowing and the sky was overcast. Sarah zipped up the front of her jacket and hurried through the rows of parked cars to her own. She felt the beginning of a dull depression and wished Beverly had been free to spend the day with her. Company might cheer her and keep her thoughts from circling hopelessly back to Brian. She tried, as she drove, to concentrate on the immediate problem, but the depression was already spreading, tingeing every avenue of thought with its greyness. She would not find Valerie. Even if she found her, Valerie would be unwilling or unable to help. After all, Valerie had fled the house after meddling in forces beyond her control. She had been able to save her own skin, but she couldn't vanquish the demon she had summoned.

Mrs. Owens' house was on a short street that ended abruptly, a ditch and a high wire fence separating it from the expressway. It was the last house on the street, covered in pale green aluminum siding, with white shutters framing the curtained front windows. The small, flat lawn was littered with the big leaves of a slippery elm and the smaller brown curls of a young ash. A car the color of tomato soup was in the driveway.

As she parked her car and got out on the street, Sarah felt uncomfortably as if she were being watched. But when she looked around she could see no one. The windows of Mrs. Owens' house presented her with the blank, cream-colored backs of long draperies. She stared hard at them, but they did not stir to reveal the presence of a watcher.

Listening to the doorbell, Sarah did not believe it rang through an empty house. There was someone inside, she thought. She could feel an intangible presence. But no one came to the door.

Finally, Sarah turned away. She had taken only a few steps towards the street when she heard the soft but unmistakable sound of a door being opened. She turned.

There was no one there. But now the door was slightly ajar, as if a breeze had pushed it.

Sarah frowned and looked around, almost expecting someone to tell her what to do. But there was no one in sight; only the open door waiting for her decision.

Wondering what she would say if challenged, Sarah stepped forward and pushed the door wide.

"Mrs. Owens?"

Sarah found herself in a small foyer which opened on one side into a living room, and onto a narrow hallway on the other. From the end of the hallway came a faint sound.

Sarah swallowed hard. She could not place the noise, which was soft and uncertain, but she knew she had heard something. She said, more loudly, "Mrs. Owens?"

There was no answer. By now, Sarah scarcely expected one. Her whole body prickled and crawled with unease, but she felt committed to going on, having come this far. She made herself step into the dim hallway and walk in the direction of the sound.

Doors opened off the hallway on either side, and Sarah glanced into each one as she approached: a bedroom, a bathroom, a sewing room, all empty and tidy and still. The last door on the right was closed. Sarah stared at the painted white wood and the glass doorknob. She raised her hand, hesitated; then raised it higher, and finally knocked.

"Mrs. Owens? Are you in there? Are you all right?"

She had come too far to go back. Her hand closed around the fluted glass knob, held tightly, then turned it.

The door opened on a white-walled bedroom with short, flowered curtains at the window and a bed with matching flower-print spread. Beside the bed, flat on the powder-blue rug, was a woman in a pale yellow dress. She lay on her back, her white hair making a halo around her head. The look on her face was one of mute, uncomprehending terror. Her bright blue eyes met Sarah's, and her lips moved, but she made no sound.

Sarah crouched beside her on the floor. "Can you speak? Can you move?"

The muscles of the woman's face contorted, as if she were struggling to scream. Her eyes conveyed an intense appeal. Sarah touched her shoulder. "All right. Take it easy. I'm going to call a doctor."

The front door slammed jarringly, and Sarah jumped up and hurried into the hall. "Who's there?"

She saw no one and heard no other sound, and when she opened the front door and looked out, there was no one in sight. The sky had grown darker, and there was a wind.

Sarah stepped back into the house and closed the door gently. Her throat was dry and her heart pounded. She went back to the bedroom hardly knowing what to expect. But nothing had changed: the white-haired woman still lay on the floor. Sarah tried to smile, hoping her expression was comforting. There was a telephone on the bedside table, and Sarah used it to call the emergency ambulance number which was given on a decal stuck to the receiver.

After the paramedics had taken the old woman away, and after Sarah had given her story to a sympathetic young policeman, she stood beside her car and debated what to do next. She had come to a dead end, no closer to Valerie than before. The only idea she could come up with was to wander around the campus in hopes of meeting her by accident—and that could take forever. Valerie might well be keeping out of her way deliberately.

Sarah looked around uneasily. The feeling of eyes watching her was not paranoia this time, she thought. She felt very conspicuous, standing in the street in the lull that followed the departure of an ambulance. Finally she got back into her car, deciding to go to the library, where at least she could work.

But at the corner of Jefferson and West 35th, Sarah took the wrong turn, realizing what she had done a few seconds later as she approached the expressway overpass. She grimaced at the mistake. It was her subconscious again, she thought—first warning her away from the house and then drawing her back.

And yet she wasn't sorry she had taken the wrong turn. Her pulse speeded up at the thought of going back to the house, and it wasn't fear she felt, but a more pleasurable anticipation. She felt a perverse desire to challenge the thing that had driven her away, to test herself against it in the same way that, as a child, she had dared herself again and again to do the things that frightened her most, deriving pleasure both from the fear and the conquering of it.

I won't go into the house, she thought. I'll just have a look at it. She turned the corner and drove towards the house.

There was a black Ferrari parked in back.

Sarah pulled up behind it, blocking it, feeling excitement knot her stomach and tighten her throat. What luck, to find her here.

But was it luck? It couldn't be luck. Suddenly wary, Sarah emerged slowly from her car. What had made Valerie come here? What did she want?

The back door opened, and Valerie came out. She looked tense and nervous, jerking her head around to give Sarah a furious, watchful look. "What are you doing here?"

Sarah stepped away from her car, leaving the door hanging open and said, in the gentle voice people affect with children and the mentally disturbed, "I live here, remember?"

Valerie snorted contemptuously. "No you don't. Not anymore. Jade scared you off. I know *that*."

"What do you mean, Jade?" Sarah felt a quickening of excitement, the sense of being on the trail. A name, she had now. *Jade*.

"Why did you erase my magic circle?" Valerie asked, her voice plaintive. "Did *he* make you do it?"

"I got rid of it because I thought it might help banish the . . . demon. You called it Jade? Is that its name? I thought it might be holding the spirit to this house, somehow, providing a link."

Valerie shrugged. "It was supposed to protect me. It didn't work well enough. But I thought I might be safer if I stayed there. Oh, well, I don't guess it matters. I'm going." She came down the steps.

Sarah moved quickly to block her way. "Wait a minute. I've got some questions . . . you've got to help me."

Valerie stopped short. She looked bewildered. "Me, help you? What do you mean?"

"You can help me get rid of the demon . . . Jade, you call it?"

"It's what he told me to call him. I don't know what it means."

"Well, it's a name, and names are important. It might be useful," Sarah said. "All right, that's a good start. I want you to tell me everything you know about Jade, and how you summoned him."

"Why do you care?"

"Because he's evil, and we have to destroy him."

Valerie shrugged. "I don't see . . . you got away."

"Yes, I got away, but the next person might not be so lucky. As long as that thing is loose in this world, it's like . . . like the germ of some horrible disease. And if his power grows, he might not be restricted to this house, as he seems to be now. There's no telling what he might not do."

A faint, unpleasant smile appeared on Valerie's narrow face. "Well, he's not in the house now," she said. "He's got a body, not that it will do him much good."

Sarah felt a mental chill, and moved away from Valerie. "What do you mean?"

"I mean he's trapped. Jade's trapped in a sick, dying body, and when it dies . . . well, I hope *he* dies, too. If he doesn't, I don't want to be here to find out what happens. I'm going."

She walked past Sarah towards her car, but Sarah grabbed her arm. "Wait a minute. You've got to tell me what you mean."

Valerie looked down at Sarah's fingers and she pulled away, her whole body seeming to shrink and recoil from contact.

"Let me go," she said sullenly. "I'll tell you."

"Not here," Sarah said. Her eyes went to the house, half expecting to find some visible sign of Jade's presence, like a face at the window. But if the demon still lurked in the form of a rat or a cat or some other animal, it was not showing itself. "We have a lot to talk about. Let's go somewhere . . . I know a coffee shop nearby."

Valerie gave her head a jerk, presumably in agreement. She was staring fixedly at the ground, her body rigidly pulling away from Sarah's grasp. Feeling a little sorry for her, Sarah let go her arm. Immediately, Valerie went to the gleaming black Ferrari.

"Let's go in my car," Sarah said quickly. "I'll bring you back here afterwards." She saw Valerie's bony shoulders hunch, and then she backed away from the car. Feeling like a teacher with a backward child, Sarah said, "Don't you want to bring your purse?" She could see the soft brown leather bag on the front seat. She remembered it from the first time she had seen Valerie because, along with Valerie's knee-high boots, it was obviously expensive, and she had envied it.

But instead of simply reaching into the car for the bag, as Sarah expected, Valerie turned around to face Sarah, a look of dumb suffering on her face. "Yes," she said. "Of course I do." As if in slow motion, she leaned back into the car and got the purse. Slipping the strap over her shoulder, she held the bag close, almost cradling it against her body.

"I'm ready," she said.

Valerie would not make a comfortable ally, Sarah

thought as she let her into her car, but she might be useful. She made no attempt to break the silence between them, but drove swiftly to the coffee shop on Lamar Boulevard. There they settled into a corner booth and, after the waitress had brought them two steaming cups of coffee, Sarah finally spoke.

"Now tell me what you mean about Jade being trapped. What did you do? What happened? And what exactly *is* Jade, anyway? How did you summon him?"

Valerie glared at her sullenly across the gold-speckled formica table top. "What do you want to know first? I don't know much about Jade . . . just what little *he* told me, which I don't believe, or what I could guess, which turns out to be mostly wrong."

"Start at the beginning," Sarah suggested. "Where did Jade come from?"

"I don't know. I just called him up and he appeared. I painted the magic circle on the floor like the books said, to protect myself, and I said some invocations, which I found in the books, and I made a blood sacrifice." Her lips twitched upward in a tight little smile.

In her lap, beneath the table, Sarah's hands clasped each other. "What sort of sacrifice?"

"I killed a rabbit. I bought it in a pet shop. And I had the most beautiful knife . . . a guy I knew, a real warlock, gave it to me once, in trade for some drugs. He said it was a genuine, sacrificial knife, real powerful . . . I never thought then that I'd use it for anything like that, though.

"But one day . . . it was after I'd moved into that house . . . I started thinking about magic. I'd always known people who were into witchcraft, but I wasn't. It always seemed, well, those covens always seemed to be into dancing naked down by the lake, and group sex and stuff." She wrinkled her nose. "I wasn't interested in that. But then I started thinking about being able to get some things . . . money, mostly, because I was always broke. And I got some books at the library, and I thought I might as well give it a try—I decided I'd try to summon a demon, if there were such things, and make him work for me. So I did the whole number, with the chanting and the rabbit and the candles and the blood, and . . . he came. Jade.

"Only it wasn't like the books said it would be. And . . . he tricked me. He made me come out of the magic circle, where I was safe, and then he—" Valerie's mouth moved but no more words emerged. She licked dry lips and looked pleadingly at Sarah.

Sympathy welled up, overwhelming Sarah's dislike of the woman. She reached across the table for her hand, but Valerie jerked it away.

"He took over," she said flatly. "Just took me over . . . just . . . snuffed me out, like I wasn't anything, like I didn't exist, so that he could use my body. And I couldn't stop him."

"But you managed to fight him off."

Valerie shook her head. "No. No. I told you . . . I couldn't do anything. He was too strong. He must've . . . I don't remember, but it was horrible. He smothered me and took over."

"Then how can you sit here and tell me about it?" Sarah asked sarcastically.

Valerie shrugged. "Because in the end he let me go. He let me have my body back. I don't know why . . . I guess I tried to kill him, or myself." She stretched her arm on the table, palm up, and peeled back the sleeve of her green sweater, revealing a tightly bandaged wrist. "I can't remember doing it, but I figure I just couldn't stand having him in my body. So my body rejected him. I couldn't drive him out, so my body tried to kill itself. Kill me, I mean. Or him. Anyway, it worked. Jade got out. He said he could have stayed, but it wasn't worth the trouble of keeping me alive. He wouldn't have been able to trust his own body." She smiled faintly.

Sarah sighed. "That's not very useful. If the only way to avoid being taken over is to kill yourself . . ." She sipped her coffee.

"Jade says I want to die. He says he'll let me die after I . . ."

"He says you want to die, so you believe him? And he'll let you die—that's some reward!" Sarah said, a little too loudly. The emptiness in Valerie's eyes, the flat, childlike way she spoke, made Sarah's skin crawl.

"I don't care," Valerie said. "Maybe I did once, but I

don't anymore. I don't care if I die, so maybe that means I want to die. I don't know anything else I want."

"You must have wanted something a lot in order to try conjuring up a demon," Sarah said. "What *did* you want? Surely not death."

"I don't remember . . . money, I think. A lot of things, maybe. It doesn't seem real to me now. Jade told me he'd give me whatever I wanted . . . but that was a joke, I guess, because by then there wasn't much of anything I wanted. But I brought you to the house for him. I did what he asked."

"And did he reward you? Did he keep his word? What did he give you?"

"Oh, there's plenty of money, now. I don't have to work anymore. I can have whatever I want," Valerie said without enthusiasm. "Jade told me the way, he said the simplest way was for me to find a rich man. He said even I could learn how to make a man be in love with me." She fell silent, then raised her eyes to Sarah's. "Only . . . I have to let him do things to me."

Sarah shuddered. Again, Valerie reminded her of a child —a molested child who did not understand. "Leave him," she said. "If you're not happy . . . do something about it. Why do you talk as if you have no control over your own life? You don't need that man's money, you don't have to obey Jade's orders, you can go away—"

"Jade won't let me go," Valerie interrupted. "I'm not like you. I'm not strong. Jade hurts me if I don't obey him. He called me back this morning, early. He said I'd made a mistake with you, that you were too much trouble, he couldn't have the patience to spend the time it would take to wear you down. Also, he thought you might have run away for good. He told me to bring him another body, any kind of body would do—any human body, that is. If I didn't, he said he'd use mine, that he could control me and my death wish for long enough to get out into the world and find himself a more suitable, permanent home. I didn't want him to do that to me again; I'm afraid of him. You don't know what it's like."

"I do," Sarah said softly, but her words made no impression.

"I kept trying to kill him," Valerie said. "I kept trying to trick him. When he was in my cat's body, I killed my cat."

The smell of the cellar was strong in Sarah's nostrils.

"But Jade didn't die. The cat did, he escaped. But I still thought . . . maybe if he was trapped in a body that was dying, a human body, away from the house and away from other people and animals, so he couldn't escape into some other animal . . . I thought maybe then he really would die, for good.

"So when he told me to bring him another victim right away, I thought of old Mrs. Owens, the landlady. She didn't know I'd moved out, and she was the only person I could think of to get to come to the house. And I thought, she was so old, she'd probably be weak . . ."

"I don't think age has anything to do with it," Sarah murmured.

"The minute she stepped into the house, he attacked. She fell on the floor like she'd been hit by lightning, stiff as a board. I thought she was dead, at first, then I looked at her eyes. And I saw *him*. Those yellow eyes. Furious. He was trapped. Something had gone wrong, something he hadn't counted on. I guess she'd had a stroke. And he couldn't get out, and he couldn't use the body." Valerie dribbled a spoonful of sugar into her untouched coffee and stirred it around. "I hoped he would die there, and never be able to get out. It was the first thing to give me hope in such a long time, seeing him trapped inside her like that. So I took the body back to Mrs. Owens' house and left her there. And I said a spell of protection around her door, just in case. And then I thought I'd better go back to the house, I thought maybe . . ."

"You just left her there?" Sarah said. "Knowing she would die? You left her helpless and alone?"

"She'll be better off dead, than having him in her body," Valerie said unemotionally. "And if he dies when she does . . . then it's worth it. Isn't that what you want, too? For Jade to die?"

Sarah remembered the helpless terror in the old woman's eyes. Her clear blue eyes. She frowned. "But you're wrong. Jade wasn't there. I'm sure of it. I'd have known it if he was."

Valerie looked confused. "You? You weren't there. What do you mean?"

"I went to Mrs. Owens' house this morning. I found her there, lying on the floor. But she wasn't possessed, I'm sure of it. I could see how absolutely terrified she was . . . there was nothing but terror in her eyes, and helplessness. Jade wasn't there. I called the ambulance, and she's in the hospital now. If she dies—"

The pupils in Valerie's eyes were dilated and her freckles seemed to blaze out of her pale face. "Damn you! You've ruined it! If you'd stayed away—if you'd left her alone—"

"If I'd left her alone she might be dead by now," Sarah said angrily.

"Yes! Dead! And he'd be dead, too, and I'd be free!"

Valerie's fury subsided back into hopelessness then, and she slumped down in her seat.

Sarah looked around. Two waitresses were staring, but at Sarah's look they turned away.

"You're wrong," Sarah said quietly. "Jade wasn't there. I don't know what you saw happen, but I know that by the time I got to the house, Jade was gone. I didn't help him escape. All I did was to help a poor old woman, another victim, like us."

Valerie twitched her shoulders; it was not quite a shrug. "Maybe you broke the spell by going inside. I cast a spell of protection around her bedroom when I closed the door, to try to keep Jade trapped there even if he left her body. And what made you go there, anyway? You don't know Mrs. Owens."

"I was looking for you. I wanted to ask you to help me. The only person I could think of who might have your address was Mrs. Owens."

"So you went there to find me," Valerie said. Her lips twisted. "*He* made you go there. He's got his hooks into you—he called you, and you didn't even know it. That's why you won't run away and stay away—you think it's your own choice, but it isn't. You can't escape from him any more than I can."

Sarah imagined invisible fingers lightly touching her mind, making her decide to go to Mrs. Owens' house, and she shivered uneasily. Why had she gone there, rather than phoning? It didn't make sense when she thought of it. And what had made her go through that open door? And what force had opened the door?

"He's playing with us," Valerie said. "Now he's got two of us, to fetch and carry for him. Maybe he couldn't take you over completely, like he could me, but he's got part of you, anyway. Give him time and he'll get more. You'll be like me. You won't even care."

"You're crazy," Sarah said sharply, to shut her up.

"Yes," Valerie said. She scooted out of her seat and dropped a five-dollar bill on the table. "Let's go. This place is getting crowded."

Feeling angry, tired, and vulnerable, Sarah followed Valerie outside to the car. Another dead end, she thought. Valerie was useless, having made up her mind that Jade could not be defeated. Valerie was not the powerful witch Sarah had imagined, but just a crazy kid who had played around with forces she did not understand.

Maybe Valerie's right, Sarah thought. Maybe all I can do is run, run away and not look back. Away from the house, it would not be her business anymore, not her fault what happened to other people.

Right, responded a bitter voice in her head. And all my life I can tell myself it wasn't my fault. Not my fault that innocent people might be destroyed, not my fault if a demon is let loose in the world. Not my fault that I turned tail and ran, doing just what Jade wanted me to do. I'd be no better than Valerie if I gave up now.

At that moment Valerie turned to face Sarah, slumping against the side of the car. She looked very small and pathetic suddenly.

"I'd help you if I could," she said. "Truly. But I've tried —I've tried everything I could think of, and none of it worked. The longer he goes on, the more powerful he gets. If he gets what he wants, he may come after us, and destroy us both. But I don't know how to stop him. He won't let me trick him again. But if there is something I can do—if you think of something—I'll help you."

This faint concession from Valerie—useless though it probably was—sparked hope in Sarah again.

"We have to try," she said. "We have to. We can't give
up. There must be a way, and we only have to find it. We'll
talk more later, after I've done some research. Maybe
there's a ritual somewhere, in some old book, which will
work. You can tell me exactly what you did to summon
him, and maybe we can figure out how to reverse what you
did. We can't give in to him. There has to be a way to beat
him, and we'll find it."

Sarah drove back to the house. During the drive, both
women were silent, lost in their own thoughts. But as she
pulled up behind the house and parked beside the Ferrari,
Sarah remembered something Valerie had said and never
explained. "When you said that Jade called you, how did
you mean? On the telephone?"

Valerie released a brief, shrill laugh. "No. He has a better
way than that. You've heard of witches' familiars?"

"You mean like cats and things?"

"Like cats . . . and things." Valerie giggled and scrabbled in her large purse. She withdrew something and held it
out towards Sarah. "Meet my familiar—Lunch the toad."

Sarah recoiled. Squatting on Valerie's open palm was a
live toad. It had bumpy, brown-mottled skin and two liquid,
yellow-brown eyes.

"Don't you like my precious Lunch, then?" As Sarah
stared in queasy fascination, Valerie pulled the toad to her
lips and kissed it.

Valerie's grey-green eyes glittered. She caught Sarah's
look and giggled again. "Jade gave him to me, to be my
companion. There's a little bit of Jade in him. He controls
Lunch, and Lunch lets me know when Jade wants me . . .
and he lets me know other things, too."

"You mean that all the while I've been talking to you
about destroying Jade, all the while you've been offering to
help me, you've had that . . . thing in your bag, listening
to us? Just what do you *want*, Valerie? Whose side are you
on?"

Valerie looked confused. Her lower lip sagged, and she
looked away from Sarah's angry face to the still, silent toad.
"Lunch? I didn't think . . ."

"A part of Jade," Sarah said bitterly. "How many parts
are there? What do we have to do to defeat him? How many

scattered parts do we have to find and destroy? Get rid of that toad, Valerie! What the hell are you thinking of, to keep it? What kind of a hold does Jade have over you?"

Valerie stared at her, confusion battling resentment in her thin, sharp face. She held the toad clutched close to her heart. "He's mine," she said at last, her voice pitched defensively high. "I won't hurt him, I love him. He doesn't do any harm. He's not powerful, not like Jade. He's only my little familiar spirit; my little Lunch." She bent her face close to the creature again and crooned, "Want your lunch, my pretty Lunch?"

She flashed Sarah a hostile, mocking glance and then, still holding the toad on one hand at chest-level, extended a finger of her free hand towards it. The toad opened its mouth and the end of Valerie's finger vanished inside. Valerie gave a small gasp, and her eyelids fluttered.

"There, dear," she murmured. "Suckle well."

A few, interminable seconds later, Valerie withdrew her finger from the toad's mouth. A drop of blood glistened on the end of her finger, like misapplied nail polish.

Sarah opened the car door violently and got out into the cool, fresh air, fighting the urge to be sick. A moment later, Valerie got out, too, and stood regarding Sarah across the top of the car.

"You see," she said. "He's like my own child, Lunch is. He's a part of me, as well."

Chapter Eight

The house haunted Sarah's thoughts, waking and sleeping, and she found it hard to stay away. Half a dozen times every day she had to fight off the temptation to return. Often it was for practical reasons—a book, or a sweater, or a pair of shoes she had left behind in her flight. In the bright October sunshine, among crowds of people on the Drag or in the cool stillness of the library, Sarah's memories of what had happened to her in that house seemed suddenly thin and vague, and she couldn't quite believe in the demon called Jade.

But if she was in any danger of forgetting, the nightmares reminded her. Once or twice every night she woke, sweating and shaking, from terrors which seemed far more real than the bed she found herself in. And so she stayed away from the house, as she had agreed, and spent long hours in the library, researching witchcraft, magic, and the little-known ways of demons. She copied out ancient spells in a spiral-bound notebook, and her confidence began to grow. She would find the way, she thought. She didn't need the untrustworthy Valerie's help at all. A long-time student, Sarah trusted in books, and felt secure, on her own ground in the familiar territory of primary and secondary sources.

Somewhere among all these printed pages lurked the answer she sought.

Pete spent nearly as much time as Sarah in this research. Magic was all they talked about in the evenings, to Beverly's growing boredom. Pete continued to maintain his detached attitude towards the subject, and the ease with which he could be distracted by tidbits of superstition and useless information annoyed Sarah, who thought he should be taking his reading as seriously as she took hers. But, she had to admit, even if he looked upon it as a diversion, he was reading as widely and intently as she was herself. It was from Pete that Sarah learned that a witch in seventeenth-century England had claimed a toad called Lunch for his familiar. She wondered if Valerie had run across that fact in her reading, or if the name originated with Jade. Familiar spirits, according to the books, were given by the devil to his converts to aid and comfort them. Did that mean that Jade was the devil? The idea sent Sarah into despair. How could she fight the devil? She didn't believe in the devil—but, then, neither had she believed in demons before she encountered Jade. What *was* Jade, exactly? And what was Lunch?

Sarah scanned book after book until she lost her bearings and simply swam in the subject, her mind a confused jumble of magic words and names, rites, rituals, powers, and horrors.

On Tuesday afternoon, as Sarah was getting into her car to go to the library, she caught the sleeve of her blouse in the door and ripped it. She swore, staring ruefully at the torn sleeve. She could go back inside and use Beverly's machine to stitch it up, or she could borrow one of Beverly's tops and go through the day feeling too tightly packaged.

She swore again and decided, getting into the car and slamming the door. Enough of this nonsense. She would go over to the house on West 35th Street right now and get the rest of her clothes.

Her skin prickled and her heart was beating faster in anticipation. Now she would see if it was all a dream, or real. Her memories of the demonic cat, the rat, the suffocating presence inside her head, the dead voice on the disconnected telephone all seemed as distant and unreal as the things she had been reading about. Had they really happened, or had she dreamed them?

But despite her doubts Sarah was cautious as she entered the house. Everything was so peaceful that she suspected a trap. The quiet, high-ceilinged rooms were filled with the cool, underwater light of sunlight through leaves, and a faint breeze freshened the air. The only sounds were those she made herself, footsteps on bare boards, her own breathing.

Sarah looked around, feeling a curious sense of loss. It was wrong for this house to be so empty. She had brought her things here and then abandoned them, making no effort to turn this place into her home. Why shouldn't she be happy here? She sat on the couch and looked around at her books and posters. I belong here, she thought. She closed her eyes, trying to sense another, alien presence, trying to discover where Jade was hiding, but she felt nothing. She was alone.

The sound of a car pulling up in back distracted her and she opened her eyes, waiting to hear the sound of it reverse. Cars often took a wrong turn, not realizing the road led only into the camp. But instead she heard the sound of an engine being shut off. She rose and went to the back door to investigate.

Pete was walking toward the house, his expression apprehensive. "Sarah! Are you all right?"

"Yes, of course. Why?"

"I didn't expect to find you here."

"It was a spur of the moment thing. I came to get some of my clothes," she began, her tone faintly apologetic. Then she realized the strangeness of what Pete had said.

"If you didn't think I was here—why did you come?" she asked.

Pete looked uncomfortable. "I wanted to have a look around," he said. "That's all."

Sarah smiled, feeling a surge of empathy. He was curious, of course. It was surprising he had waited so long. In his position, she would have done the same thing. "Come on in," she said. "I'll show you around. Don't get your hopes up, though. The place feels pretty empty to me. I'm starting to wonder if—"

He was looking at her curiously. "You're not having doubts?"

Sarah shrugged, uncomfortable. "It just seems so silly now. In the light of day, as it were. I was just sitting in the front room thinking how comfortable I was here, and what a nice place it was to live . . ."

"That doesn't make what happened before any less real."

"I know." She laughed. "It seems odd, having me be the skeptic, and you arguing for the supernatural."

"I wasn't—"

"Come on in."

He followed her into the house and she closed the door. "Would you like a beer?"

He hesitated long enough that she had turned back towards the refrigerator to get one when he stopped her. "I thought there was a pentacle drawn on the bedroom floor?" His voice was sharp.

Sarah looked through the bedroom door, following his gaze. "There was. I got rid of it. I couldn't stand looking at it anymore. I thought I told you."

"No. I kind of wish you'd left it, though. We could have used it for protection."

Sarah tensed. "What do you mean? It's not good to leave them after they've been used—the spirits might turn them to their own uses. I thought you might have run across that piece of information in your reading."

He shrugged, still staring into the bedroom, a thoughtful look on his face.

"What are you thinking, Pete?"

Without looking around at her, Pete reached into the pocket of his corduroy jacket and pulled out a small, paperback book. "There's a License to Depart given here —that's the spell to send spirits away again. I thought I might recite it and see what happens."

Like an atheist making a prayer and then waiting impatiently for God's answer, she thought. She was annoyed.

"Why do that now? Why waste energy on the small stuff?" she asked. "I thought the plan was to learn as much as we could from all the experts, read all the books, and then work up a ritual and put everything we had into it—to give it our best shot."

"But what have we got to lose by saying a simple License to Depart? It may be the only thing necessary. It's the sort of thing that Valerie might have forgotten to do." He was looking at her now, so calmly and earnestly that she wanted to shake him.

"What we've got to lose is our *faith*," Sarah said. She sighed. "Not that you have any to begin with. You think of all this as very unreal, don't you? Just something to do to humor Sarah. Do you think that by saying a few magic words you can make me feel all better?"

"Is that what you think?"

"Pete, will you quit that? Quit being so detached! You can't have it both ways—you can't be involved without believing. You're the one who keeps telling me that magic requires belief. At least Valerie believes—she may be crazy, but she knows that Jade is for real. She knows that she summoned him up with words and ritual, so it makes sense to believe that some other words and rituals will send him back. I don't trust Valerie, but I think that working together we might have a chance. But you . . ." She bit her lip. "I don't know, Pete. I really appreciate your help and your friendship and everything, but I don't know if you can help me now. Sometimes you even make me doubt Jade's existence—and that's no good. You make me doubt what I *know*."

Pete looked distracted. "Did you hear that?" He asked. "A voice. Is there someone else in the house?"

Sarah shook her head, and then went cold as Pete turned his head rapidly from side to side as if expecting to catch someone trying to sneak past. "There is someone here," he said softly. "Spying on us. And whispering and laughing, as if we couldn't hear! Now where the hell is he hiding?"

"Let's get out of here," Sarah said.

A broad smile spread over Pete's face; he looked much as he did when he won at cards. "It's *Jade*," he said, scarcely above a whisper. "That's it, isn't it? It's him. There really is someone here. It's amazing." He sounded fascinated.

"Pete, let's go. Now."

He shook his head and gazed around the room, still with

that expectant, pleased look on his face. "Hello," he murmured. "Hello, hello. Will it manifest itself physically?"

"Christ," Sarah muttered. She took Pete's arm and tugged, but with no effect. "Pete, *please*. It's not a game —you don't understand what could happen—you don't realize its power—"

"No, I don't, but I'm starting to. I'm ready for him." He looked down at her with a kindly expression and patted her hand. "Go on, if it upsets you. There's no need for you to stay through this. Wait out in the car."

"Pete, please!"

"I can't leave now, Sarah. A few minutes ago you were accusing me of being detached, and not believing. Well, now I believe. I can feel another presence in the room with us. Now I know what you felt. I'm on the verge of understanding. If he comes closer, I'll know more. I'll know—" His face changed; his nose wrinkled as if he had caught a whiff of something foul. Then his eyes widened and he looked startled, almost frightened. "Christ," he said, his voice alarmed and disbelieving. He pulled his arm out of Sarah's grasp and backed away. "That's—"

He was staring in horror at something behind her. Sarah whirled, but saw nothing. She turned back.

Pete had gone chalky-white, and his tall, thin body swayed. Before Sarah could reach him, his eyes fluttered closed and he rocked, then fell forward, catching himself on his hands and knees, hard on the floor.

"Pete!"

Sarah dropped to the ground and caught hold of his shoulders, pulling him to her. "Pete, what's wrong? What's happened? Can I help you? Let me help you outside."

His whole body shook as he labored for breath, and he had broken out into a sweat. He didn't have to answer. Sarah knew what had happened. Jade had attacked again, just as she had been lulled almost into disbelieving in his existence.

She wrapped her arms tightly around Pete and pressed her head against his and concentrated, trying to reach Pete, trying to sense Jade. She could not feel Jade's presence at all, and that frustrated her. It must mean the demon was concentrating all its energy on Pete, and that left her helpless, without an enemy to fight and with no idea how to help her friend.

"Pete," she said urgently. "I'm here, Pete. I want to help you. Let me help you."

His only answer was a moan and a racking shudder.

Jade, she thought grimly, trying to aim her thoughts like an arrow. Get out, get away. Leave him alone.

She felt Pete tense suddenly, within her embrace and then, before she could think about it or try to fight back, Sarah was lying flat on her back. Pete crouched over her, a look of demented courage on his tortured face, and his long, strong fingers were at her throat, choking her.

Sarah twisted wildly, feeling his fingers grip her more tightly, and clawed at his wrists, trying to pull them away. The pain intensified; she thought her chest would explode; the world turned red and purple. Despairing, Sarah brought up one knee as hard as she could, and connected.

With a cry, Pete jerked up and away from her, his fingers momentarily releasing their grasp. Sarah rolled away on the hard floor and scrambled to her feet, panting and watching Pete warily. As one part of her mind screamed at her to run, another part refused to leave him here alone, so totally at Jade's mercy.

"Pete," she said. It came out a whisper. She touched her throbbing neck, swallowed painfully and tried again. "Pete."

He looked wildly around the room, and Sarah wondered what he saw and what he heard and if he was aware of her at all. She had never seen such terror on a human being's face.

"No," he said. "Get away from me! Leave me alone!"

Anything she said or did might add to his terror, Sarah realized. She had no idea what hell Jade had put him in. Again she tried to sense the demon and could not. For her, the room was normal and empty except for Pete, who was behaving like a madman.

And then Pete saw her. At least, he looked directly at her. But whatever he saw, standing in her place, made his face twist with a loathing so strong that it frightened her, and she backed away from her friend, realizing she was retreating only when she bumped into the wall.

"Pete," she said yet again. "It's me, Sarah. I don't know what you're seeing, but if you can hear me—"

"No!" he shouted. He shut his eyes. "You're not real, I don't believe it, none of this is happening. I'm hallucinating, that's all. This is not real. I'll get out of this—I'll prove—" He began to walk forward with his arms outstretched, fingers seeking although his eyes were still tightly shut. Sarah trembled, wondering what to do. Should she run? If he found her, would he know her, or would he again try to kill her?

Abruptly, before he reached her, Pete stopped and recoiled, drawing his arms in to his chest as if he had touched something.

"No, no," he said, his voice a whimper and his face contorted. "No! It's not real, none of it is. This is an empty house and I'm all alone . . . . Sarah? Sarah, where did you go? Why did you leave me here?"

"I'm here, Pete."

"Why am I here? What have I done? How do I get out?"

Sarah saw that he was crying. He slumped to the ground and wrapped his arms around himself, the sobs shaking him. Feeling a painful lump in her own throat, Sarah went to him and touched his arm.

He screamed and shoved her away, his eyes wide open now. "Get away, don't touch me, you're not real; I won't believe in you, I won't be one of you, get away!" He panted the words out in ragged gasps, staring directly at Sarah. Then, as if unable to bear the sight any longer, he clamped his eyes shut and cried out three words that Sarah did not understand.

And then there was peace.

As Sarah watched, Pete cautiously opened his eyes again, looking dazed and frightened. His gaze fell on her, and Sarah tensed for another outburst. But instead relief flooded his face and the terror began to recede.

"Oh, thank God," he said. "Sarah, is it really you? I'm back? It's over now?"

She nodded tentatively and stepped forward to embrace him, but he made a sudden, frantic gesture and a long shudder rocked him. He turned his head to one side and was sick on the floor.

Feeling slightly sick herself, but relieved by the obvious return to reality, Sarah hurried away to fetch a towel and a bowl of water. But when she returned, Pete pushed her aside and cleaned up after himself. Afraid to argue, still shaken by the violence and hatred he had turned on her earlier, Sarah leaned against the wall and watched without speaking. She had never seen Pete look so ill and exhausted; he suddenly seemed very old and frail.

"Shall I make you some tea?" she asked, watching his unsteady progress to the kitchen sink. He shook his head.

Sarah bit her lip. She wanted to go to him and put her arms around him and comfort him, but she did not dare. He would probably push her away again, or worse . . . She touched her throat.

But that wasn't Pete, she thought. At least—it wasn't Pete seeing *me*.

"What happened?" she asked.

"I don't want to talk about it," he said sharply. "All right? I just want to get out of here."

"I'll take you home."

He looked at her with pained, exhausted eyes, and slowly nodded. "Please." Then, as they were leaving the house, he stopped her. "I'm sorry, Sarah."

"That's all right," she said quickly.

"No. I'm sorry I doubted you. I just didn't know. I thought of it as a kind of game, or as something *you* were overreacting to. I'm sorry, now, that I didn't believe you. You tried to protect me, and I still walked right into it."

"You couldn't have known," Sarah said. "I'm not so sure I would have believed it, if anyone had told me."

"I wish to God I'd never gone in there."

"Well, it's over now," Sarah said briskly, helping him into her car. "You never have to go in there again."

"Of course I will," Pete said dully.

Sarah looked at him but started the car without speaking.

"I have to go back for the same reason that you do," he said. "We can't leave that—thing—in there, alive. Somehow, we have to destroy it. Otherwise the next person who goes in there may not come out the same."

"You were the one who told me I wasn't responsible," Sarah pointed out.

"That was before I *knew*." He sighed and rubbed his face. "I wish to God I didn't. But knowing, I can't pretend I don't, anymore than you can. That thing is too dangerous, too horrible. We have to stop it, somehow. We have to find out how to get rid of it. If we don't, who will?"

Sarah was silent, feeling a sense of relief so powerful it made her eyes sting. She wasn't alone anymore. She wasn't crazy. Pete *knew*. He had been through it, just as she had, and he understood, and he was united with her in a common fight. And together they would win. They would conquer the demon.

"One thing," said Pete. "One thing that gives me hope —it isn't much, but it is something—is those words."

"Words?"

"Arabic words of protection against evil. I'd seen them in a reference book and copied them down. I didn't really expect to remember them off the top of my head, but suddenly, when I couldn't think of any way out, I saw those words, just as if they were on a page in front of my face. And I said them aloud and then . . . it was all over. I was out of hell and back in the house with you. So it must have been the words. They must have worked."

Sarah said nothing, but she wondered. Were words that powerful? Had they really had an effect? Or had Jade simply come to the end of his repertoire of tricks for the moment? Had Pete simply been stronger than Jade anticipated, as Sarah had been herself? Could words really be enough to fend off, and ultimately destroy, the demon?

"Did you see anything?" Pete asked.

Sarah glanced at him and saw that he was staring away from her, out the window. She cleared her throat. "Only you."

"So none of it was real. It was all just hallucination." His tone was bitter. "But it didn't do me any good to tell myself that."

"Believe me, it was real enough," Sarah said. "I went through it myself, or something like it."

"I suppose it didn't really take much time? It felt like days, inside. It was like being smothered. There was the most horrible smell. And nasty, sharp claws scraping at my head, trying to scoop out my brain. And those things, all around me. Gibbering at me, trying to touch me. I was turning into one of them. I couldn't get away. I—" From the corner of her eye, Sarah saw Pete shudder and press a hand to his mouth. After a moment he took it away again, leaned back in his seat, and breathed in a shaky sigh. "It was all so real. And then, at the end, to have been able to make it all vanish with a few magic words. Hell!" He lurched forward in his seat.

"What is it?"

"The License to Depart. I forgot all about it. That's what I went over there to do. Let's go back."

"Pete, not now! You're in no shape to face Jade again. You need to rest. Tomorrow, or the next day—"

"Now, Sarah. We have to strike now." She could feel his excitement filling the car. He was revitalized, his former sickness forgotten, pushed aside, by a sudden surge of hope and energy.

"My God, Pete, after what just happened to you? What if he attacks again? You might not be able to—"

"If anything, I feel stronger now than I did before, because I know what to expect. But the same won't be true for Jade. I think that attack must have taken a lot out of him. He won't be expecting us back. We're probably safer right now than we would be if we gave him a few days to recover."

Sarah turned and drove into the parking lot of a convenience store. There she stopped, letting the car idle. She looked at Pete, seeing how his weariness seemed to have been burned away. She wondered how far his excitement could propel him before he collapsed. She remembered the profound sleep which had followed her own battle with Jade.

"This is the time to strike," Pete said. "I think we've got a damn good chance of winning. Why did Jade attack when he did? I think it was to keep me from saying the License to Depart. It was self-preservation, to distract me. If we go back now, we may catch him off guard—say the right words, and he'll have to obey. If we give him more time to recover—"

Sarah nodded and shifted into drive. It made sense, what

Pete had said, and they had to try anything that might work. She pulled back into traffic, now heading west.

Pete reached over and put his hand on top of Sarah's, where it rested on the steering wheel. "We'll do it," he said.

While Sarah drove, Pete explained his plan. They would draw a protective circle on the floor with chalk, stand within it and recite the License to Depart and some other Words of Power that Pete had copied into his notebook. As he spoke, Sarah felt her spirits rise, and by the time they reached the house she was almost giddy with hope. They would do it, she thought. Of course they would do it! She had Pete with her now, actively believing. She wasn't alone anymore. With the magic words and their combined strengths, they would send Jade back where he had come from.

As they got out of the car, Pete handed Sarah a piece of ruled paper covered with his neat, black printing. "These are Words of Power," he said. "You might try to remember them—they could be useful."

The words were many-syllabled, like children's nonsense: *Anrehakatha-sataiu*, *Senentuta-batetsataiu*, *Sabaoth* . . . Sarah doubted that in a moment of crisis any such words would come to her lips. One, however, was simple enough. "Bast." Beside it, in parentheses, Pete had written "to make all spirits depart." That sounded promising, and the word was easy enough to remember. *Bast*. She moved her lips, pronouncing it silently.

Pete had already gone ahead of her, into the house, and Sarah followed after, in no hurry. She found him on the living room floor, crouching with a stick of chalk in one hand and an open book before him, copying a magic protective figure. She stood a moment, watching him, feeling detached. The house was quiet and peaceful, the sun filtered through leaves, making patterns on the wall. The air was humid, but it was not unpleasantly warm. Autumn afternoon edging towards a cool evening, her favorite time, her favorite season. It would be so nice, she thought, to sit on the porch and drink a glass of wine, enjoying the end of the day and waiting for the sun to go down. No worries, nothing to do. And afterwards, she and Brian, wrapped in one another's arms—

Brian looked up from whatever he was doing on the floor and smiled at her seductively. "Come over here," he said.

She couldn't move.

It wasn't Brian, she told herself; although she heard Brian's voice and saw him there, and ached to touch him —that wasn't Brian. Hard to believe that when she saw him smiling at her; hard to remember that she had come into the house with Pete, and that there was no one else in the house, when memory shifted and she saw Brian.

"Pete," she said, pleading.

"What is it?"

It wasn't Brian. It was Pete. Had been, all along. Pete crouching on the floor, drawing a rather wavering freehand circle.

Sarah sighed, relieved but saddened, and joined him on the floor, squatting nearby, within the parameter of the circle. "I thought you were Brian," she said. "I saw him, I even heard his voice. That's Jade's doing. He's already working against us, fighting back. He's trying to distract us." She put her hand on Pete's arm. "Be careful."

He pulled away as if her touch had scalded him. "You don't have to tell me to be careful!"

The hostility in his voice shocked her. Nerves, she thought, trying not to be hurt. She watched him complete the circle by writing Latin words around the rim, and she said nothing. Let it be his show. She wouldn't interfere.

Pete rose and gestured for Sarah to do the same. The circle was not large, and of necessity they stood very close together. They were not touching, but Sarah could feel Pete's tension, his body giving off excitement like heat.

He began to read from his notebook: a formula for consecration of the circle, he had told her. She recognized it as a translation from an Assyrian tablet, said to be the oldest known formula for such consecration. Most of the formulae Sarah had found called repeatedly upon the Christian God. Pete's attitude towards the religion he had been raised in was so antagonistic that Sarah had wondered how he could read an invocation praising God the Father, God the Son, and God the Holy Spirit with anything like the proper reverence and conviction. He had side-stepped that difficulty by looking to the older gods—beings he could believe in with the same unresentful interest he had for ghosts and demons and familiar spirits.

"Ban! Ban! Barrier that none may pass,
Barrier of the Gods that none may break,
Barrier of heaven and earth that none can change,
Which no God may annul,
Nor God nor man can loose,
A snare without escape, set for evil,
A net whence none can issue forth, spread for evil,
Whether it be Evil Spirit or Evil Demon or Evil
  Ghost,
Or Evil Devil or Evil God or Evil Fiend,
Or Hag-Demon, or Ghoul, or Robber-Sprite,
Or Phantom, or Night-Wraith, or Handmaid of the
  Phantom . . ."

Pete's voice, instead of growing stronger as he threw himself into the mood of the exorcism, was growing more uncertain. Sarah watched him, puzzled, wondering what was wrong. Suddenly he broke off his recitation and half-turned to face her. On his face was a strange mixture of pain and longing which Sarah did not understand, but which made her uneasy.

"Pete? Is it Jade?"

He made a sound low in his throat.

"Pete—" She reached out and suddenly she was in his arms. He clung to her tightly, trembling.

"It's all right," she murmured. "Fight him, Pete. I'm here; I'll help you."

He gripped her more tightly. "Pete," she said. "Let me read the rest of the formula, if you can't. We can't let him stop us. Maybe if we consecrate the circle he won't be able to touch us."

His arms loosened somewhat, and Sarah was able to draw back far enough to see his face. And suddenly she knew the name for the expression on his face. Desire. Her stomach lurched. Not Pete. Not for her.

And then he was kissing her, or trying to. She writhed in his grasp, eluding his mouth. "Pete! For heaven's sake!"

He still pressed her close. Denied her mouth, he was

kissing her hair, sniffing it, murmuring her name. She could feel his erection.

"Pete, stop it." She didn't want to hurt him. She didn't want to hit him. "Let me go," she said, trying to make her voice calm and reasonable. She pulled away and this time, although he did not let go of her, he did not pull her back.

"Pete, this is crazy," she said gently.

"I don't care," he said. He looked drunk, dazed. She had never seen him like this. "I want you, Sarah. I can't stand it any more. I can't fight it any more. Don't you feel it too? I know you do—you must."

Suddenly it wasn't Pete but Brian who was talking, Brian who had his arms around her, Brian who begged her to love him. Reality slipped and shifted and Sarah felt that she had fallen into a dream. She put her arms around him and hugged him tightly. Brian was a bigger man, more solidly built, than Pete. She knew the feel of him in her arms so well, too well to be fooled; too well to be mistaken. She pressed her face against his chest and closed her eyes. If this was a dream, she would go on dreaming. This man in her arms was real, and the only thing that mattered.

She felt him moving, trying to disengage himself and gently push her away. She looked up at his face, her heart pounding, afraid that she would see that weak-willed apology, that pained look that said he was thinking of Melanie and feeling sorry for himself. But instead Brian was smiling at her, and there was love in his eyes. She felt weak, and turned her face up as if to the sun, closing her eyes and straining to kiss him.

His mouth met hers and they kissed hungrily. But it wasn't Brian's mouth; it wasn't Brian's kiss. And, she realized, it wasn't Brian's familiar body she was pressed against. In the space of less than a second everything had changed again.

Sarah broke away from the kiss, her breath coming hard, and she stared at Pete, hating him because he wasn't Brian. Pete reached out for her, and she wondered who he saw, who inspired that longing on his face.

"Stop it," she said sharply. She pulled his hands away from her breasts. "Pete, stop it! You're letting Jade control you. Fight it!"

"I don't want to fight it, Sarah," he said. "I want you." His fingers tightened on hers and he pulled her to him again, his head coming down to kiss her.

Perhaps he would turn to Brian again in her arms, she thought, first letting him kiss her and then kissing back. It would be only an illusion, but an illusion was better than emptiness. Her arms slipped up his back—Pete's back —and pulled him closer, and their kiss increased in passion. He wasn't Brian, but that wasn't important. She had always liked Pete, and now his mouth on hers was compelling, his desire sparking her own. She couldn't help responding to his hand on her breast, his tongue in her mouth. He wanted her and she wanted him, and where was the harm in that?

Beverly, she thought. There was the harm. Easy enough to give in now to the moment's desire, but what about later, when they had to look at each other, and put their clothes back on, and go home and lie to Beverly?

She broke away from him. "Pete," she said breathlessly. "Pete, listen to me. We can't do this. It isn't fair—it isn't fair to Beverly!"

Passion made his face a stranger's. "Is it fair to *me?*" he asked. "Are you being fair to me?" He caught her hand and pressed it against the bulge in his pants.

She jerked her hand away, angry for the first time. "We didn't come here for this! Use your head, Pete! You wanted to come here to say the License to Depart. Let's do that, then, and—"

"Later," he said, reaching for her. "Later, we can do anything you like."

"Not later! Now, before it's too late!" She pushed him away, and bent to pick up the book he had dropped. When she came up, he caught her to him and kissed her hair and the back of her neck. Sarah squirmed, trying to avoid his caresses, and paged through the book, looking for the marked page.

"Sarah," he murmured into her hair. "You're driving me crazy. If you only knew how much I want you . . ."

She found the page with the License to Depart. She prayed that it would work, without the consecrated circle and without both their minds concentrated on it. She shifted and twisted away from Pete's lips and hands and hoped that she, at least, would be safe from Jade. He can only fight us one at a time, she thought. In a trembling voice she began to read.

"O Spirit . . . Jade, because thou has diligently answered me—answered Valerie's—demands, I do hereby license and command thee to depart, without injury to man or beast. Depart, I say, and be thou very willing and ready"—she slapped at Pete's hands—"to come, whensoever duly exorcised and conjured—"

Pete grabbed her head and held it still, kissing her mouth, silencing her. Sarah brought the book up in both hands into his stomach, but it was a weak and ineffective blow. Still, she managed to break away from him, and moved backwards hastily out of his reach.

"Depart, I say," she resumed breathlessly. She looked for her place on the page. "And . . . be thou very willing and ready to come, whensoever duly exorcised and conjured by the sacred rites of magic. I conjure thee to withdraw peaceably and quietly, and may the peace of God continue for ever and ever, between me and thee. Amen."

She looked up and saw Brian standing in the center of the chalked circle. Looking at the floor, she saw that she was outside the circle, and that her footsteps had smeared and broken the line. She bit her lip. She would not give up. Not yet. Perhaps it wasn't spoiled. It might not be too late. Quickly she found the second marked page in the book—an exhortation if the spirit be reluctant to leave, and began to read it aloud. She was painfully aware of the man standing only a few feet away.

"I command you by all the holy names, by Adonay, Amay, Horta, Vegadoro, Ysion, Ysey, by the Holy Name by which Solomon did bind up the devils and lock them up, Ethrack, Evener, Agla, Goth, Joth, Othie, Veneck, Nabrack, by all the holy names and powers that be, Beroald, Berald, Balbin, Gab, Gabor, Agaba, by the grace and power of God, depart and leave us in peace."

She looked up. She still saw Brian. Tears filled her eyes. She dropped the book on the floor, raised her arms above her head and shouted at the top of her lungs, hopelessly yet still hoping, "BAST!"

She opened her eyes and saw Pete. Relief flooded her. Tentatively she smiled at him.

He smiled back, but it was the wrong smile. He was looking at her still with desire, still controlled by Jade, tricked into seeing some other Sarah. Sarah felt cold and very much alone. She backed away from him when he held out his arms to her.

"I'm leaving," she said. She turned away.

"Sarah."

It was Brian's voice.

She trembled but did not look back.

"Sarah, sweetheart, I love you. Come here and let me kiss you."

She made herself walk away. She could not look back. If she looked back, she knew she would be lost. If she saw Brian she would go to him, even knowing that he was really Pete, even knowing that he was an illusion. She would make love to him gladly, greedily, accepting the illusion since that was all she had.

"Sarah, please. Come back to me. I need you."

She broke into a run, then, through the kitchen and onto the porch and outside, down the three wooden steps. She was crying.

Outside, she slumped against the side of her car and wept. When the worst of it passed, she looked up and saw that Pete was sitting on the top step, head buried in his hands. She wiped her face with a tissue, watching him, but he did not move or speak.

"Pete," she said at last.

He looked up, cautiously, giving her a hunted look. His face was haggard, and the expression on it might have been guilt or it might have been fear. He did not speak.

Sarah sighed, pushing herself away from the car. She felt like an empty shell, and it was an effort to move. "Come on," she said wearily. "Let's get out of here."

Pete rose, moving like an invalid, and walked towards her. He stopped short while there was still quite a distance between them and said in a whisper, "I'm sorry."

"Don't," Sarah said. "It wasn't you. It wasn't your fault." She hated the stricken look on Pete's face. She wanted to forget what had happened—and what had not happened—but there was still this problem to be worked out between them. She sighed. "Let's go," she said.

They got into Pete's car, Sarah again taking the wheel. She didn't quite trust Pete to drive; she didn't trust what his guilt and exhaustion might make him do.

"It was Jade," she said again. "You don't have to feel guilty." She looked at him. "It was just another kind of attack. He was playing with us. I kept seeing you as Brian, and I wanted . . . all I wanted to do . . . Jade made me feel that, just as he made you feel . . ."

"But you saw Brian," Pete said dully. "That's why . . ." He drew a deep breath and rubbed his face fiercely with the palm of one hand. Not looking at her, he said, "I didn't see anyone but you. I didn't imagine that you were Bev, or anyone else. I knew what I was doing the whole time; I knew it was you. I don't have an excuse, you see. I've always been attracted to you, Sarah. I love Bev. I would never do anything to hurt her. And there I was . . . acting out my fantasies about you. I don't know what came over me—"

"Of course you do," Sarah said sharply. "We both know that it was Jade. You wouldn't have done that on your own. You don't have to be ashamed of your fantasies—you would never have thought of trying to act them out except for Jade."

Pete went on as if she had said nothing. "It was as if nothing else mattered, as if there was nothing else in the world except the two of us. And all I wanted was to make love to you. I didn't want to think about what I was doing —hell, I didn't even try to fight it! I can't justify what I did."

"You don't have to. Pete, you're talking as if you were alone in there—I was there, too, and I—"

"You thought I was Brian. Jade tricked you into seeing Brian," Pete said. "He didn't trick me."

"Of course he did! Will you stop pitying yourself and be logical? I knew Brian wasn't there—I knew it had to be you —but I didn't want to argue against my own senses, and it was Brian I saw and Brian I felt in my arms," Sarah said. "You could tell yourself you loved Beverly, but how could you argue against the lust Jade was making you feel? Jade was speeding up your pulse, muddying your thoughts, feeding your fantasies—how could you be expected to fight against that? He was playing on you physically and mentally—you didn't have a chance. It wasn't *you*, Pete!"

"The classic excuse," he said dryly.

The hint of humor in his voice cheered her. "And it's over now," she said. "We're out of the house, and out of that whole fantasy. Jade can't touch us here. It's over. Let's forget it and go on, O.K.?"

He sighed, not looking at her. "I can't shrug it off like that."

"Why not? You have to. There's no point in torturing yourself over it—it wasn't your fault. Anyway, nothing happened." She paused, watching him for some response, but he continued to gaze out the window. "Nothing happened," she said again. "You kissed me. I kissed you. All right. We went a little crazy, at Jade's command. That's all. And it's over now. If you'd been drunk and made a pass at me we could forget it and go on as friends."

He didn't answer.

"Give me the key," Sarah said wearily.

He dug into his pocket and handed her the key-chain, still not meeting her eyes.

Sarah started the car, feeling hollow inside. She missed Brian with a physical ache, remembering too well how he had felt in her arms. It didn't help much to tell herself that she had held only Pete. However it had been done, Jade had given her a fresh reminder of what she had lost, and life was newly bleak without him. The wall of guilt and unease that had sprung up between her and Pete made her feel even more alone. She thought of the hopelessness of trying to confide in Beverly, of trying to make her understand what had happened.

As if he read her thoughts, Pete said suddenly, urgently, "You won't tell Bev?"

Sarah looked at him pityingly and shook her head.

"I don't know how I could explain it to her," he said miserably. "When I can't even explain it to myself. It would only hurt her. She wouldn't understand it."

Sarah nodded, dismissing the matter from her mind, and backed the car into the street. Looking up at the house before driving away, Sarah felt a rush of despair that swept away her earlier worries as insignificant. They had failed. Jade held all the weapons, and she and Pete were ignorant even of the rules of battle. She had no reason to imagine that she could do any better in their next encounter. It was hopeless. She had lost.

Chapter Nine

Sarah sat at the Marchants' table with the newspaper and a pen, going quickly and methodically through the rental listings, circling all the possibilities. They were all more expensive than her house, all smaller, and not one of them sparked any real interest in Sarah. But it had to be done. Sarah had made up her mind to get out of the house on West 35th Street as soon as possible.

She had accepted defeat. Earlier, she had been almost eager for battle, driven by a stubborn need to prove herself, against her fear. Now Sarah even mistrusted her own emotions, afraid they might be used against her. Jade didn't fight fair; she didn't even understand his strategy. She had brooded endlessly over what had happened at the house with Pete, the madness which had come over them both, and she wasn't satisfied with the explanation that it had just been Jade's way of distracting them from the spell they were trying to cast. Something more must have been intended—she was certain there was some meaning in Jade's choice of weapons. What was it, though? What would have happened if she had given in to Jade's illusions, if she and Pete had actually made love?

Sarah was on edge. How much of what she felt was fear,

how much simply sexual frustration, she couldn't judge. Her own emotions were suddenly as opaque to her understanding as those of the creature called Jade.

She had spent an uneasy night, full of vivid, fragmentary dreams. They were dreams full of sexual longing, but the man in her dreams was not Brian. The man was a stranger to her conscious mind, but in her dreams she knew him.

At one point, Sarah woke up to find herself out of bed, halfway across the Marchants' guest room, hand outstretched to open the door. The one compelling thought in her mind was that she must get home to join her husband. But where that home was, or who she thought was her husband, Sarah could not remember.

She jumped at a sound behind her, and turned quickly away from the table. But it was only Beverly emerging from the bedroom.

"Peter's still asleep," Beverly said. "Poor thing, I guess he needs the rest." She looked down at the page of newspaper Sarah had been marking, and nodded. "I'm sure you're doing the right thing."

Sarah sighed. "I'm not. Oh, yes, the right thing for me, but I'm still worried about someone else moving into that house . . . I still feel responsible in a way. But I'm going to talk to the woman who owns the house, and see if I can explain the situation. Maybe she'll believe me, maybe she'll understand." An image of the old woman's terrified face flashed into her mind. "I'm hoping she'll agree to let the house stand empty."

"Is she all right?" Beverly asked.

"I think so. I called the hospital, and they're letting her receive visitors." She sipped her coffee and found it cold. She pushed the cup away and folded the newspaper. "Do you think you'd have time to take me by the house so I can pick up my car?"

"You're not coming to class?"

Sarah grimaced and shook her head. "I couldn't concentrate. I'll catch up once this stuff is out of the way."

Beverly nodded. "We can leave now. I'm going to let Peter sleep. He looked terrible when he came in yesterday —I'd never seen him look so sick. What happened to him, Sarah?"

Sarah sighed, feeling guilty, and waited until they were out of the apartment before she answered. "He must have told you," she said. "I don't know how to describe it to you any better, even though it happened to me."

"He said he didn't want to think about it, he didn't want to remember it, and anyway, he couldn't describe it to me so I'd really understand," Beverly said. "I didn't want to nag him about it, but I want to *know*."

Sarah nodded but said nothing. They walked out to the parking lot. "Peter told me that Jade tried to kill him," Beverly said. "That even though it was all in his mind it was very real and seemed physical."

"Yeah."

Beverly looked at her as they got into the car. "You don't want to talk about it either," she said. "You know and Peter knows, but I don't. I can't. You won't tell me."

Sarah winced at the accusation, alert to a trace of jealousy in Beverly's voice. "It's hard to talk about," she said. "Partly because it sounds crazy, partly because words don't communicate what it was really like, and partly . . . because talking about it stirs up memories I'd rather forget. Pete may be able to discuss it with you after he's rested more—after he's feeling more himself. We're not trying to leave you out, believe me."

"I know," said Beverly. "You're just trying to protect me, both of you. But I wish it had happened to me. I wish I could have been there!"

Sarah looked at her uneasily. "No you don't," she said. "Believe me—you don't ever want that to happen to you. Stay away from the house, Bev. It couldn't have helped any of us if Jade had attacked you, too."

"No, I suppose not. But then at least I'd *know*. I'd understand what Peter is going through. I know it's selfish of me, but—I want to share everything with Peter. I feel so cut off from him now, Sarah! I look at him, and I see the pain in his eyes—and then he looks away from me, and I have no idea what he's feeling, why he's suffering so! I don't know how to help him—maybe I can't help him."

"Just accept it, Bev," Sarah said quickly. "Just be there for him. That's a help. It helped me, to have you and Pete caring about me. It would have helped more if—"

"I know." Beverly took one hand from the wheel to touch Sarah's arm. "It's just that being here feels too much like doing nothing. I hate to see Peter in pain, but the worst part is that I don't understand it. It's so hard to accept. I mean, demons . . ." She cast Sarah an apologetic glance, then looked back at the road.

"It does sound crazy," Sarah admitted. "I'm grateful for your belief—it's more than I could have expected. I didn't believe my own experience, at first. I thought I was going crazy, because that made more sense than the idea of evil spirits at large. But I experienced Jade's power at firsthand. You've had to accept it all on faith."

"I never thought you were crazy, Sarah," Beverly said earnestly. "I believed everything you told us."

"Pete didn't. He had to experience it for himself before he could believe. My word wasn't enough."

"Peter's like that," Beverly said. "He can't take anything on faith—he always wants to see the proof."

"Well, it nearly destroyed him this time," Sarah said. "I hope it was worth it to him."

Beverly pulled up behind Sarah's house. Her face was tense and unhappy. "I don't like leaving you here," she said.

"Don't worry, I'm not going inside. I don't want to give Jade another chance. Although . . . I'll have to go in to get my things when I move. I wonder if he'll let me go, or try to stop me?"

"We'll come with you then," said Beverly.

"No!" Sarah looked at Beverly uneasily and then managed to smile. "I'd be more worried about you than about myself, you see. Jade would see you as a new victim. Or he might try to use us against each other, to hurt ourselves. It'll be a problem, moving out, but I think it would be best if I did it all myself."

"But the furniture . . . you couldn't move that couch by yourself."

"All right. We'll talk about it later. Maybe there's still something we can do . . ." She glanced up at the house and twitched her shoulders uneasily. Then she leaned across to give Beverly a hug. "You go on now. Don't worry about me—I'm not going in there. I'll probably be out late, so don't bother fixing dinner for me. I'll get a bite to eat somewhere and then probably head over to the library."

"You've still got your key?"

"Yeah, so don't wait up for me, Mom." Sarah gave Beverly a big, mocking grin as she got out of the car and was pleased when her friend returned it. Still, it was a relief to watch Beverly drive away. In conversation with her, Sarah had felt she was walking a mine field, afraid at any moment a chance word would set off an explosion of insecurity. It was obvious that Beverly had picked up reverberations of Pete's guilt, and knew, without understanding, that he was hiding something from her.

Sarah stopped as she was about to mount the wooden steps leading to the back porch. Preoccupied with thoughts of Beverly, she had walked towards the house unconsciously, realizing what she was doing just in time to stop herself from going in.

Was it an unconscious mistake? Or was Jade calling her, reeling in the line? Sarah shivered, remembering Valerie's words again. Was it true? Did Jade have a hold over her that she had not recognized? Looking at the house, Sarah realized that she still felt the desire to go inside, although she could not justify it to herself.

A dream-fragment flashed vividly into her mind. She had been married, and living in this house. The house had been furnished differently, with chintz curtains and rag rugs on polished, new wooden floors, and there had been an open fireplace, and, in the dining room, behind the glass-fronted doors, pink and white china had been on display. And in that proper, old-fashioned household, she, Sarah, she, the dreamer, had been down on the floor, on her hands and knees on one of the rag rugs, her skirt and petticoat pushed up to her waist while behind her, thrusting himself into her with groans and curses, was a man she could feel but not see, a stranger, her husband.

"You whore," he whispered furiously. "You like this, don't you?"

Yes, yes, she did. She liked this brutal act, being driven like an engine, every thrust pushing her closer to the edge, to the end, when she would take leave of her senses, fly out of herself . . .

Her hand was on the kitchen door.

Sarah came back to herself with a shudder, almost leaping off the porch in her haste to get away. Her heart was pounding painfully and she felt feverish. It was a dream, that was all, only a dream. It had never happened.

You need a new boyfriend, she told herself grimly. Celibacy is driving you crazy.

Keeping her thoughts under strict control, Sarah went to her car, got in, and drove away from the house to Seton Hospital, where Mrs. Owens was resting in a private room.

"She's doing much better, but she tires easily and her mind wanders," explained the nurse who escorted Sarah. "So you mustn't get upset if she seems to forget who you are, or talks about the past as if it has just happened."

"Does she remember what happened to her? When she had her stroke."

"No. She understands what has happened to her because we told her, but her memories are confused and mixed up with dreams. I'm not certain whether or not she'll ever remember exactly what happened, but it won't hurt to ask. It may come back to her. It's often the case that stroke and accident victims suffer a partial amnesia."

The door to the room was open. Knocking lightly on it, the nurse led Sarah inside.

"Well, Helen," she said brightly. "You have a visitor this morning! This is Sarah Cole, the young lady who found you and called the ambulance when you had your stroke."

Sarah stepped forward and saw a frail, white-haired woman lying in bed. She looked smaller than Sarah remembered, and her skin was grey against the white sheets. But her blue eyes were still bright and alert in the old, sagging face.

At a nod from the smiling nurse, Sarah reached out and lifted a limp hand from the bed. "Hello, Mrs. Owens," she said. "I'm Sarah. Do you remember me?"

"I'll leave you two alone," the nurse said softly. And, pressing Sarah's shoulder quickly, she was gone.

Mrs. Owens moved her head on the pillow: a bare shake of negation. There was no recognition in her eyes.

Sarah said, "I live in the house on West Thirty-fifth Street. The one you rented to Valerie."

Something sparked in the eyes: alarm. "Valerie," said the woman in a faint voice. She shuddered. "Valerie, the spiders! They're on my face—" Her voice rose in pitch, although not in strength, and she pulled her hand out of Sarah's and made swiping motions at her face, as if brushing something away.

"It's all right," Sarah said. "There aren't any spiders here. You're safe—you're in the hospital."

The panic faded. "I know."

"But you were remembering something just now, something that happened to you. Something about Valerie. What did you mean about the spiders?"

"All over me," Mrs. Owens murmured. "On my face, spinning . . . I couldn't breathe. I couldn't move. I fell down, and they were all over me . . ."

"Where was this?"

"The house . . . my husband's house. On West Thirty-fifth Street. The rent-house. We always rented it out. He would never go there, because of the awful things that happened there when he was a child. You couldn't blame him. Such things make a terrible impression on a young mind. And it was his own mother, after all. He never would live there, afterwards. But he didn't want to sell it, either. So we always rented it out."

"Why? What awful things happened there?"

"There was never any trouble. We rented it out for years and years without any complaints or trouble. And why should there be? I don't believe in ghosts. Only memories can haunt, and they don't haunt places—they haunt people. My husband doesn't believe—didn't—" Her eyes filled with tears. "Oh, my dear. I forgot. I'm always forgetting. I can see him so clearly, still, in my mind, that it's like he's alive. But my husband has been dead for five years. I'm alone now. All alone."

Sarah squeezed the old woman's hand, trying to be sympathetic, trying to control her impatience. But she had to know. "Mrs. Owens. You were telling me about the house on West Thirty-fifth Street. What was it that happened there? What awful thing frightened your husband?"

"He was only a child then, of course."

"Yes."

"I'm sorry." Mrs. Owens smiled—a crooked smile, since only the right half of her mouth lifted. "I keep forgetting. So foolish of me. What's your name again?"

"Sarah."

"Sarah. Yes. Of course. And you're a friend of . . ."

Sarah sighed. "I live in the house on West Thirty-fifth Street," she said. "I rent from you. You were going to tell me about the house."

Mrs. Owens frowned. "Now, what stories did you hear? We don't generally tell people. You know how it is. Rumors and gossip. And people don't feel comfortable. Although there has never been any trouble. Some people won't live in a house where there has been a murder. They just don't like the idea. But the house isn't haunted, you know. It was only my late husband who felt that. It was a personal thing, because it was his mother. And his father."

"When did this happen?"

"Oh, a long time ago. Back in the Twenties. And no one who lived there ever since—although it was empty for awhile after, I believe—ever had any trouble. There was never any reliable report of . . . ghosts, or anything like that. My husband found it too painful to go back to the house where his parents had died so horribly, but that was understandable. No one else ever saw or felt anything in the house, despite all the talk about witchcraft and black magic, and the nasty rumors . . ." Mrs. Owens moved up on her pillows slightly, seeming more alert than she had been yet.

Sarah stared at her, questions bubbling in her mind, but did not speak. She was afraid of asking the wrong question and sending Mrs. Owens off on a tangent, slipping and sliding among all her memories of years past.

"You mentioned black magic and witchcraft," Sarah said carefully. "What did that have to do with the murders?"

"It was the reason for it. That's what they said. She —Albert's mother—she was involved in some sort of magical practices." Mrs. Owens sighed and closed her eyes. Then she opened them again and smiled her lopsided smile at Sarah. "Sorry, dear. I don't mean to bore you."

"You aren't boring me. I want to know about it," Sarah said. "You were telling me about your husband's mother. Was she a witch?"

"Oh, my, no, she was a very sweet woman, from what I understand. But different. Perhaps over-educated for her time. Interested in things which weren't common for Texas in the Twenties. Imaginative, sensitive, but very strong-willed. When her husband ran off she took it very hard, and the people she turned to for friendship were not . . . ordinary folks. They involved her in strange things. Magic, they called it. Shocking things . . . It's all in her diary. What happened, or what she thought happened. Perhaps she was crazy, but it wasn't her own craziness. It was those people, that man she got involved with, a sorcerer or magician or whatever he was. That man who called himself Jade."

It changed everything. Mrs. Owens' story created a new picture. A man called Jade in the 1920s—a demon called Jade nearly sixty years later—they were connected, possibly even the same being. What did it mean?

Sarah hoped the diary Mrs. Owens had spoken of would tell her more. Perhaps it held the clue to what Jade was, and how he could be destroyed.

Mrs. Owens had expressed a sleepy, drifting surprise at Sarah's interest but had agreed that she might borrow and read the diary. Impulsively, Sarah planted a kiss on Mrs. Owens' thin, dry cheek.

"Thank you," she said. "You don't know how this may help! I'll be back to see you after I've read it. Maybe I'll have a story to tell you!"

But in spite of her impatience to read the diary, Sarah had to wait. Several hours passed before she was able to find the neighbor who could open Mrs. Owens' house for her, and then she spent a frustrating half-hour searching for the book. She found it at last, not in the drawer where Mrs. Owens had thought it would be, but on a shelf between two *Reader's Digest* Condensed Books. It was a small volume covered in dark red leather. The diary of Nancy Willis Owens for the year 1923.

Sarah felt excitement rising in her as she held the book. Flipping through it, the name *Jade* seemed to leap off the handwritten pages at her. But she restrained herself; she didn't want to read it in bits and pieces, but all at once.

There was an answer in this book; maybe the answer she was looking for. Just as it had seemed most hopeless, she had been presented with a new weapon against her enemy.

Realizing she'd had nothing to eat all day, Sarah drove by the Burger King. Impatience to read the diary made her eat quickly, but something still nagged at her mind.

And then she had it. That photograph—the torn snapshot which she had found the day she had taken the house. She remembered now where she had seen the face of the man in her dream, the stranger she had recognized. He had been the man in the photograph.

But what had she done with it? Sarah scrabbled through her purse without success before remembering—seeing the image so clearly she could not doubt it—that she had put the torn picture away in her desk drawer. It was in the house.

Shoving aside her half-eaten hamburger, Sarah gnawed her lip instead. Now that she had thought of it, she was certain that the photograph was yet another connection—not merely with her dream, but with Nancy Willis Owens and the murders that had taken place there decades earlier, and with the man or the spirit called Jade. She had to see it again. Clear as it was in her memory, Sarah knew she would not be content until she had held it in her hand again.

So despite her promise to Beverly, despite her promise to herself, Sarah drove back to the house on West 35th Street, and this time she went inside.

Nothing happened. All was calm.

Sarah looked around the familiar, empty kitchen, her mind alert for signals of another presence. Jade, wherever he was, made no sign. Sarah wandered through the house, wondering where he was. In the air? In the walls? As well ask where the soul resided in the body, she thought, and yet the mind demanded a material answer.

She found the photograph in the desk drawer where she remembered putting it, and she gazed at it eagerly. The shadowed face, the faintly glinting eyes, told her nothing, did not even mock her.

Sarah suppressed a faint feeling of disappointment, and made another slow circuit of the house, both the diary and the snapshot clutched together in one hand. It was still daylight, and the slanting rays of the sun lit the high-ceilinged rooms gently, making the worn wooden floors gleam. It was a comfortable house, Sarah thought with regret, but it wasn't hers. It belonged to Jade, even if she could not feel his presence.

She told herself to go. She knew she should leave the house, drive across town to the library, find a comfortable chair and settle down to read the diary. But the stifled, public air of a library did not appeal to her; nor did the idea of returning to the Marchants' apartment to face Pete's guilty hostility and Beverly's bewilderment.

What she wanted was to stay here. To curl up on her own couch in her own house, in comfort and privacy. Why shouldn't she do something so simple? She felt safe, and why shouldn't she trust her own feelings? If there was a trap in her logic, Sarah didn't want to know about it. She would stay.

Feeling pleased with herself, Sarah took a beer from the refrigerator and settled down on the couch to read.

Chapter Ten

February 2

I can delay no longer. Tomorrow I must take my children and move into the new house. To think that once I longed for this day . . . It was to have been our home, but now it is merely another trial to bear, a strange place, without warmth or meaning. Walter and I planned that house together, watched it grow as we watched our children. Without him, it means less than nothing to me. Somehow I imagined that when the house was finished he would come back to me, and we would be a family once again in our new home. Foolish of me, I know, but even now, as I write, sitting in this room for the last time, spending the last night in the house where I was once so happy, I still expect a reprieve. I still strain my ears for the sound of his footstep outside, the sound of his voice calling the children as he enters. I tell myself that he is gone forever, but I cannot believe it. I cannot believe that I mean so little to him, that the years we spent together, the love we had, has all been for nothing. To be thrown away as if I meant nothing to him. My pride, I suppose. Aunt Gena said as much, although I was not meant to hear; said that it was my haughty ways, my pride in my good education, my constant talk of books and art that drove Walter to the arms of a simpler, more properly submissive woman. But Walter liked my learning, and my pride, when he met me, and he must have known—surely I proved, in all the years we were together—that I never thought of anything more, any higher calling, than to be his wife and the mother of his children? I would have done anything he asked. I would still do anything. Anything, to have him back.

February 10

Caught up in the chores of moving, I have been remiss in writing. But perhaps it is just as well. This will be a boring legacy to read over in my old age, if ever I should read it again. Only one thing I want to write about or talk about; only one subject on my mind: Walter. I feel dead inside, like a ghost in this house that was to have been ours. How can this be my home, when Walter is gone and has never lived here, will never live here?

How bored my friends are with me, with my silent misery. I try not to weary them with my constant complaints, my eternal longing for Walter, but then I find that I have nothing to say to them beyond a few, mechanical comments on the weather and the rate at which children grow. They say—so obviously eager to offer some positive advice—that the new house will be good for me. In new surroundings, I will find it easier to forget. Forget. They all want me to forget him. That is the sum of their advice, the patent medicine they offer. Face reality, Nancy. Admit he is gone. Forget him.

Such good, sensible, realistic advice, and I can no more follow it than I can fly. I continue to hope and wait for Walter's return because I know of no other way to live. I cannot give up the only man I have ever loved. Without him, I scarcely exist. Only the children give me a reason to go on living—for what would they do without me?

My stubbornness in clinging to foolish hopes—my stubbornness, too, has been offered as a reason for why Walter left me—makes my friends sigh for me. It can do no good, they say. Refusing to forget will only make life harder for me.

But one person agrees with me. I met someone today who believes that stubbornness can do wonders. Who believes that all is not lost, so long as I truly want Walter back. Someone who thinks that I can accomplish something by refusing to forget and refusing to give up.

Who is this person? Oh—only Yolanda Ferris, Ursula's strange sister, back from an extended stay in Europe and as out of place in our quiet little community as an eagle in a hen house.

February 13

Yolanda called today.

I find myself fascinated by her, drawn to her where others are repelled or frightened. She is "not our sort," of course. Poor Ursula is shamed by her, but she is family and can hardly disown her, despite her loose talk, her public smoking, fast ways and bold way of looking. She is rather contemptuous of us all—she finds us slow and provincial and boring. I was flattered that she sought me out, that she found me different enough from the common herd to be worth knowing.

She talked about her life in Europe, and about books and music and art—the sort of conversation I have been starved for. I did worry about keeping up my end of the conversation—my life has been devoted to the children and to Walter for so many years that I have not had much time for literature or music, dearly though I love them—but she did not seem to mind. She seemed as happy to talk as I was to listen—grateful, I suppose, for a sympathetic ear. The things she told me! The things she has done, the places she has been, the famous people she has glimpsed or even spoken to in the great cities of the world! She talked about her life in London and Paris and Berne. I am tempted to set down some of the things she told me here—they were so much more interesting than my poor, dull life. The stuff of an exciting novel. She made me forget my troubles in my interest. My spirits were lifted higher than they have been in six months. She made me remember those exhilarating conversations of my school-days, when everything seemed possible, and the whole world might be attained with a little effort. How my world has shrunk—although I let it go willingly, gladly, for love. Only to lose even that. A depressing note to end on, after those bright hours with Yolanda. And yet I always come round to that in the end.

February 15

If only there were something I could *do*. Something positive. Forgetting is a negation, and I don't want that. I want to cling to my memories and my love for Walter and make them real again. I don't want to lose myself in wishes, but to make use of them. I want my love to be so strong that it will compel his return, that it cannot be denied. If I had been strong enough, if I had loved him enough, would he have ever left me? But now that he is gone, why should it be forever? Men do leave their wives and then return to them, just as they take leave of their senses, only to return to them when the liquor wears off. If I could make Walter feel the power of my love, surely he would return?

February 17

God bless Yolanda. She listens to me and understands as no one else does. She may look bold and hard as brass, but when she presses my hand and tells me not to give up hope . . .

February 18

I told Yolanda, a little timidly, my thoughts on love, and my perhaps foolish dream of compelling Walter's return. She did not think it foolish. She was very interested. She encouraged me to go on thinking of Walter. She said that if

I could learn how to *will*, how to use my will for what I wanted—

And then she broke off, and looked very mysterious. And when I pressed her she hedged and seemed reluctant. At last she said that I had stumbled upon a very important principle without understanding it, out of my own need. But that she knew someone who—Again, she stopped as if she had said too much. Finally she told me that she would bring me some books to read, and that afterwards we could discuss them. I am eaten up with curiosity.

February 22

I have been reading and thinking these past few days; nothing but reading and thinking. At first I was disappointed by the books Yolanda brought to me. They were books about Magic! Superstition, I thought. It was all crazy. Skimming through them did not change my mind. But I believe that Yolanda is too intelligent to be taken in by nonsense, so there must be something to this. So I set myself to reading without preconceptions. And now I wonder . . . it seems mad, but there is something more to it. The things hinted at make my skin prickle with anticipation.

February 23

Yolanda knows Crowley, the one they call The Great Beast. She met him in Paris. And she understands his writings because she has seen what he writes about! Oh, the things Yolanda knows . . . the things she has done . . . are much stranger than anyone in Austin could imagine! It is another world entirely that she belongs to. And yet within my grasp. I reread Crowley with new attention. Much of what he writes is deliberately obscure, as a challenge and a caution.

He proclaims in his writings and his self the power of the directed human will. "Do what thou wilt shall be the whole of the law." Want something strongly and purely enough, and it will come to pass.

How much more exhilarating that is than the tame, weary advice to forget, to adjust to reality! To take the world, and shape it closer to the heart's desire!

March 1

A whole new life stretches before me; a whole new world. Yes, it *is* within my grasp! Yolanda has told me so much, deciding that I can be trusted, now, to understand the truth. She has told me of certain things she has done, rituals she has taken part in with others, how she accomplished things that would normally be considered impossible. She showed me certain proofs which I should not write about, not even here. But it is true, I know. I have glimpsed the Truth.

Yolanda has told me about a man she says is even greater than Crowley, a powerful magician who is her lover; who is here in Austin even now. Crowley has the popular fame, but this man has the real power, she says. He has put into practice things Crowley scarcely dares hint at. He has achieved the ultimate. He can dissociate his soul from his body and send it travelling—in other forms, or disincarnate. He leads more than the one life we are normally allotted. I fell into a kind of a dream as she told me about him. I envisioned him changing bodies like suits of clothes, dispossessing the previous owners and then discarding their husks. He is the Superman Nietzsche dreamed of, beyond questions of Good and Evil. I must meet this man, and I tremble at the thought. He could help me, teach me, as he has Yolanda, or he could as easily destroy me.

March 6

Today I met him, the man Yolanda told me about; the great magus who calls himself "Jade."

Never before have I been so struck by the sheer force of a

personality. It is as if he has a great fire burning inside him, whereas the rest of us are only matches, easily extinguished by any passing breeze, or even by *his* breath.

Physically, he is rather small, muscular but small-boned. His eyes are strange. They are brown with golden flecks in them, like bits of flame. His hair is short and dark, his hands manicured, his dress quiet but fashionable. I took him for a Yankee by his speech—his voice is soft and easy, but every word is absolutely precise.

Describing him physically does not describe him. I was aware of his power as soon as I entered the room, even before I actually saw him. I *felt* him, his will, his attention turned towards me, like a great heat, like a force of nature. I concentrated on details, clinging to solid reality, afraid that otherwise I would be swept away.

"Jade is my magical name," he told me, smiling, when I made the *faux pas* of addressing him as "Mr. Jade."

"It is a name with a special meaning for me, the name I chose for myself," he said. "You must have a magical name, too, now that you have joined us."

I was flattered and frightened by that. So I had joined them. He has accepted me. He stared at me—he stared at my bosom, at my legs, at my face, and at my middle, frankly inspecting me. I was afraid of failing some test. I felt my cheeks heating and I struggled with my embarrassment, but I was afraid to meet his eyes. I felt—I *knew*—that if he concentrated his will upon me I would do anything, no matter how out of character or morally repugnant. I was almost paralyzed by his presence. I saw that even Yolanda, normally so bold and sure of herself, faded away to a quiet grey mouse, eager to please her master and afraid of failing him. Someday, I thought, he will break her and cast her aside. Can I expect anything better?

"We will call you Lilith," Jade said. "It is a good name, and a powerful one."

I wanted to ask why I should not choose my own name, as he had done; to ask why Yolanda did not have a magical name; to protest against the name. I did not want to be called after Adam's first, disobedient wife, cast aside for Eve, changed into a demon. But I said nothing, afraid to challenge him. Perhaps I should have; perhaps he was testing me and would have had more respect for me if I had spoken up and asserted my own will.

March 7

Jade came to see me today. In my own house. He stood very close to me, touching me now and again as if accidentally, but always looking at me to show me it was deliberate. Always testing me. I did not move away. I let him test me.

"The love spells are the easiest," he said. "To compel desire in a woman or a man, to bring back a straying lover, to wrap the web of passion tightly. Even those who lack the strength of will to succeed in other aspects of the Art often manage to work such love spells. It is a very ancient and widely used magic, the way of a man with a maid, or a woman with her lover."

Was he telling me that it will not be hard to win back Walter? Telling me I could do it myself if I had any willpower at all? Or teasing me, letting me know that he could make me fall in love with *him* if he cared to? But I could never love Jade. I will do whatever he tells me—I will give myself to him, if necessary—but all that I do is for the love of Walter. Because my life is unimportant without him. I will do whatever I must, whatever I can, to win Walter back.

So I did not flinch when Jade put his hand flat on my breast. I looked at him as coolly as I could, thinking he was more like a man judging horseflesh than a man wanting a woman, but his hard, bright eyes were too much for me and I dropped my gaze. He laughed, scoring a point, and then walked around the parlor, assessing it. The windows were open, the day was warm and windy. From the fields outside rose my son's voice as he ran and played.

"I could make you want me," he said. "No matter how you think of your lost Walter, if I cared to, I could make you shiver with desire for me."

It startled me, that he knew my husband's name when I

had not told him. I wondered if Yolanda had told him, or if he had picked it out of my mind, lying unspoken on my lips.

"You are an attractive woman," he went on. "If you were taught how to dress and do your hair and wore a bit of paint, you would draw many compliments."

"I do not care to," I said, wondering what he meant to do with me.

"I could make you care to, if I willed it."

"And if I did not will it?"

"Would you care to test yourself against me?" He sounded amused, as well he might. During our talk he had been backing me across the room by subtle inches. I could feel myself perspiring. I did not dare meet his eyes. I was terrified that he would make me do something humiliating, to degrade me, to teach me a lesson. I did not doubt that he could break me, but I sought some way out.

"Crowley said that 'Do as thou wilt' did not include the license to overwhelm others," I said. "Even the weak have wills which should not be violated, even though it is possible."

"You've been reading Crowley, have you?" Suddenly he released me, and flung himself down in the easy chair. "Crowley's a coward and an ass. If it *can* be done, it *should* be done. He tries to have it both ways—the law of the strong mixed with some kind of golden rule for the benefit of the weak. Crowley has seen the truth, and he is afraid of it, for all his posturing. Weak wills demand to be destroyed. That is their nature. The weak beg for mastery. Like you, my Lilith. You're waiting for a master."

"I'm waiting for my husband."

"No. He didn't want you. He left you. If you had really wanted him, really loved him with all your soul, he could not have done that. If you were stronger—" He watched me closely. He ran his tongue over his lips. "What do you think of Crowley's attitude about the sexual nature of magic? Do you believe that? That results are obtained only when the magician lets himself go in a kind of cosmic orgasm?"

I did not flinch at his language. Talking with Yolanda has made me less shockable. "You would know better than I," I said.

He laughed. "Such humility! You have no interest in it, I suppose? It was not that aspect which attracted you, I suppose? I tell you, my Lilith, the spiritual ecstasy, the shooting forth of the unstoppable Will, is the greatest experience of all. Sex is a dim reflection, but not a poor analogy. For lesser mortals, the sexual coupling releases the greatest force they shall ever know, this side of death. But they all stop there, unaware of how to harness this energy so as to reach even greater heights of pleasure and power.

"I think Yolanda has told you that our rituals involve sexual congress. The coupling builds up energy which the properly disciplined Will can feed upon and grow strong. There is nothing else to match the power inherent in sexual intercourse, save violent death. And death has its drawbacks. Sexuality is endlessly renewing, while the blood sacrifice . . ." He shrugged, smiling like a devil at me.

"The spurting of blood or the spurting of semen—one or the other is necessary for a ritual to succeed, for the magic to work. Sex or death, to focus the power of the Will."

He talked on and on and I sat numb and entranced, both repelled and fascinated. He may be the most powerful man on earth, and I want, I need, some part of that power for myself. I am weak, I know how weak I am, but I have my love to give me strength. I love Walter, and for that love I will do anything. I will do whatever I must to learn how to win my husband back.

And before he left—again, seeming to read my thoughts —Jade promised me: "I shall give you what you truly want, my Lilith. Your heart's desire. Blessed art thou among women."

The devil quoting scripture. His words should have pleased me, but they made me shiver with a sudden dread.

March 12

I am in it now, well and truly in it. I could not escape if I wanted to.

They need me for something, although I do not know what. I am to help them and, in return, I shall have what I most want. I know they can teach me how to get Walter back, and I will do anything for that.

Although I am afraid of what is to come, I am impatient for it to begin. I think about the days *after*, when Jade and Yolanda will have gone away and left me to resume my life with Walter.

I have already begun, on my own, to will his return.

At night, every night, I place his picture beneath my pillow and dream of him. During the day I carry a photograph with me, in my apron pocket while I do my chores, and I stare at it and kiss it and touch it many times. Walter is never out of my thoughts. Thoughts, properly directed, can compel. Unskilled as I am, I *can* concentrate. The force of my thoughts must reach Walter, wherever he is. Eventually they will draw him to me, like a magnet pulling steel.

March 15

Today Ursula came by to warn me against Yolanda. I nearly laughed out loud.

"She means you no good. She's a dangerous, untrustworthy creature—I say it even though she is my own sister. You do not understand her, and she will harm you. She has dangerous friends and vicious habits. She means you harm, I fear." Etc. etc.

I scarcely remember what she said. During her visit I was thinking about Walter, as I always do. I saw Walter sitting in the chair where Ursula perched; saw Walter walking in through the door as she walked out. Walter, filling my vision like the sight of God.

March 20

At night I can feel him beside me in our bed. When I open my eyes, the illusion vanishes, but for just a few moments it is so *real*. Only a matter of time, now. My will is almost too strong to deny. While Walter sleeps, my soul flies to him and takes stitches in his skin. I pull the threads, and his astral body flies to me, to nestle in my arms. His physical body will not be long in following.

Soon he will return. Soon he will be here beside me. And then Jade will tell me how to keep him, how to bind his soul to mine with bonds he cannot break in this world or any other.

March 27

I gather hints and try to guess what they want of me, for they won't tell me what I must do or what they need me for. I know that the date set for the ritual is in April; that is all I know. I think of Walter and try not to worry.

March 29

Yolanda took me to Jade's lodgings today—a suite in the Driskill Hotel. I don't think Jade was expecting us—although he showed no surprise—and I don't know what Yolanda intended by the visit. Jade had coffee sent up and we sat around sipping it and making small talk, as if we were in society. It was very peculiar.

Eventually, almost as if he were at a loss for anything else to do, Jade took something out of a case. He unwrapped a piece of silk from it and put it into my hands. "What do you make of her?"

I held a dark green carved stone—jade, I think—about six or seven inches high and no more than three across. It was in the likeness of a naked woman.

Oddly, it felt warm, almost hot, to my touch. And as I looked at it I felt the most powerful sensation. It was a blast of pure evil, as if the thing had been a poisonous snake, uncoiling in my hand. I was so frightened I nearly dropped it. But Jade must have anticipated such a response because his hands had closed around it before it could fall.

He set it down on a small table. I looked at it out of the corner of my eye, not liking to look at it but not feeling safe leaving it unwatched, either. I was too shaken to speak. Yolanda, too, was staring at it. She was very pale, although with fear or simply excitement I could not tell. Jade was watching both of us with his usual calm amusement.

I felt he was challenging me. Frightened but determined to prove my courage, I rose and walked to the table. I heard Yolanda gasp. I reached out and touched the figure for only a moment. It was enough. I knew I had not imagined it—the thing was alive. No, that's not true. The stone was merely stone; the woman merely a carved representation. But there was life *within* it, like electricity glowing in a glass bulb, like lightning caught in a jar. Some spirit, some living spirit, had been put into the figure. It did not belong there; it was trapped there, unnaturally preserved within the solid stone.

I looked at Jade and saw him watching me.

"I must leave now," I said. I was terrified, so frightened that I felt ill. The life in that stone was so wrong, so unnatural, that I could not stay in the same room with it. I did not know if it was evil or dangerous, but it horrified me.

When we were away, I questioned Yolanda about the little figure. But she was evasive, claiming to know nothing.

"You had seen it before," I said. "It didn't surprise you."

She admitted that Jade had shown it to her, had her hold it, some time past. But I suspected that she knew more and I was determined to have it out of her. So all the way home I persisted in talking about it—even though I would rather have forgotten it—speculating on what the thing in the stone was. At last I hit upon something.

"It wants to get out," I said. "I could feel that. It is trapped in the stone and wants out. Do you suppose Jade can keep it trapped?"

"Oh, yes! He—" She stopped short but my imagination finished the sentence for her. "He put it there." Was that right? As casually as if I knew what I was talking about, I said, "Of course, he will call it out again, with our help."

She turned her head to look at me, making me fear for our safety as she was driving a poorly paved road. "What has he been telling you?" she demanded.

I smiled, smug as a cat. "What hasn't he told *you*?"

A silly trick, but it made her uneasy. "Why should he tell you anything?" she wondered aloud.

"I know how powerful Jade is," I said. "But I wonder if he's powerful enough. The spirit in that stone—I could sense the strength of it. It must be awfully powerful. Once we set it free, will Jade be able to control it?"

Yolanda laughed, and I knew I had said something wrong, revealed my ignorance.

"You don't know anything," she said, pleased. "You're only fishing." After that, I couldn't get anything out of her.

I have been trying to puzzle it out with the clues I have. Jade's name—that must be a clue, since the figure is made of jade. Or is that just one of Jade's jokes? I wish I knew more. I would be stronger if I knew what was to happen.

March 30

Jade has sent a small black dog to watch me.

It isn't a dog.

Its eyes are not a dog's eyes. When it looks at me, I see a flicker of that yellow-brown gleam and a suggestion of the heat that glows out of Jade's eyes, and I know that it is not a dog but Jade who is looking at me.

Superficially, it is a small, shaggy mongrel, one ear torn from a fight, friendly and hungry. The children beg to keep it and are enamored of it. It doesn't matter what I do—it *will* stay.

According to Crowley, "You can always use the body inhabited by an elemental, such as an eagle, hare, wolf or any convenient animal, by making a very simple compact."

April 1

I wait like a dumb animal, knowing that Jade will not let me escape. I am afraid he means to kill me, not merely to use me sexually as I had thought. I am to be the victim, the lure, the bait.

I reread Crowley and think of Walter. I pray to Walter,

not to God. I pray that Walter will come before it is too late, come and take me away from here. I am frightened, and my fear makes my will waver. But I must do it. I must call Walter to me.

The dog keeps getting into the house, no matter what I do. I have forbidden the children to let it in, but time and again I turn to find it behind me, watching. I put it outside again, and it does not protest or fight. It only looks at me, and we know each other.

April 2

I dreamed of Walter last night. He had come home. I heard his voice in the parlor, heard his footsteps on the floorboards. He called my name, but when I woke and rushed from my bed to find him there was no one there but the little black dog, curled up in Walter's favorite chair, watching me.

April 3

I told Yolanda about the dog. She was not surprised. She told me that Jade had had other "familiar spirits" in the past —chiefly, a lizard and a cat, which he sent out to spy for him.

I asked her if these "familiar spirits" were not rather animals who had been taken over by Jade, possessed by him; creatures which housed some fragment of his will and personality and were extensions of himself. She seemed surprised, and somewhat suspicious, that I should know this, but she did not deny it. When I asked her how many such beings Jade could control at one time, she seemed agitated. She asked me how I knew such things, and I quoted Crowley to her.

"I thought you didn't understand his books," she said, rather peevishly. Could it be that I am smarter and stronger than Yolanda—and Jade—expected? I think I make Yolanda uneasy now, and I wonder if it is because she realizes that I am not the simple, unwitting victim she must have thought I would be. I don't know enough, but I know too much—more than I was expected to know.

"Has Jade ever managed to possess another human being without losing consciousness in his own body?" I asked. "Can he split his soul and be in two places at once?"

Not such an unusual question, I thought. We used to discuss such things, back when she confided in me, before I was truly drawn into the web. That Jade could leave his body and take on other forms was something she had boasted of to me.

"I don't know," she said nervously. "What a strange idea."

"Not so strange," I said. "When Jade is watching me through the eyes of that dog, he is not fully *here*. He is also somewhere else, in his own body, doing something else. You told me once he could take on other forms. Did you mean only animals? Or can he possess other human bodies —perhaps survive his own bodily death that way?"

My questioning shook her badly, and she soon made an excuse and left, telling me nothing except what I might deduce from her nervousness.

April 6

Walter is in town, so I have heard. He has not tried to contact me, but he will come to me soon, I am certain. I know why he is here. He has come in response to my will. I have drawn him back to town, and soon I will draw him back to my arms.

April 9

They came for me in the middle of the night. Jade and Yolanda both wore long black gowns, and had me dress in one. Jade would not let me wake my children, nor even leave them a note of explanation.

We drove through the blackness in Jade's saloon car,

heading south out of the city, then west on the Bee Caves
road. Yolanda was tense and silent. Jade was as relaxed and
powerful as ever. I fancied that he gave off a kind of glow,
there in the coolness and dark of the closed car.

"Don't worry and don't think," he said to me. "Simply
feel. I will tell you what to do. You must trust me."

But I knew that was the last thing I could do. I would not
trust him, even though I might obey him. I would do what I
had to do. I reminded myself that although no man but
Walter had ever held me in his arms, although I loved only
Walter, I was no virgin. I have borne children and known
suffering and pain, and I could bear what Jade would do. I
would not be his blood sacrifice, but I would be his altar, his
ritual tool, the focus of his will, his sexual receptacle. I
would survive, and return home, and Walter would respond
to *my* will.

Outside the city we travelled narrow, rutted farm roads.
At last, Jade pulled the car to the side and announced that
we would walk. Branches whipped my face and high weeds
slowed my progress, and as I stumbled through the darkness
I prayed I would not tread on a snake or twist my ankle. Out
here, away from the city, anything might happen. I did not
want to be made any more helpless than I already was. The
sky had lightened to grey by the time we reached our
destination, and the approaching dawn was some relief. In
the pale morning light I saw that Jade had led us to the
mouth of a small cave.

I knew there were many caves in the region, most of
them unexplored and likely to remain that way. The
entrance to one had been boarded up after two children met
their deaths playing there.

To my relief, Jade showed no interest in entering the
cave. He set Yolanda and myself to work clearing away
brush and sweeping at the ground to clear a limestone arena.
On the stone surface of the ground he drew a figure in
colored chalk—a star within a circle.

Yolanda had been carrying a small, wooden chest which
Jade now took from her. He took out three things: something I could not see, which he put in his mouth and
chewed; a small leather bag; and a small, silk-wrapped

package which I knew must be the stone figure. Then Jade looked at me. "Come," he said.

The very possibility of resistance seemed to drain out of me, and I went to him and followed him into the center of the chalk circle. I knew then that I had been fooling myself. I was his victim; he would do whatever he chose to me and I could not stop him. My previous experience of his power was as nothing. I realized then that he had never before concentrated more than the smallest fraction of his will upon me. I had been intimidated by his surface; now I was perceiving the power that lay within his depths.

"Disrobe, and cast your gown outside the circle," he said, and I did so, standing naked in the dawn.

His eyes left mine for a moment as he removed his own gown, and I had time to feel afraid and cold. I shivered, and he caught me, fixed me with his gaze again, stilling me.

He put the jade figure—although it was wrapped in silk, I could feel the living heat of the thing—into my hand. "Unwrap her and gaze upon her," he said.

I did not want to, but I could not stop my hands from fumbling at the cloth, or stop my eyes from turning down to look. Only in a tiny part of my mind was I screaming and struggling and imagining escape.

The tiny figure throbbed with an evil, unnatural life.

"There is my immortality," said Jade. "That is what you hold in your hands."

I stroked it, as if it were a part of him and I his lover.

Jade laughed, a low sound like a purr. "And yours, too, my dear," he said. "As long as that stone survives, we both shall live. Imagine being stone, my Lilith. Immortal, unfeeling stone."

Although I struggled to end the repetitive motion, my hands went on caressing the thing. The little green face leered up at me, and the tiny, slanting eyes seemed to sparkle with a hint of the fire I knew from Jade's. I stared at it, feeling that I was turning to stone while the stone in my hand turned to flesh.

"But, while stone is very useful, and very strong, human bodies were made for pleasure," Jade said. I realized then that he had moved closer to me and that he was touching me, stroking my body even as I stroked the tiny figure. My body was responding to his touch, and I knew that I was not turning to stone at all. I was flesh, I was alive, and the pleasure I felt beneath his hands frightened me. I felt his breath on my face, and then his tongue in my mouth, flickering like a snake's. But the venom was so sweet. I was willing to die for it. I closed my eyes.

"No. Look at me. Know me," he commanded.

I had to obey. I didn't want to see him, but I had to look. I did not want to feel his mouth or his hands upon my naked body, but at the same time my body cried out in desire. I was torn in two: my body hovering on the brink of ecstasy while my mind was in torment. I stood accepting all his caresses and hardly knew if I obeyed his will or my own.

Then he pulled me to the ground. His hard, naked body pressed the length of mine, and the small stone figure was trapped between us. I could not free my hands. I held the statue and could neither embrace Jade nor try to push him away. Only a small discomfort, feeling the stone pressed against my ribs, but that tiny discomfort was enough to keep me from drowning in his arms. I turned my head slightly and saw Yolanda. She was standing outside the circle watching us, her face a study in mixed passion: desire, fear, hope, jealousy.

Then Jade's eyes caught mine again. I looked into those brown and golden depths and I could not look away again. I felt as if they were burning into my soul.

"You are my bride, Lilith," he said. "I have chosen you as my mate. We will be bound together forever, inseparable." His tongue moved into my mouth, exploring it lazily. I could no longer differentiate his body from my own, we were so tangled together. I felt that he knew my thoughts as well as his own, as well as he knew my body. And still I wanted to escape.

He answered that thought as I had it, pulling his lips away and murmuring, "No, Lilith. You cannot escape your fate. You cannot escape yourself. They are not *your* thoughts, not any longer. They are mine. We shall be one mind in two bodies. Soon you will be a part of me, and I a part of you, and there will be no more talk of 'me' and 'you,' and no more thoughts of escape."

I was scarcely certain that I had heard his words—they

seemed to flow directly into my mind. I felt half-asleep, drugged. Only my body was still alive, demanding, set on fire by the light in his eyes. I didn't care for thoughts or words. I pressed my lips against his.

His arms tightened around me and with his knee he parted my too-willing legs. I could feel him laughing into my open mouth: a weird, triumphant laughter that filled me up and rattled loose all thoughts. Who was I? I felt breasts soft against my hard chest, knew the feeling of a woman's body crushed against me, felt her legs part beneath me and then clasp me—

He thrust himself into me, and fire blazed all along my spine. But his sudden movement jarred the stone figure, pressing it sharply, bruisingly into my ribs. I cried out, abruptly back in my own body, and terrified. "Walter!" I cried.

"No." Jade raised himself on his arms above me, panting, and thrust again. At the sudden lifting of his weight, the small jade statue fell off my middle and to the ground beside me. Jade, pounding viciously into me, neither noticed nor cared. "Look at me. Feel me. No one else but *me!*"

I clung to the thought of Walter, knowing that he could save me. But his beloved face wavered in my mind. I could see no face but Jade's, blazing above me like a sign from Hell.

My body responded distantly to Jade's assault. I knew what had nearly happened, and my fear diluted the passion my body still felt. Realizing that he was losing me, Jade became more careful. He slowed his rhythm and began to kiss me again. "Let go," he said, between kisses. His hands worked on me, insinuating, arousing my flesh. "Enjoy it. Don't think; just feel. Let yourself feel this pleasure fully. You'll have such ecstasy, now and forever. Relax. Let me take you, Lilith. Give yourself to me."

As I struggled to hold on to my own awareness, to think of anything but Jade, Yolanda helped me by moving within my range of vision. Jade saw her, too, and he turned his blazing eyes on her for a moment.

"The statue," she whispered, pointing at the ground.

The relaxing of Jade's attention let me find my voice.

"Take *her*," I said, meaning Yolanda. "Take her instead. She wants you. She would give in to you. I only want Walter. She loves you."

"It isn't love I want," he said. But his blazing eyes went from me to Yolanda and back again, and then he said, "Yolanda. Fetch the bag and come into the circle."

Still joined to me, supporting himself above me on his arms, Jade gestured Yolanda to his side. From my helpless position I stared up at them, knowing that Jade was not done with me and wondering what new indignities he had in mind for us. Yolanda looked dazed.

Looking down on me as if from a very great height, Jade said, "If you won't give yourself to me, I shall have to take you."

It all happened so quickly after that—so smoothly.

From the soft leather bag Yolanda had brought him, Jade drew a knife. With his other hand, he grasped her hair and yanked her head back to expose the neck. Then, with one hard, brutal stroke, Jade cut open Yolanda's throat.

There was not even time for her face to register fear. The blood spurted out, more than I would have imagined there would be, spattering Jade's face, spattering me. All this time, Jade was still, obscenely, inside me. His eyes looked down at me, twin fires blazing through the carnage.

I opened my mouth to scream, but I had no breath. Jade was on me, full-length, his weight pressing me into the ground, his mouth sucking greedily at mine as if he could draw the life out of me.

The whole world was his. There was nothing that was not Jade, nothing happened that Jade did not will. My body rocked back and forth under his control. I felt his heart pumping mine, breathed his breath in through my lungs, moved to his command. My own thoughts were snuffed out one by one. Every individualistic impulse was suffocated. I was his.

And still, something that might be called Nancy Owens, some dim part that remained of me, fought on. I clung to the idea of myself, refused to become a part of Jade. I was not-Jade, in Jade's world.

Yolanda's blood greased our bodies and mingled with our sweat. Blood and semen—I remembered Jade's words. The act of destruction and the act of creation. How could I fight against those twin powers? When he climaxed, I knew, his will would be a tidal wave, sweeping mine out of existence.

Why not? Did it really matter? Did my survival really matter to anyone?

Yes, it did. It mattered to me, even if I could not have said why. And so I went on struggling. I have been trying to find physical analogies for the battle, but there is no point. It was a war of souls, more painful, more bitter and more difficult than anything I have ever endured. Physically he raped me; mentally I continued to resist. And as I went on resisting, holding out against all the odds, Jade had to shift more and more power to our spiritual struggle, leaving our bodies to sweat and grapple as they would, leaving them as unimportant.

And so it was that I could act. So it was that my hand, moving helplessly on the ground, flopped like a beached fish, grazed the knife that Jade had used to kill Yolanda. It was a very sharp knife. I scarcely felt it cut me, although from the corner of my eye I saw the fresh red bead the surface of skin already stained with another's blood.

I didn't think. I was too occupied with holding my own against Jade to be able to plan. My hand grasped the knife almost of its own volition. My arm rose languidly into the air and came down on Jade's back as if I wished to pull him closer to me. But the hand held a knife, and the knife plunged deep into Jade's naked, laboring back.

The shock of it made him pull out of my mind, although not my body.

We stared at each other. His eyes were only a man's eyes now. No fire, no strength, only pain and bewilderment at the approach of death. I felt new strength. He pulled away from me and tried to rise. I stabbed him again.

I don't remember much about going away from that place.

I remember the two bodies lying in the chalked circle, their blood eating away at the boundaries of it and seeping into the porous rock. I remember bending over Jade, feeling for breath or pulse, needing to know for certain that he was dead.

It is nearly night, now. I sent the children to Hannah's

house. This is my confession: I killed the man called Jade. It was self-defense, although I do not expect anyone to understand that. I suppose I shall pay for my actions.

It is hard to direct my thoughts, and yet I know I must plan. There are so many things I must think of now. But I am weary unto death from my struggle with Jade, a weariness sleep cannot help.

I find myself thinking of Walter, almost as if nothing happened. It is easy to think of him, to let my mind slip back into old patterns. It is such a habit to think of him and to want him back. I want him still but, ironically, I hope he does not come back. I am not fit for any man now. I thought once that Walter could save me, but it is far too late for that, now. I can't remember why I wanted Walter. I don't know what I would say to him if he came tonight.

Who am I? I am not who I once was. I have been changed. I am not Jade, although he tried to take me, to make me another part of himself, to fill me with his own spirit. I fought him off. I survived. But having survived, where do I go now?

I kept the small jade figure and took it away with me, back to town. It lives, still, warm to the touch and tingling with the same energy. I have it wrapped in silk on the table before me as I write. What is it that lives within the stone? Can I make use of it? If I could turn that power to my own use . . . Some instinct warns me not to try. Perhaps I should destroy it, and end this whole affair. But I am afraid to—and I don't want to. I want to know more. What life is it that heats the smooth stone? Would it give me Jade's powers if I knew how to use it?

Why shouldn't I use it, as Jade tried? Why shouldn't I be more successful? If Walter comes

Chapter Eleven

And there the journal ended, in the middle of a line. Sarah flipped through the book's remaining pages, hoping for some postscript, some last thoughts, but the creamy blankness was unmarred by ink. She stared at the page she had just read, wanting more from it. She felt frustrated and muddled, emerging into her own world again.

What had happened next? Had her husband knocked at the door? Had the stone figure come to life in her hands? Sarah thought of Mrs. Owens. What had she said? There had been murders in the house—plural. Both Nancy and Walter Owens had died here. But who had killed them? And why?

Sarah became aware of the silence.

It was not a natural silence. It was as if the whole house had been wrapped in a muffling cloth, isolated from the rest of the world. Sarah got to her feet, her body already tensing for the expected attack, and then the world was plunged into darkness.

The darkness was as absolute as the silence, and the suddenness of it was dizzying, as if the room had fallen away. Sarah clutched the diary to her chest and remained standing, feeling the couch against the backs of her legs. Her eyes strained against the blackness, but there was nothing to see, no shapes or shades to grade the darkness. She was blind. Her heart pounded loudly in her ears, and the darkness seemed to throb around her. It was as if she'd been swallowed alive by some huge animal.

It wouldn't do her any good to think like that. Sarah forced herself to be calm and breathed slowly and deeply. She had to get out of the house, to safety. There was no reason why she had to stay here—she could find her way to the door even in total darkness. To her left was the dining room; beyond that, the kitchen, the back porch, and safety. It seemed an awfully long way to walk blind, but she had no real choice.

She had taken only the first step when she heard the breathing. She took another step and did not turn back, although her skin crawled with the awareness that there was someone behind her.

There was a sibilant whisper, scarcely louder than the breathing. Had someone spoken her name? Boards creaked, across the room, as if someone was coming towards her. Her skin prickled, electrified, as if a hand had brushed her as a teasing threat.

Sarah walked more quickly, stumbled, and cried out, bruising her hip against a doorframe. Her own breath was coming so quickly that she couldn't hear anything else above the sound of it rasping in her ears. Her hand trembled as she stretched it out, and she had to grit her teeth, but her fingers found the edge of the kitchen doorway and she oriented herself again.

Behind her—but she wouldn't think about that. There was nothing behind her. There was no one else in the house —only Jade. And Jade could not hurt her. Jade was not a person, not a thing, not a demon, but only the leftover echo of someone who had once lived. He had powers, still, but they were not physical powers. He could only use her own mind, her fears, against herself. All he had was trickery, and she would not let herself be tricked by him again. Feeling a little more secure in her own strength, Sarah stepped through the doorway, and into the solid, immovable body of a man. Powerful arms crushed her in an embrace.

She should have been frightened, but, for a moment, all Sarah wanted to do was to relax, to give herself up to sensation, to be stroked by knowing hands. She had turned her face up to be kissed, straining forward, when her own response, the betrayal by her own body, suddenly frightened her far more than any invisible stranger. She jerked away, flailing out with her arms and shouting incoherently. Her blows did not connect. There was no one there.

Panting, her shoulders slumped. "No," Sarah said, in case her point had not been taken. "I won't—I don't want you. Stay away from me."

Jade's voice came out of the darkness, cold and distinct. "You have not learned yet, have you, Sarah? A woman has the right to play coy, but there are limits. There comes a time to say yes instead of no. And if you will not . . . if you still reject me . . . then I shall have to show you what I do to those who reject me, to those who try to escape me."

"You can't," said Sarah. "You're not so powerful. I know what you are. I'm not afraid of you."

"Aren't you?"

"You're not a demon, at all. You're just a man—just what's left of a man—a man who somehow didn't die when his body did."

"Ah," said the voice, mocking. Laughter bubbled just below the surface. "Is that all that I am? And is that so little? To be a man who did not die—who *will not* die?"

"You will die," Sarah said stubbornly. It was a feeble challenge, and she knew her voice must betray her own uncertainty and fear. "There's a way you can be destroyed . . . there must be."

"But you will never find it," said the voice, still so close to her ear that she had to restrain herself from flinching away. "Nancy Owens thought she understood. She thought she could trick me. And do you know what happened to Nancy Owens? She could not save herself in the end."

Sarah saw a light. It was a thin, wavering line of yellow seeping beneath the bedroom door. She was puzzled by it

—she didn't remember turning on any light in the bedroom. And there was something about the quality of the light—it made her think of candles. Candles burning in the bedroom?

"Go and see," said Jade softly. "Go and see for yourself what happened . . . what will happen to you, if you continue to fight me."

Sarah walked slowly across the floor, took hold of the doorknob, and opened the door.

Half a dozen candle-ends flickered and guttered on the floor, filling the room with a watery light that made the blood glisten like black ink. There were two bodies on the floor, a man and a woman, their throats gashed open. In the far corner crouched a small, black beast, the only living thing in the room. Its eyes reflected the candle flames and, as it saw Sarah in the doorway, its tail began to thump the floor.

Sarah shuddered and gripped the edge of the door hard, trying to anchor herself to reality. No, it's not real, she told herself, and strained to see beyond the illusion—beyond the candles, the bodies, the animal—to the empty bedroom that she knew was there.

But even as she told herself that she was seeing only a scene from the vanished past, even as she tried to disperse the horror with the strength of her own will, the dead began to stir. There was a horrible, heavy, sliding sound, and tangled limbs and bloody clothing moved. The woman, her head flopping and lolling as if it would fall off, pushed herself up off the floor. Now she was on her hands and knees; now, horribly, rising. The blood on her face and dress and arms looked like dark paint. Her eyes stared glassily through a gore-streaked face, and she turned slowly towards Sarah.

Sarah's chest hurt with fear. She stepped back quickly and pulled the door shut. Her heart was pushing up into her throat, and she saw stars of light circling in the blackness before her eyes.

"I don't want to hurt you, Sarah," said a man's voice, Jade's voice, mocking and easy and low. "It would be such a waste. You and I should be together. I can teach you so much."

"No! I told you before—I don't want to have anything to do with you. I won't help you, I won't bring you someone else to destroy."

"Then you'd better run, Sarah. You'd better try to escape. It may already be too late." There was an indescribably menacing tone to the voice.

Sarah had no inclination to argue. In two swift steps she had reached the door to the porch. The big metal knob turned loosely in her hand, and she rattled it impatiently, then tugged. But nothing happened. Impossible though it was, the door seemed to be locked.

From the darkness behind her, she heard Jade's laughter.

Sarah reached up and pressed the light switch beside the door, and the kitchen was flooded with yellow light. She saw the skeleton key where it hung, still, on a nail behind the door, and although she knew she had never taken it down to use it, perhaps someone else had.

She heard the doorknob of the bedroom door rattle loosely, as if some weak, will-less hand grasped but could not hold it firmly enough to turn it.

"I told you it might be too late," said Jade.

Sarah clenched her teeth. I won't be afraid, she thought. None of this is real. Without much hope, she took the skeleton key down. But she could not use it, for the keyhole seemed to have vanished.

It is there, Sarah thought. It must be. Or maybe the door is already open, only I can't see it. Jade keeps me from seeing it.

The bedroom door was opening. Despite herself, Sarah turned to look, and she saw the gory figure of the dead woman shuffle forward to slump against the doorframe.

Sarah backed away, and her shoulder jarred the back door. No illusion, this—it was solidly shut. She could not walk through it.

Filled with horror, she stared at the thing in the doorway. It was even more gruesome in full light, even more real. The flesh was mottled grey, the blood a harsh, violent red.

Where it leaned against the doorframe it left red smears. Sarah could hardly take her eyes from the source of all that red, the raw, gaping wound in the throat.

As if galvanized by Sarah's scrutiny, the thing began to move again, pushing itself away from the wall and taking a staggering, uncertain step forward. It made a sound—a terrible, high, wheezing gasp. Sarah shuddered, horrified, realizing that she was hearing the corpse breathe, the sound the helpless lungs made as they sucked air through the bloody rip in the neck.

One dragging, bare foot streaked blood on the light-colored linoleum.

Run, screamed all her instincts. But Sarah could not move. Her back was pressing against the door. One hand grasped the useless knob and rattled it desperately, willing it to turn.

Sarah noticed the dress beneath the bloodstains was white, patterned with small, lilac flowers. The thing which had once been a woman, the thing inside the bloody dress, moved its arms, opening them to embrace, and Sarah thought she would faint.

Then she heard Jade's voice in her ear, feeling the warmth of a man's breath against the side of her face.

"Run, Sarah. Run away now," he said.

Her hand still grappled with the useless doorknob, but now, as Jade spoke, Sarah felt it respond, and turn in her hand. She jumped aside, pulling the door open, and as she did so, she brushed up against the staggering corpse. She caught her breath in fear, and then gagged as the stench hit her: the faint, sickly, sweet smell of blood and the much more powerful odor of rotting meat, the smell of inner flesh exposed to air.

But there was no time to be sick. The door was open, her way was clear, and she could run away from the rotting embrace of those dead, clumsy arms. So she ran. And as she ran, she heard Jade's voice still close to her ear.

"Run away, Sarah. And stay away. If you come back, I'll never let you go."

Sarah tumbled down the steps, crying, running faster than she had ever done before.

At last she leaned against her car and in between her sobs drew in long, ragged breaths of the clean, crisp air. Her stomach clenched, and she swallowed hard, willing herself not to be sick. Her mind was blessedly blank. For a while she simply wept. It was a relief to be out in the open air alone, a relief too great for anything but tears. Gradually her sobs died away and she began to recover, to allow herself to think again. Sniffing, she took a tissue from her pocket, wiped her eyes and blew her nose. She stared up at the house, at the light from the kitchen. She couldn't see anyone in the house, but from this angle she might have been fooled. The bedroom window was dark and showed nothing.

Calmer now, Sarah reflected on what had happened to her. Once again Jade had been victorious. He had chased her out of the house, and she had not been able to oppose him. So much for her strength of will, and her boasts that he could not control her. He knew how to play her. Her fears were all he had, but they were all he needed. He knew what would make her run, and what would make her fight. He could make her see Brian, or a walking corpse, or a rat with glowing eyes; create sights, sounds, voices, and smells out of empty air.

He might as well be inside my mind, she thought with dull horror. She sagged against the car again, feeling weak and helpless. Might as well give up and go away. That was her only chance to save herself—to run like hell. The longer she stayed here, the more he would know of her, the more he would have of her, while she would grow weaker as she saw her plans batted aside and faced more of the things she most feared.

But Jade wanted her to run away. He wanted her to give up, to leave the house and not return. Surely that meant that she posed some threat to him? That she *did* stand a chance of defeating him? Knowingly or not, she must have the knowledge and the power to destroy him, or he would not expend so much energy in frightening her away. If she were truly powerless, Jade would not have to try to convince her of that.

Sarah stared up at the house, imagining it in flames. Her hands tightened on the diary she still held, and she knew she could not walk away forever. She could not let Jade win. She would not. She was leaving now, but she would return when she had a plan. Just then, that time seemed distant and unimaginable.

But it was only a few minutes later, as she was driving across town on 38th Street, that the idea came to her, and Sarah realized what it was that the diary had told her; what she knew about Jade and the way in which he might be destroyed.

Chapter Twelve

Pete and Beverly looked up from their dinner in surprise as Sarah burst in. The apartment was dimly lit, with candles on the glass-topped table, so as she crossed the room Sarah turned on a lamp, then flung herself into the large chair that faced the dining area.

"I thought you were going to eat out," Beverly said. She moved in her chair as if uncertain whether to rise.

Sarah waved a hand at her. "Dinner? Sure, I had a hamburger. Don't worry about it." She grinned broadly, feeling she was about to burst with her discovery. "You're not going to believe what I just found out. It's fantastic—"

"Sarah," Pete said. "Do you think it could wait until after dinner? We've just started eating and Beverly went to some trouble with this meal."

Sarah looked at him, unperturbed by his coolness. Wait until he heard. "Don't mind me," she said. "You guys go ahead and eat, and I'll do all the talking. You can listen while you chew, can't you?"

Beverly moved her mouth the way she did when she was nervous, and darted a glance at her husband, then looked at Sarah. "We didn't expect you until much later," she said. "You said you'd be out late."

"God, isn't it late?" Sarah said. "I've lost all track of time. I suppose it is still early, but after what I went through —Jade just tried another of his games on me. Ambulatory corpses. Really horror-movie stuff. Straight out of my own, sick, predictable imagination, and of course I fell for it." She laughed and got to her feet. She was feeling good, the fear far away and unreal in these familiar surroundings, among friends. "Could I have some of that wine?" She saw Pete and Beverly exchange a look before she went into the kitchen for a glass.

Pete filled her glass in silence, and Sarah looked at the dishes spread out on the table: chicken kiev, wild rice, rolls, artichokes with drawn butter. Beverly was wearing a long, slinky, blue velvet dress Sarah had seen her wear only a few times before. Raising the full glass of wine to her lips, Sarah suddenly understood. Pete and Beverly wanted a quiet, romantic evening alone together. Judy Collins on the stereo. Candles on the table. She took a too-large gulp of wine, wondering if she were blushing, and backed away from the table.

"So what's this exciting discovery?" Pete asked.

She could excuse herself, go spend a few hours at the library, and talk to them in the morning. She knew she should—they had put up with her moods and intrusions for so long that she owed them at least one evening to themselves.

But she didn't want to wait; she couldn't. She wanted to bounce her ideas off them, wanted to have her cleverness applauded. She *needed* to talk about it, to discover if there were flaws she hadn't thought of. It was important, damn it. Certainly more important in the long run than the spoiling of one romantic evening. Surely they would see it that way once they knew.

More restrained now, Sarah settled back in the big chair, placing the diary on her knees. She tapped it. "This is the diary of Nancy Owens, who was the original owner and inhabiter of the house on West Thirty-fifth Street. Her daughter-in-law, my landlady, let me have it, and I read it today. And now I know that the trouble in that house didn't start with Valerie's witchcraft—in fact, I wonder now if that witchcraft was Valerie's idea in the first place. I think she was used. This woman, Nancy Owens, had the house built in the nineteen-twenties. Her husband had left her, and she was miserable about it. She met some people who were into magic—some kind of disciples of Aleister Crowley, I think—and they let her believe that if she helped them in their rituals that they would teach her how to win her husband back. One of these people was a woman called Yolanda Ferris, and the other was a man, a powerful magician who called himself Jade."

She paused for effect, watching Pete expectantly. He went on eating methodically, dipping artichoke leaves in butter and biting the ends off. Sarah grimaced. Perhaps she should have let them finish their dinner in peace. But she had started and could not stop now, merely because Pete was refusing to respond. Beverly met her eyes and nodded encouragingly.

"Nancy Owens became more and more involved with Jade, and more convinced of his tremendous powers. He was supposed to be more powerful than Crowley, and less cautious. He was ready to crush anyone who got in his way —he was the only being in the world who mattered to himself. His plan, which he kept from Nancy until the last minute, was to survive death. To inhabit more than one body and, that way, to become immortal. Through a sexual and magical ritual he meant to destroy her soul. Or to absorb it. Anyway, he meant to become her while still remaining himself. One mind in two bodies. He'd had some practice with splitting off a part of himself to take over the bodies of various animals, but this was to be his first trial with another human being. Either he overestimated his own power, or he underestimated hers. It didn't work.

"She managed to fend him off with her mind, the way you and I did, Pete. And then she killed him—killed his body, anyway. She stabbed him to death. That should have been the end of it, but it wasn't.

"Jade survived his own death."

Again Sarah paused, and again she was disappointed. Pete simply ate, as if there were nothing more important on his mind, and she could see by the stiff way he held himself that he was still angry with her for altering the mood of the evening. Beverly had been listening with her usual sympathy, but Sarah could tell by her anxious glances at her husband that she longed to placate him.

"Was that a pause for our gasps of amazement?" Pete asked sourly, not looking at Sarah.

"I thought you would be interested in this," Sarah said. "I thought it concerned you, too."

Pete swallowed some wine and then looked around at her. "Sarah, of course I'm interested in your concerns. But this hardly seems the time—I don't see the overwhelming importance of this diary. So the woman who used to live in your house was involved in magic rituals, like Valerie. So what?"

"It's about *Jade*," Sarah said, annoyed by his obtuseness. "That's what I've been telling you! It explains everything."

"Does it?" He raised his eyebrows. "Really?" He pushed his chair away from the table and moved around to face her. "What do you think it explains?"

"Jade. It explains who he is, what he is. He's not a demon. He's not the devil. He's a spirit, the left-over force of a very powerful man who lived in the 1920s." Her voice softened then, pleading. "Pete, this book explains what we experienced."

He looked at her calmly and as he spoke Sarah realized how far he had distanced himself from the events of the previous day. "I doubt it. Perhaps it explains it to *you*, but I don't think it would help me. I don't deny that I experienced something very disturbing and completely outside my usual experiences. I don't pretend I can explain it. I can't label it. But I don't know that having a name for what happened would help very much."

"Of course it would help," Sarah said desperately. "Naming is the first step. If you don't know who your enemies are, how can you fight them?"

Pete shrugged. "If it is a matter of enemies . . . But I don't see that it helps very much to say that your enemy is a demon."

"No!" Sarah shouted.

Beverly flinched and silverware rattled against the glass.

"I'm sorry," Sarah said quietly. She looked at Pete, wondering how she could reach him, and if he would let her. "Jade is not a demon," she said. "That was my mistake.

Our mistake. We tried to deal with him as if he were a traditional demon, something that would obey a set of rules and respond to traditional spells. But we were wrong. Valerie thought he was a demon—it was in Jade's interest to mislead us, to make us all feel powerless against him. It wasn't that Valerie called him up—he must have been there all the time, in a kind of hibernation, waiting for someone who was receptive to him, someone who could give him what he needed. I think he probably fed off of Valerie somehow—and he's probably been doing the same thing to me. He's been gaining power from his contact with us. But he's not all-powerful—he has limitations and weaknesses —he must. He was human once, and he can be destroyed."

"How did he survive?" Beverly asked. "After she stabbed him."

"There was a little stone figure, a woman carved out of jade. He called it his immortality. Somehow, he put a part of himself into that figure. He trapped a spark of his soul, or whatever you want to call it, in the stone, so that no matter how many bodies died—and I'm sure he had no intention of stopping at two!—he would go on, ready to be reborn again and again. He preserved the essence of himself in stone."

"Have you seen it?" asked Pete.

"No. But I'm sure it exists. And I think it must be in the house somewhere. Maybe it's in the cellar, buried under the house. I think it's there, and it is holding Jade to the house. That has to be it. Nancy Owens took it away with her after she killed the man called Jade. If she had destroyed the statue—but she thought that she could use its power for herself. It destroyed her. I don't think she realized that as long as it existed, so would Jade. I'm going to find it, if I have to dig up the whole cellar. And then I'll smash it. There won't be anything left of Jade."

"In other words, you've found your excuse to stay on in the house," Pete said flatly.

Sarah stared at him. "You don't believe me. You think I've created this whole thing out of my head, that Jade is a fantasy of mine, don't you? Did you just forget what happened to you? How *could* you forget? Yesterday you believed me—yesterday you *knew*."

He sighed. "I believe you, Sarah. I know this is very real to you—"

"Will you stop playing psychiatrist for a minute and tell me how you explain what happened to *you*? Or did you conveniently forget all that?"

"I haven't forgotten anything," he said. His voice had taken on an edge. "But I don't think it explains anything or does any good for me to say that I was possessed by a demon, or by the spirit of a dead man! That's just not . . . very useful, Sarah. I don't live my life according to the dictates of devils and angels; they may be real to other people, but not to me. I had some kind of hallucinatory experience, some sort of mental . . . aberration. I don't know what to call it, or where it came from. Possibly it was suggestion—I might have picked it up from you, somehow. I was in a weak and suggestible state—"

"You were weak *afterwards*—you were perfectly okay when you came over meaning to exorcise the demon. If you're denying it now, I don't know what to—" She chewed her lip, trying not to cry.

Pete started to reach out for her, then drew his arm back. "Look, Sarah, don't get upset. What I think doesn't matter. If you've figured out a way of handling this thing, whatever it is, fine. You have to do what feels right to you. It's not my fight. I think you should leave the house, but if you feel you have to stay, if you think there is something you have to do to conquer this demon, then do it. You don't need my approval."

Sarah thrust the leather-bound book at him. "Here. Read it. Please. It explains everything. Even what happened to us when we tried to say the License to Depart. Jade believed magic was sexual in nature, that for a magic ritual to work there must be a kind of orgasm—either in sex, or in a violent action. He focused his will through sexual energy —he had sex with Nancy Owens while he was trying to possess her. When that didn't work, he killed another woman who was there. Both sex and violence made him more powerful—and that's still true. The part of Jade that's left has to increase his power however he can. He was trying to use us—he excited us, trying to get us to make love because he could feed on our sexual energies and grow stronger. That's why we—" She faltered. Pete's look was ice, and Beverly was much too still.

Beverly broke the silence. "I knew there was something," she said in a small voice, not looking at either of them. "I knew there was something." She stood up, jarring the edge of the table.

"Sweetheart," said Pete. Beverly evaded his arms and ran from the room. The bedroom door slammed. Pete stood up, nearly overturning his chair, and disappeared down the hall without looking at Sarah. She heard the door open and close again quietly, and she was alone.

Chapter Thirteen

The next morning they were as polite and indifferent to one another as strangers. Tension hummed beneath every word and gesture, and none of them dared break the surface.

Instead of lingering to talk, as she usually did on mornings when she didn't have an early class, Beverly was brisk and efficient, out the door after only half a cup of coffee. Pete hurried after her as if afraid of being alone with Sarah.

Sarah had no appetite for breakfast. When the Marchants had gone, she made herself a cup of tea and sat watching the steam rise from the cup. She told herself that it would pass. Beverly would listen to her, and understand, and the wounds would quickly heal. Their friendship would survive. It was very hard, now, to be so alone, but the misunderstanding—the hurt in Beverly's eyes and the guilt in Pete's—was not the worst of it. Much worse was Pete's defection, his disbelief and retreat to the role of rational, uninvolved observer. She understood, recalling her own initial refusals, that he had found forgetting to be the simplest way of coping with his experience, but understanding made it no easier to bear. She felt abandoned.

She pushed her untasted tea away and stood up. Feeling sorry for herself wouldn't change anything. She had something to do, and she might as well do it now.

During the night, lying awake and brooding, Sarah had realized that the cellar was not the only possible hiding place for Jade's statue. The image of the two red-brick chimneys, chimneys without fireplaces, had leaped vividly to mind. The fireplaces which had been there in Nancy Owens' day must still exist beneath sheetrock and plaster. There might have been a loose brick, or a hidden ledge within the chimney, where a small carved figure might have been hidden away. There was also, she reflected, that built-in cabinet in the dining room, and the drawer where she had found the old photograph. But it was the image of the fireplace that drew her.

She would need tools to smash through the wall to the old fireplace. Brian had tools.

Sarah was nervous and excited as she left the Marchants' apartment, but less with the thought of the battle ahead of her than with the prospect of seeing Brian again.

The morning was bright, clear, and warm, the promise of more heat in the air. The chill of the previous week was gone as if it had never been, and it was summer once more. It would be another hot Halloween, Sarah thought, remembering the year past. She and Brian had gone to a costume party held at a house out on the lake. The heavier, more elaborate costumes were early sacrifices to the heat, and around midnight there had been a mass exodus into the water. Sarah could still almost feel the cold water and the soft night air on her naked skin. She remembered how she and Brian had teased each other, playing like dolphins in the water, and later dragging an air mattress up the rocky slope into the woods, where they had played other games.

Why think of that now? And why did she feel so ridiculously hopeful, like a woman going to meet her lover? Melanie would probably be there, Sarah told herself, being deliberately cruel. Melanie would be lying late abed with Brian, as she used to do.

But Brian's truck was parked alone. He answered the door a brief while after she knocked, such a familiar sight in his old red plaid bathrobe, his hair still tousled from bed, that Sarah wanted to kiss him. She bit her lip.

A smile spread across his face, slow and sweet. "Hello," he said softly, sounding pleased.

She smiled back in spite of herself. "Hello."

"Come in? Have some coffee?"

"I came to borrow some tools."

"Oh, O.K., fine. But coffee first?"

"If it's made."

"It always is."

The look they exchanged felt almost like old times. He turned, and Sarah followed him up the stairs. So close behind him, she caught a whiff of his unwashed, sleepy, morning smell, and tenderness surged up in her like sickness. She wanted to grab him and hold on for dear life. She wanted things to be normal and ordinary again.

"Sit down," Brian said. "I'll just be a minute." They were both aware of the awkwardness of this game of host and guest. Sarah remembered their first date, the first time she had come to this apartment. She looked around at the walls, at the familiar Utrillo street scene, and at a print she hadn't seen before: kittens on a rug. Her mouth quirked in a condescending smile. Melanie, of course.

Brian emerged from the closet-sized kitchen with two mugs and set them down on the low table. "I didn't put any sugar in the blue one," he said. He hesitated a moment, then sat on the couch. Sarah could feel his discomfort at the fact that she was still standing, so, after a moment's uncertainty, she walked around the table and also took a seat on the couch, although at the far end from Brian.

"So how you doing?" she asked.

"Oh, fine. You?"

"Fine. Great."

Things had suddenly become unbearably awkward. They both nodded at coffee which was too hot to drink, and avoided each other's eyes. Sarah searched desperately for something to say, something neutral. But all she wanted to do was to shout at him to stop being awkward, to stop pretending they were strangers. She wanted to grab him, and burrow into his side, and pull off his bathrobe, and tickle him until his warm, rich chuckle flowed out and he responded, and hugged and kissed her as she wanted, and was hers again.

"What sort of tools do you need?" Brian asked. "You need something fixed? I can do it—I don't have a class until after lunch."

She stiffened. "I can do it myself."

He smiled. "Sarah," he said, in his gentle, pleasant voice.

The sound of her name, spoken like that, paralyzed her, and she stared at him helplessly.

Brian dropped his eyes, blushing slightly, and bent down to fish a pair of tennis shoes from under the table.

"I didn't mean you couldn't do it yourself," he muttered. "Whatever it is. I just meant . . . I'd be glad to help, you know." He busied himself putting on his shoes.

For a moment Sarah was tempted to take up his offer, to tell him all about the house, and about Jade. But only for a moment.

"It's only a small thing I wanted to do," she said coolly.

"It looked like a nice house," Brian said. "I envy you all that space."

"Oh? I thought you liked it here."

"I do. But it is a little cramped. There's nowhere to put the records, for one thing."

It would be so easy, Sarah thought, to move a little closer to him on the couch. To slip her hands up under his robe —she could almost feel the warmth of his flesh now. Looking at him, watching the way he sat, the way he raised his cup of coffee to his lips, she knew how easy it would be to seduce him.

"Now you know the truth about me," he'd whispered close to her ear some time during the first night they had spent together. "I'm easy." It had been a joke, but it was true. He *was* easy. He never said no. He liked to please her. And she'd never had to seduce him, before—before, he'd always picked up her earliest signals, responding almost before she knew she wanted him, before—

Before Melanie.

Now, after Melanie, things were different. She could sit here all day willing him to touch her, and he would not respond. Had that special channel between them been jammed, or was he just pretending not to hear?

"So what tools did you want to borrow?"

Sarah looked at him, meeting his gentle brown eyes. She didn't speak. She concentrated all her thoughts, all her will, on making him speak to *her*. Let him say something, or do something that could not be misunderstood. Let him make the first move, as he always had before. Surely the passion she felt couldn't be one-sided—he couldn't have forgotten her, and forgotten how he had felt about her, so soon. If he still wanted her, he must know he could have her, for an hour or a day or forever. All he had to do was make a move.

He set his mug down too hard, splashing coffee onto the table. He stood up, not looking at her, and said, "Let's go get those tools you wanted."

Through her bereavement, staring at his back, Sarah managed to speak in something like a normal voice. "Don't you want—shouldn't you get dressed first?"

But he mistrusted her now—or, she thought, with a glimmer of hope, he mistrusted himself. "No, it doesn't matter. There's no one to see." He started down the stairs without looking back.

He wants me, Sarah thought, but there was no triumph in the thought, because he was still rejecting her. He was hurrying away to safety, not daring to take a chance.

How long would I need alone with him, Sarah wondered, to break through his defenses, to make him forget Melanie?

It was a useless question, because the moment was past. Wearily, Sarah got to her feet and went after him.

She found him standing in the narrow doorway of the storage shed, looking in, and she stood beside him, feeling the heat of his body all along one side as intently as if they were actually touching. He moved uneasily away, and Sarah took a painful pleasure in moving after him, maintaining the closeness he was afraid of. She was physically hungry for him. Standing beside him, greedily feasting on his presence, did not satisfy her any more than a starving man is eased by the odor of baking bread, but it was all she had.

"What do you want?" he asked, impatience sounding like self-pity in his voice.

She restrained herself. "I'll need a crowbar and a hammer."

He moved away from her into the dimness of the shed and returned with the items she had asked for.

"And I guess I'd better have the shovel, too, just in case."

Now he looked at her. "What are you going to do? Smash somebody in the head and bury him?"

"Yeah, you got it." She waited for him to repeat his offer of help. This time she would accept it.

"Well, good luck," he said. "Have fun."

Walking away from him was like pulling tape off tender skin. "Thanks for this stuff. I'll get it all back to you in a couple of days."

"There's no hurry."

She felt the pressure of his gaze on her back. Call me back, she thought fiercely. Tell me you still want me. I know you do. It isn't too late. Call me back. Don't let me go, you bastard.

"Sarah."

She turned to face him, her mouth dry, wondering if she should drop the tools and rush across the grass that separated them, into his arms.

But his arms were folded tight against his chest. "Sarah, I'm glad you came by. I know it's hard . . . I've felt you've been avoiding me, and I never wanted that. I know you have every right to be angry, to hate me, but I want us still to be friends."

Her throat and stomach hurt. She couldn't even swallow.

"I just want you to know that if you need anything, you can always come to me. I hope we can be friends."

She waited for something more. Surely he knew what she needed from him. He wouldn't have been able to express such pious sentiments if she had been standing close enough to touch him. Suddenly she was furious with him. She shrugged, her throat still too tight for speech, and turned and walked to her car. The weight of the tools she carried made her stagger slightly, but Brian did not come rushing after to offer his assistance. From the car she watched him go back into his house. Tears blurred her vision for a moment.

"I can't be your friend," she muttered. "I don't want to be. Because I don't like you. I just love you."

* _ * *

There was a dead bird at the foot of the steps.

It had been a big, black grackle, now silenced forever. It had been violently killed, the head nearly wrenched off, and feathers speckled the pale, dusty ground, dark as spilled blood.

Sarah stared down at it. Another death, she thought. What did this one mean?

She looked around uneasily, feeling watched. But if there were eyes glaring at her out of the tall weeds at the side of the house, she could not see them. Was the dead bird a warning? Had Jade gained new strength from this act?

She leaned the shovel against the house and cradled the crowbar and hammer awkwardly in one arm. As she let herself into the house she was tense, already anticipating some attack.

But the house felt empty. Sarah went through it nevertheless, holding the crowbar like a weapon as she looked inside closets and peered under furniture. But she was being silly, she thought, looking for some physical danger. It was being alone that made her so nervous. If Brian were here—

She remembered how he had looked at her, and how he had avoided looking at her. The thought of that sleepy, seductive glance and the sound of his voice saying her name made her weak with desire. She leaned against the bedroom wall. She remembered how charged the atmosphere between them had been, and she cursed the missed opportunity. Why had she waited? I could have had him, she thought. He wanted me.

She wondered if he was thinking of her now. She could almost see him as he must be, still in his bathrobe, slouching on the couch, his coffee grown cold while he brooded.

It would have been so easy, she thought, there in that apartment where shared memories conspired to bring them together, to forget the recent past and heal all the hurts by the movement of their bodies together.

Dazed, half in a dream, Sarah walked slowly into the kitchen and stared at the bright red telephone. It wasn't too late. He would come if she called him.

Call him. Call him now. Get him over here.

Swallowing hard, Sarah crouched by the telephone. She had to call Brian. He could make things right. He wouldn't reject her again, he couldn't, not here in her own house. Here, she would be the strong one, and she had desire enough for both of them. She knew how to please him, she knew what to do. And she would do anything, say anything to have him again, to be able to wrap her arms and legs around him, and feel him inside her, their two bodies straining to become one, just as it had been before, as it should be now.

All she had to do was to get him over here. Sarah drew a long, shuddering breath and picked up the telephone and dialed the well-remembered number.

The telephone rang in her ear.

She tried to think of what she could say: something plausible, not too threatening.

"Hello?"

"Brian," she said. Her mind had gone blank. She couldn't even remember why she had called him.

"Oh, Sarah, hello, is anything the matter?"

"I wondered if you'd help me. You said you'd help me."

"Sure," he said cautiously. "What did you want?"

"I need you . . ." Her imagination balked, and she couldn't think beyond that simple fact.

"Sarah? Are you all right?"

"Yes, of course. Why?"

"You sound strange."

"Could you come over?"

"Why?" There was a sharp note of suspicion in his voice.

Sarah balanced the receiver between chin and shoulder and wiped sweaty palms on her jeans. "Look, I can't really explain on the phone . . . if you could just come over . . ."

"Can't you give me some idea of what you want me to do?"

She chewed her lip with frustration. "Look, I need you to help me. It's complicated to explain . . . I need to knock in a wall."

"Wow, does your landlord know?"

"I don't want to get into all that—I told you, I'll explain

after you're here. It'll be easier." When he did not reply immediately she said, "You *did* offer to help."

He sighed. "All right. When . . ."

"Now."

"Now? Oh, look, Sarah, I've got a class this afternoon . . ."

"That's hours off. It won't take long."

"I could come over tomorrow afternoon, or Saturday morning . . ."

"I want to do it now."

"Well, I'm sorry, Sarah, but—"

"Brian, *please*." Her frustration, her sheer physical need blazed out of the word, and across the distance Sarah sensed his withdrawal.

"I just can't manage it today, Sarah." A door had closed.

"Oh, Brian, please, please." She was crying. "Please let's try again. I can't stand it without you. I've tried, and I can't."

"Sarah, don't. You're just making it harder."

It was hopeless. The telephone was the worst possible connection: it allowed him a safe distance, and deprived her of all weapons except naked words. She didn't have a chance. She hung up without saying goodbye.

Trembling with frustration, Sarah remained sitting on the floor, staring at the telephone. If only she'd kept her cool, she thought, she might have had him, she might have tricked him into coming over.

With a sudden, shocking sense of dislocation, Sarah saw her thoughts as if they belonged to someone else. Why this desperation? Why such a frantic need for Brian here, in this house, immediately?

Reason shone with a cold, hard light. It wasn't she who wanted Brian that badly. It was Jade.

It was Jade who wanted Brian here, who wanted them to make love within these walls, to fill the air with sexual tension and sexual satisfaction, providing the power he needed. He had failed with Pete, and so he was using Sarah even more deviously, still trying to turn her desires to his own benefit. If she had been successful, how would Jade have used that power, she wondered. Would it have provided the last key he needed to unlock Sarah's mind, to allow him to possess her utterly?

Sarah shuddered and stood up, appalled by how willingly she would have gone to her doom. Even now her body wanted Brian, and would have risked all Jade's terrors for him, would have risked hell.

But she wasn't going to. She was going to destroy Jade now, forever. She picked up the hammer and walked into the living room. At the sight of that oddly jutting wall came the image of a carved statue wrapped in silk, hidden beneath a loose brick—it was so vivid that for a moment Sarah almost thought she had already found it. But no, it was waiting for her, waiting to be found.

Her own certainty made her hesitate. How did she know? How *could* she know—unless Jade had put the knowledge in her mind. Could it be that he wanted the statue to be found? Was he tricking her again, playing some subtle game of control?

Staring at the wall, Sarah agonized over the problem, hesitating and fidgeting and rationalizing until finally, annoyed by her own uncertainty, she stopped thinking and simply acted.

Sarah took the hammer firmly in both hands and swung at the wall. At the last minute, unconsciously, she pulled her swing, and the blow merely dented the wall, sending a few cream-colored chips flying. Sarah clenched her jaw angrily and swung again, this time giving the blow everything she had. The hammer cracked into the wall, spraying out fragments of powdery white sheetrock, and leaving a jagged hole.

She grinned, feeling a rush of power. There was something remarkably satisfying about smashing a wall; something liberating in the act of destruction. Jade couldn't stop her now. She felt powerful and pleased with her thoughts, all doubts vanished. She swung again, splintering the wall and enlarging the hole.

After three more satisfying blows, Sarah put down the hammer and lifted the crowbar. She thought of the darkness behind the wall, and fetched her flashlight. Then she thrust one end of the crowbar into the hole and used it as a lever to pry away the shattered section of wall. She was panting and dripping sweat in a matter of seconds, but finally, with a groaning of nails, the newer section came away from the original wall, and Sarah could look into the cavity.

Her work had revealed a small brick fireplace filled with dust, white flakes of gypsum, dead insects, twigs, and the tiny, fragile bones of birds. Sarah picked out the details in the beam of the flashlight, not quite daring to stick her head instead for a better look. She saw a hairy, brown tarantula and nearly dropped the flashlight. On closer inspection, it was clearly dead—but nearly as big as her hand. When she felt fairly certain that nothing living waited for her in the rubble, Sarah used a broom to sweep out the fireplace.

She found nothing of value and the feeling of having been cheated began to rise within her when common sense intervened. Of course the jade figure wouldn't have been left in the open fireplace. Whoever had blocked it up had almost certainly done so years after the little statue had been hidden. If it was indeed in the fireplace, the only possibility was a loose brick, or perhaps a ledge within the chimney. So when she had swept the hearth clear, Sarah got a butter knife from the kitchen and began to test the spaces between the bricks with it, searching for a brick that could be moved.

She had finished with the floor and started on the brick-lined walls when she found it: a brick gave slightly under the probing blade. Sarah caught her breath and poked the brick more aggressively. It shifted. She ran the knife blade all around the edges and then used the blade to pry the brick up. Finally she had to drop the knife and grasp the protruding brick with her fingers, pulling with all her strength. She ignored the gritty shower of mortar in her face.

A hollow was left, a space deeper than the brick alone could fill. And in that recess was something wrapped in a fraying, yellow cloth; something perhaps six inches long and two across. Scarcely breathing, Sarah reached into the hole and her hand closed about the treasure. She withdrew it and moved away from the fireplace, squatting on her heels and staring at the thing she held. She was afraid to unwrap it. Then she caught a piece of the old, fraying silk between two fingers and unwound it.

An ancient, evil face leered up at her.

The thing was warm in her hand; she felt it move. All over her body the tiny hairs rose, electrified. It was alive. As she stared at it, she saw the tiny face change, just like a living face. The expression now was one of gleeful lust.

"So you've seen me at last. What do you think of me?" A man's voice, right behind her.

Sarah almost fell over in surprise. Her fingers closed tightly over the little figure and she stood up and whirled around. There was no one there.

"You hold my immortality in your hand. Does it please you?" asked the same silky voice.

Sarah felt the thing she held change within her grasp. Her fingers recognized it first, but she stared down in disbelief and saw that she was holding a man's penis: alive, engorged with blood, attached to nothing.

She cried out at the sight of it and almost flung it away in repugnance. But she stopped herself. It was a trick. A trick to make her drop it. And she did not intend to let Jade trick her again. Now that she had found the statue she would not let it go until she destroyed it, and destroyed him.

"Don't you like me? Isn't this what you wanted? Surely I don't shock you, my Sarah. You must remember your dreams of me?"

Something flashed in her mind at his words, a kind of *déjà entendu*, memory without details. Yes, she had dreamed of Jade, she had dreamed of a stranger who knew her better even than she knew herself, and who made endless, potent, intoxicating love to her. Feeling herself blush, Sarah shook her head stubbornly. She didn't have to admit to her dreams.

"You remember me, Sarah," said Jade, and she felt his hands caressing her breasts. Sarah caught her breath sharply and looked down in disbelief. There were no hands. No one touched her. And yet she felt the teasing, pleasurable stroking and she could see her nipples stiffening against the fabric of her shirt.

"Stop it," she said sharply, stepping back. It made no difference to the invisible hands. The thing she held throbbed within her grasp and, absently, she caressed it with her thumb. An instant later she realized what she was doing, and she stopped, but her hand tightened around what still felt like a man's erect penis. She wouldn't look at it; she told herself it was illusion, just as when Pete had seemed to become Brian. She tried to remember what the piece of carved jade had looked like and what it should feel like.

"Sarah." His breath was hot in her ear and she shuddered. "Sarah, I want you."

The invisible hands moved down to caress her hips, to insinuate themselves between her legs to caress her inner thighs. Even through blue jeans their touch was arousing. Sarah tried to move away, to escape, but there was nowhere to escape to. It wasn't fair, she thought. Jade was just distracting her, playing on her desires as he had once played on her fears, dividing her body from her mind and leading her astray.

"You want me, Sarah. If you didn't want me, I wouldn't be able to come to you like this." She felt lips on her neck, the grazing nibble of teeth, and jerked away.

"No! I don't want you! Leave me alone!"

"You want me, Sarah. Your breasts are aching to feel my touch. Undo your blouse and let me suckle."

Sarah's empty hand went to her breasts, but it was not to obey Jade but to shield herself. "No."

"Why do you tremble, if not with desire? You are empty, Sarah, and I can fill you."

"No!" she cried again. "I won't let you—you want to destroy me!"

"Ah, no, Sarah," the voice chided. "Do you think that still? After you have fought me off so bravely, and proved yourself worthy of me? I want more than your body, Sarah. I want more than your shell. I want *you*. I want you as my bride."

Her legs were suddenly too weak to hold her. Abruptly, Sarah sat down on the couch. "I don't want you," she said stubbornly.

"Your body tells me another story." He chuckled intimately. "How lovely to feel you respond!"

It was true, she was responding, her body betraying her. Sarah clamped her thighs together and twisted back and forth on the couch. The hands were everywhere, unavoidable, and her attempts to avoid them seemed useless.

Sarah looked down at the thing in her hand. It was horrible: a naked, ugly organ attached to nothing, out of context, alive when it should not be, like some fat, blind worm. The distaste she felt tempered her body's excitement. Newly hopeful, Sarah went on staring at it, concentrating. The outlines of it blurred, and suddenly it was only an old, oriental stone carving that she held.

The groping fingers took on more urgency—he must realize he was losing her, Sarah thought—but now she could feel their touch more as a nuisance than as a danger. She had been tempted, but she wasn't going to fall. She could hold out by thinking of other things. By thinking, for example, of what she meant to do. She held the statue in her hand; the hammer was across the room.

"Don't, Sarah. Don't fight me." Lips at the back of her neck, hands that knew her body. "I won't hurt you. As my bride, you can have everything you have ever wanted. Power, and strength, and pleasure, and fulfillment. We'll share such a life—"

"I don't want to be your bride," Sarah said. She stood up and looked across the room at the hammer. She could smash the statue—that was what she must do. The deep reluctance she felt was Jade's inhibition, not her own. This pleasure was too seductive. The sooner she ended it, the safer she would be. Afterwards—

But the thought of afterwards was so bleak and empty and lonely it didn't bear thinking of. There would be no reward for her then, no pleasure, no one waiting. If she went to Brian he would only reject her again. There would be no fulfillment like the one the stroking, teasing fingers promised, if she would just relax, just give in . . .

"Stop it!" she shouted, and whirled around, trying to pull away from the sensations. She must not think, she must not feel—everywhere there were traps. She had to act. Find the hammer, smash Jade's statue *now*.

The room went dark.

I know where the hammer is, Sarah thought. It's in the same place. The room is the same, everything is the same, even though I can't see. She took a careful step ahead into blindness.

"Sarah," said Jade's soft, caressing voice. "Stop and

think. Don't be hasty. Think of what I'm offering you
—think of the power, the passion, the immortality."

"No." She took another cautious step forward. In a
moment, she knew, she would bump the hammer with her
foot.

"At least know what you are giving up. Know me first,
and then decide."

She took another step, and then couldn't move any more
because she had run into someone. A man, who put his
arms around her. She gasped, and would have cried out, but
his lips met hers. Then she wasn't afraid anymore. He was
real, whoever he was, and she belonged here in his arms. It
felt so right that she could only relax against him, almost
melt into him as his tongue teased at her lips and his hands
moved down to fondle her bottom.

And then she realized who held her, and what this
embrace meant, and she began to struggle. She broke away.
Tears sprang to her eyes, and her body throbbed with
frustration. She had wanted to give in. To let herself be
seduced by a ghost.

"You're not real," she said bitterly. "It's a trick."

"I am real," said the voice. "You know me. I am Jade."

Jade. And Jade was not the monster she had thought, but
a man, a real man. She had felt his hands, his lips, his
breath in her ear . . . his mind in her mind.

Sarah shuddered. Nothing had changed except the tenor
of his attacks. He *was* still the monster she had first thought,
even if he had once walked as a man. And he wanted her.
He would destroy her if she didn't destroy him first.

"No, Sarah, I have no wish to destroy you. I have other
plans for you, if you'll only be sensible. You can't destroy
me. You must realize that even if you smash that bit of
stone that I will live on. I have more than one home for my
soul, even now."

"But the statue is your only hope of immortality," Sarah
said. "If I smash it, you'll die."

"Eventually, as everything on earth dies . . . not immediately. I'll find you again, Sarah, whatever you do. I'll
come to you in another body."

"Then I'll kill that body, too," Sarah said bitterly. "I'll
kill them all."

"Why, Sarah? Why this hatred? Why won't you let me please you? Have you forgotten so soon how you loved me?"

The hands seemed to be everywhere, caressing her, parting her legs, urgently stroking and kneading her flesh. Sarah cried out and slapped at herself, trying to brush away the intangible fingers. The small statue fell from her open hands. She heard it strike the floor.

The teasing hands were unimportant compared to that piece of jade. Sarah dropped to her hands and knees, gasping as the probing hands touched her even more intimately, and scrabbled around on the floor. She found it, but as she grasped the smooth stone she felt it turn in her hands to warm flesh. The touch of it sent a rush of sheer desire through her. In the darkness it did not seem so horrible. In the darkness, she could believe she grasped a part of her lover.

How could she smash it, even if she could find the hammer? How could she destroy this . . . thing . . . which throbbed in her hands, promising joy?

She shivered, responding to his caresses like a cat. In this total, suffocating darkness the only thing that tied her to life, the only proof that she existed, was her body's response to the hands that petted and tickled and teased, soothed and aroused by turns.

She rocked back and forth in response. Coherent thought had fled. In such darkness, only the body was real, only touch mattered. Hands fumbled at her jeans, and unzipped them. Sarah gasped as fingers touched wetness. Were they her own fingers? In the darkness, it did not matter.

Her clothes chafed and stifled her, and she longed to be naked, to be enveloped by the soothing darkness, to let the fingers touch her everywhere.

Someone unbuttoned her blouse. Sarah tugged down her jeans, stumbling back until she fell onto the couch, feeling herself pushed back onto it by the welcome weight of a man's nakedness.

Somewhere, beyond the thick, slow, greedy thoughts of flesh and touch which preoccupied Sarah, somewhere deep within her mind, a small voice was screaming, warning her.

But the sound of the voice did not penetrate, as the hands

did, making her gasp. She could not hear her own voice above Jade's wicked whisperings in her ear. She had no more will to fight. In the battle between body and mind, mind had too often had its sterile victories. Now, let body win. She would be satisfied, for once. She wanted to forget everything, and simply be. This was a dream, not life. The darkness absolved her.

Hands stroked her, made her liquid. Pleasure was infinitely prolonged.

"Kiss me, Sarah."

Moving slowly, feeling as if she was floating in black water, Sarah brought Jade's penis to her lips. It was warm and smooth and alive, the only thing she knew of Jade and the only thing she wanted to know. Was this the thing she had feared? It inspired affection in her now, and desire. She pressed her lips to it, and her tongue found and licked away the one salty, bitter drop at the tip. She slipped the warm, throbbing flesh into her mouth and held it there, her tongue learning and savoring the contours as her body arched and twisted in response to the hands that played her.

She parted her legs for him. She thrust with her hips and strained to meet something that wasn't there. Why wouldn't he take her, why wouldn't he end it? She was no longer afraid he meant to destroy her—she no longer cared. Her single-minded concentration on achieving her body's pleasure was so intense that she didn't care if she died attaining it. Let the fire consume her utterly—so long as it consumed her.

"Now," she muttered through dry, parched lips. "Damn you, now."

Why did he torture her? Why did he delay and leave her empty?

The darkness had lifted, but Sarah didn't want to see. She kept her eyes tightly closed, concentrating only on what she could feel, on the tides that rocked her body. Her ears were filled with the sound of her own ragged breathing as she twisted and sweated and begged for release.

If you want me, you know what to do.

Had he spoken, or had she imagined those words? It didn't matter—she knew. She held Jade in her hand, cradled between her breasts. Jade. A man. A small, carved stone. A penis. She could feel it throbbing. She had seen it smile. She had heard him speak.

She brought the thing to the juncture of her thighs, and opened her body for Jade. She gasped and bit her lip, feeling the head of the penis butting against her, seeking entry. For one clear moment she was terrified, aware of the terrible danger she was in, and she twisted away.

"No," she said. "I won't let you. You can't make me."

But her body twisted back, eager for the penetration, giving the lie to her words, and, knowing herself in mortal danger, feeling both terrified and ecstatic, Sarah jerked her hand up, and stabbed herself with the weapon Jade had given her. She gasped as she felt him enter her, and thought she might faint, and lay very still.

Jade took control, pounding against her, thrusting and withdrawing again and again. Lost, Sarah's body moved to his command in that ancient, demanding dance. All thoughts were gone, and with them all feelings of terror or anticipation. There was only the moment. There was only the need. There was only the will. The room flew away, and there was nothing left but her body, the world, and that became one tiny, glowing, flickering flame of being, of feeling. She was motion, she was fire, she was water, a tide that rose and fell and rose, and she was torn apart, painlessly, stretched and scattered, her body flung into the ocean. She *was* the ocean. She was molten, liquid, flaming, searing, and she exploded.

Cast ashore, the waves still lapped at her body, warming her, rekindling her, reminding her in ever-diminishing rushes of the pleasure she had known. Her muscles were water. She could not move. Finally, she opened her eyes.

White ceiling. Sunlight and shadow. The room was empty and silent around her. She turned her head slightly and saw the wrecked wall, jeering at her like an open mouth. Gradually, her breathing and her heartbeat were slowing to normal. Soon, she thought, they might stop altogether, and she wouldn't ever have to think again. She didn't want to think. Her hand still lay loosely between her legs. Sarah shifted to a more comfortable position after a moment, withdrawing her hand. She saw what she held.

It was the likeness of a nude, oriental woman, carefully

carved from a piece of dark green jade. It was slick, slimy to the touch, covered with—

Self-disgust twisted Sarah's face, and she hurled the stone figure across the room, shuddering. She heard it strike the wooden floor.

She ached. Moving slowly, afraid she would be sick, Sarah raised herself on her elbows. Her jeans were lying pooled on the floor and her blouse hung open. She had done it all herself, to herself. He had made her do it. She could imagine how it had really been: lying there, masturbating, lost in a fantasy of his devising, at his command. The peace and pleasure were all gone now; even the memory of them made her feel feverish, made her skin crawl and her stomach cramp with self-loathing. Forcing herself to move against the gravity pull of misery, Sarah sat up and dressed herself. She looked across the room at the jade figure, lying now among the chips and shards of sheetrock. Jade had kept her from destroying it, she thought—he had done that much. But what else had he done to her? How much had she lost?

She could still think, she could still move, she could still plan—perhaps it wasn't too late. She could still destroy the little figure. She wanted to destroy it, to turn her hatred against that one thing and smash it. She wanted never to see it again. Hammer-blows, reducing the thing to green dust, could set her free, she thought.

She meant to stand up and cross the room, to pick up the hammer. She remembered the last time she had risen to do that same thing. Her muscles failed her. She could not rise. She began to shake, and her teeth chattered. She lowered her head in her hands and began to cry.

Somewhere, someone was laughing.

Chapter Fourteen

How long she might have remained like that, weeping and helpless, Sarah never knew. Why didn't Jade take her? Why didn't he destroy her? He must be strong enough now, and she too weak to resist. She wished that he would take her, that he would snuff out her consciousness so she wouldn't have to remember. She was roused from her miserable stupor by a pounding that rattled the back door.

Mechanically Sarah rose, found that her legs would hold her this time, and wiped her eyes and nose with a tissue. Then she walked slowly back to answer the door.

Valerie was there, looking thinner and paler and madder than ever.

"What's happened?" she demanded, pushing past Sarah into the house. She looked around, almost sniffing the air like a wild animal. "What happened? What did you do?"

Sarah shook her head. "Nothing."

Valerie glared at her. "Don't lie to me! Do you think I don't know? Something happened; I could feel it. I knew it. For the first time I could—I was *free*, he wasn't controlling me. For the first time I could think, I could see what he'd done to me. He left, he actually left, and I was myself again. And I knew then—I won't, I won't be *his* anymore; I won't let him control me anymore."

Sarah stared at her blankly, unable to follow the torrent of words.

"Tell me," Valerie insisted, her voice becoming a childish whine. "You don't trust me, but it's true—I'm not *his* anymore. I want to help you, I'm on your side. Look, look what I did. This will prove what I say; look what I did." She reached into her large leather shoulder bag and pulled out a handkerchief. She held it out, unfolding it almost under Sarah's nose.

The once-white handkerchief held a squashed, messily slaughtered toad. The remains of Lunch. Repulsed, Sarah staggered back. She looked at Valerie and saw that the other woman had tears in her eyes, and her forehead was beaded with sweat.

"You see?" said Valerie. "I am free. I killed my own, my little Lunch . . . I had to kill a part of myself, but I killed a part of Jade as well. And he doesn't own me anymore. And I'll help you." Suddenly she frowned and looked more sharply at Sarah. "What happened to you? What did he do?"

Sarah shrugged. She wouldn't admit to anyone what had just happened to her, but at the moment she lacked the energy even to think up a plausible story.

"Tell me, you have to tell me. Tell me and I'll help you. Isn't that what you want?"

"Oh, go away," Sarah said wearily. "I don't need your help; you can't help me. If you've escaped from Jade, so much the better for you. You'd better run for it—isn't that the advice you gave me, once? Run for it, before he calls you back?"

"He's done something to you, oh, what's he done?" Valerie stared wildly around, and a faint, warning pang struck through Sarah's haze of misery. Get her out of here.

"Just get out," she said to Valerie. "It's not your problem. You can't help me. I was safer here alone—don't you know he could use us against each other?" She had a sudden, vivid image of herself, out of control, attacking Valerie, killing her, and she clenched her fists. No. She had succumbed to Jade sexually, but that did not make her his creature. She was not his instrument, she would not kill, and she would not bring him any victims. She would not.

"We can help each other," Valerie said. "Two of us have to be stronger than one."

"Not against Jade."

"Yes. Why not? He's not invulnerable—I realized that when I killed Lunch." She sniffed, and blinked, and rewrapped the toad's remains, placing the small bundle carefully back inside her purse. "We can draw a new circle to protect ourselves, and say all the spells just right, and—"

"You don't know what you're talking about," Sarah interrupted. Valerie's presence was rubbing at her tender nerves. She moved away from her, but Valerie came after, once again standing too close, pressuring her.

"Spells and magic circles won't work," Sarah said. "Jade isn't a demon, and it doesn't make any sense to act as if he were. That sort of thing is just a joke to him."

"What do you mean? What do you know?"

Where was Jade, Sarah wondered. What was he waiting for? When would he strike? She decided to tell Valerie the truth. Jade could try to stop her if he wanted.

"He's a man," she said. "Or at least he was. He was a magician who didn't die when his human body did, because he had managed to imprint a part of his personality into a carved stone. And as long as it survives, he survives. So the reason we can't kill him by killing the cat or the toad or whatever animal he's lodged in is that another part of him, his essence, is still preserved in a piece of jade.

"Jade," said Valerie, wonderingly. "But . . . I called him up, out of nothing. I recited an invocation to spirits, and he came. He must be a spirit."

"Oh, he's a spirit, but not the sort he made you think he was. And you didn't call him up out of nothing . . . he was using you, getting you to focus your will by reciting spells and all that nonsense. Where do you suppose you first got the idea of using witchcraft?"

Valerie shook her head dumbly. "It was . . . after I moved into this house."

"That's right. And it was Jade who put that idea into your head. You must have been especially susceptible . . . and he was trapped, and he needed someone to help him escape. You were the focus for his powers."

"But how do you know this? Did Jade tell you? Why should you believe what he says?" Suddenly her face sharpened, like that of a dog who has caught a scent. "You found it. You found that piece of jade. Where is it?"

Sarah shook her head swiftly, feeling it imperative not to let Valerie know. "No. I didn't."

But Valerie had pushed past Sarah into the next room, where the shattered wall told a story. "Where is it?" she asked again.

Sarah hurried after, to the jade figure where it lay among the rubble. She looked at it, afraid to touch it, afraid of bringing it to life again.

"That?" Valerie leaned down, reaching for it, and Sarah had to swoop and scrabble to get there first. Her fingers closed around the slightly sticky stone and she ground her teeth, repressing a shudder. At least she had rescued it from Valerie.

When she straightened up, she saw that Valerie was staring at her, a frightened look on her face. "You're *his* now," Valerie said in a low voice.

Sarah shook her head in a hard, nervous negation. Her body prickled with goosebumps; for a moment she seemed to feel invisible hands stroking her.

Panic flared in Valerie's eyes and she backed away. Then, with an obvious effort of will, she stopped. "You tried to help me," she said. "I didn't think there was any hope, and I didn't care. But you did. You wanted to fight, for me as well as for yourself. And . . . now it's not fair if I'm free but Jade's got *you*."

For the first time Sarah felt she was seeing the person Valerie had been once, before the madness and the slavery inflicted by Jade. The emotion in Valerie's voice reached her, seemed to cut through the fog in her mind. She shook her head. "No, Jade hasn't got me," she said. And, although it was an effort, she managed to laugh. "In fact, you might say that it's the other way around. I've got Jade."

She extended her hand and opened the fingers slowly to reveal the small, carved figure. Before she could say or do anything else, Valerie had snatched up the little object.

Then, with a cry of fear, Valerie flung it away from her. She was trembling violently. "It *is*," she whispered, her terror-stricken eyes fastening on Sarah's face. "It *is* Jade—I could feel him! Oh, what are we going to do?"

"It's his immortality," Sarah explained. "As long as it exists, he can't die. It's what allows him to go from body to body. It's why killing the bodies doesn't kill him. If we destroyed the statue—"

"He'd die," Valerie said, her voice soft and gloating. "Oh, yes." She looked around the room. "What can we use? We'll smash it to bits."

But Sarah was having second thoughts. "Wait a minute. What if we're wrong? What if by smashing the thing we actually set Jade free, release his power?"

Valerie considered this, then shook her head. "Can't be. If that was what he wanted, he would have gotten me or you to smash it long ago. It's been hidden away just to keep him safe."

Yes, of course. And Jade wouldn't have tried so hard to keep her from smashing it when she found it. Another sensual memory made her shiver. Valerie was right, she told herself. The statue must be destroyed.

But still she was reluctant. She saw Valerie pick the hammer off the floor and, feeling drawn against her will, Sarah crossed the room and picked up the carved figure.

Holding it made her feel better, stronger, and more secure. Power throbbed within the stone, but it was a muted, quiescent power, no threat to her. Jade was waiting. For what?

"Sarah?"

Sarah turned to face Valerie. The hand holding the figure pulled it close to her breast, protectively.

"Let's not do anything too quickly," Sarah said. "There might be a way we could use this power for ourselves. And we can't afford to make any mistakes. After all, even if the stone is destroyed, Jade will go on existing in some animal body somewhere, and it could be difficult to find."

"We'll worry about that later," Valerie said. "Anyway, how much harm can one little rat do? Rats don't live very long, do they? Wherever else Jade is now, his real power is in that stone, that thing you're holding."

Sarah stood still holding the statue against her breast, trying to put her uneasiness, her reason for hesitating into words that would convince Valerie.

"Give it to me," Valerie said. She stared at Sarah, a trace of the old madness in her eyes. "Oh, I see. You don't want to destroy him at all, do you? You've made some kind of deal with him. What did he promise you? It's all lies, you know. You won't get anything from him—you're better off without him—I know."

"Of course I haven't made any deal," Sarah said firmly. "I just . . . don't think we should do anything rash. We know so little about Jade, after all."

But Valerie went on staring. "No," she muttered. "Not a deal, but something else, something else . . . You're different. It wasn't like it was for me, was it, for you? You *want* Jade."

It was true. Once again Sarah felt her body charged with desire, and she knew who could satisfy it. The thing in her hand changed: she held Jade's power, Jade's immortal soul, Jade's sex throbbing against her. And she wanted to feel it inside her again. Sarah started to smile at the delicious memories which filled her mind, and then she saw the uncomprehending horror on Valerie's face. That look cut right through her moody, sensual daze and she realized what was happening to her.

"No," Sarah said hoarsely as disgust and self-hatred rose up in her. She opened her numbed fingers, letting the jade figure drop away from her. Pleasure was just another trap, far more dangerous than pain. But she could still think, she could still make decisions, no matter what her flesh wanted. She turned her self-loathing instead against Jade. It was Jade she hated, and always had. Jade was her enemy. She made the decision to save herself.

"Give me the hammer," she said to Valerie. "I won't be his slave."

A low, eerie howl close by froze them both.

"The cat," said Valerie. "It's him." She put the hammer in Sarah's hand and strode towards the front door.

"No," said Sarah, suddenly alarmed. "Valerie, don't!"

But she was too late. Valerie had the front door open, and

something came flying in. Something moving so fast it was scarcely more than a blur, aimed straight at Valerie's head.

Valerie screamed. Lines of blood streaked her face. A black cat hit the ground, recovered itself immediately, and again launched itself at Valerie, this time trying to claw its way up her leg.

"Kill it! Get it off me!" Valerie shrieked. She kicked her legs wildly, trying to dislodge the animal, and began to bash at it with her heavy purse.

Sarah hesitated. There was something wrong here, she thought. Was it only another distraction, to keep them from destroying the figure? But if the cat was Jade's other form, then here was the chance they had hoped for.

Wishing for gloves or a blanket to protect herself but aware that she had no time to get anything, Sarah dropped the hammer and jammed the stone figure into a pocket of her jeans and stepped forward. She grabbed hold of the animal by the scruff of its neck and the bony ridge of its back and, although it twisted and writhed in her grasp, it could not reach her, and she was able to dislodge it from Valerie's thigh.

"Get me something," Sarah said. "A blanket or something—I don't know how long I can hold it."

The cat was possessed, howling again and writhing madly.

Valerie dug into her purse. The blood flowed freely down her face, staining her blouse with bright red flowers. She looked up, tossing her head back in an impatient movement to clear both blood and hair from her eyes. She withdrew a curved, shining knife from her purse. The sight of it made Sarah's stomach lurch and she almost thought she remembered the knife from some other time, or perhaps a dream. A dream of blood and carnage. Holding the knife seemed to calm Valerie. She smiled, and the mad, tense face relaxed beneath the stripes of blood.

"This time he won't get away," Valerie said.

Sarah looked down at the cat, realizing that it had stopped struggling and was silent. When she looked down at it, it twisted its head within her grasp to look up at her, and Sarah saw that familiar golden stare again.

As those golden eyes burned into hers, she felt her

nostrils stop up, her mouth become sealed, and she realized that she had stopped breathing. She couldn't remember how to breathe.

"Don't look at it, you idiot," Valerie said harshly.

With a gasp, Sarah broke away.

"I thought you knew so much," Valerie said contemptuously. "I thought you were being so careful. He's got you, doesn't he? You'd never have been able to break away or smash the statue if I hadn't come over. You'd be helpless by yourself. You still have the stone?"

Sarah nodded, staring at Valerie.

With the hand not holding the knife, Valerie caught hold of the cat's throat. The tips of her fingers met the tips of Sarah's through the smooth fur. She was smiling.

"Shall we make it watch while we smash the stone?" Valerie asked, her voice heavily playful. "Teach it about impending doom. Let Jade know we've won—that he's trapped inside one very scrawny cat until we decide to end all his lives with this very sharp blade."

The cat lay as still in their shared grasp as if already dead. Sarah longed to look at it, to look at its eyes and see if Jade was still there, but she controlled herself. That would be foolish. He could still destroy her, if she let him. But all the same, she could not shake the disturbing thought that Jade might have fled this limp body for a safer one.

"Do you want to hold him while I kill him?" Valerie asked. "Or do you want me to do it all? A little more blood won't make any difference to my clothes."

Sarah did not like the idea of holding the cat while it was slaughtered, but she did not relinquish her grasp. "Valerie," she said urgently. "We need to think this through. There's something wrong here. Why did he come to us? He must have known what we were planning, so why did he come running straight into a trap? We should wait—"

"*You* wait," said Valerie. The hand that had encircled the cat's neck pulled away; the hand that held the knife swung in close. The sharp blade bit into the furred throat and there was a sudden, thick rush of blood—bright and oddly beautiful against the sleek blackness.

Sarah stared at the limp, warm mass in her hands. Then,

as the blood began to crawl down her arm, she threw the cat away, crying out her disgust.

She turned to Valerie, then, meaning to curse her furiously, but the words died unspoken. Something was terribly wrong.

Valerie's eyes had rolled up so that only the whites showed beneath fluttering lids. Always pale, she was now so dead white that the welts on her face stood out lividly and seemed to pulse. The muscles in her neck were taut and corded, and her lips stretched back from her teeth. Her chest labored; she was breathing, but seemed unable to draw a breath deep enough to satisfy.

Jade.

For a moment Sarah was frozen, staring, and then she remembered what she had to do.

She had to destroy the statue.

Trembling, she pulled it from her pocket, feeling as if she had been carrying a venomous snake in her jeans. Why had she waited so long? Why hadn't she destroyed it when she found it? Was she so weak, so controlled by Jade?

Still she paused, holding the thing in her hands, looking carefully at it. It was oddly beautiful, and yet undeniably disturbing. A naked woman carved with great skill from a piece of jade, with such attention to detail that the lines and hollows that made up the tiny face became an expression of gleeful, individual evil. But it did not move as she stared at it, and she was aware, as she held it, that Jade had left only the faintest trace of himself in the stone, only an anchor. He must be focusing all his power on Valerie, struggling with her for possession of her body, hoping to win after all.

Sarah backed away from Valerie, recovered her hammer, and crouched on the floor, setting the stone figure carefully down. She gripped the hammer with both hands, then, and raised it high, and brought it down with all her might.

The hammer struck the wooden floor, the impact sending a teeth-jarring shock through her body. Sarah stared down in disbelief, but she knew she had seen it. As the hammer descended, the green stone had seemed to become pliable, semi-liquid, and it had squirmed to one side, just far enough to avoid the blow.

Valerie screamed.

Sarah looked around in time to see Valerie rushing at her, knife raised and threatening, her eyes wide. No time even to stand. With Valerie nearly on top of her, Sarah tackled her legs and leaned sharply to one side, toppling Valerie to the ground. Fearful of the knife, the blood pulsing loudly in her ears, Sarah managed to push Valerie onto her back without losing hold of the hammer.

"Valerie!" Sarah said sharply. "It's me, Sarah. Don't hurt me—I want to help you!"

Valerie's face was contorted, confused, her eyes unfocused. Sarah imagined she could see Jade's mastery coming and going, first one persona and then the other flickering out of Valerie's eyes.

Sarah left her, and scrabbled desperately on the floor to find the figure. Again she raised the hammer and brought it down. She heard Valerie behind her, but did not waver. The hammer landed hard and unerringly on the stone and cracked it in two, severing the head from the body.

Valerie screamed again, and Sarah felt a painful wrenching at her left shoulder, then a burning sensation in her upper arm. She whirled around and saw Valerie tottering and waving a bloody knife, her eyes glittering.

A quick glance sideways and down told Sarah that she had been cut; blood was soaking the blue cotton of her sleeve. She didn't stop to think about it—time enough to hurt later. She could still use her arm, and she needed it. She took a firmer grip on the hammer, hoping she would not be forced to use it against Valerie.

But Valerie was no longer attacking. The deadly glitter had gone out of her eyes and she was terrified again. She still clutched the knife, but the arm that had held it aloft dropped to her side. She began to back away from Sarah, whimpering quietly. Sarah wondered what she saw.

The figure was in two pieces on the floor. Sarah bent to her work again, determined to pulverize it, to leave Jade no safe harbor. Her next blow knocked off another piece of stone. She pounded again and again, reducing the finely wrought figure to sharp fragments of stone amid a pile of pale green dust.

Her arm ached with a sharpness that brought distracting tears to her eyes. Sarah set her teeth and concentrated on each hammer blow. When she paused, she could hear Valerie's breathing, loud and painful even from across the room. She risked a glance to see that Valerie was crouched on the floor behind the front door, her back to the wall, her eyes closed, her body hunched and tense. She was no threat.

Where was the head? The body was rubble, but the head was missing. After a moment's fear she found it where it had rolled a few inches away, and brought her hammer down hard on it, wiping out those evil features forever. It was gone. Destroyed utterly.

She paused then, and let herself savor her triumph. She was weak and sweating and weary, and her arm ached intolerably, but she had won. Jade was gone. Holding the hammer in her right hand and letting her left arm dangle, throbbing, by her side, Sarah turned towards Valerie.

She was still in the corner, curled almost into a fetal position, her breathing shallow, her face closed.

If Jade won, after all this—

She couldn't stand to be inactive, passively awaiting the outcome of the battle between Valerie and Jade. There had to be some way she could help, some way she could tip the scales and add her strength to Valerie's. She remembered Pete's battle with Jade, and how she had tried, desperately ignorant of how, to help him. And she had helped; Pete had said so. She had been like an anchor, Pete had said. She had kept him from sinking.

Sarah crossed the room and crouched beside Valerie. She touched Valerie's shoulder and leaned close. "Valerie, this is Sarah. I'm here with you, right beside you. Can you hear me? Can you understand? I want to help you. Let me help you."

Valerie's eyes opened and she stared at Sarah. Then the bloodshot, grey-green eyes focused, and Sarah knew that Valerie was seeing her. Her heart leaped up in hope.

Then Valerie's eyes narrowed and her teeth showed in a snarl. She let out an inarticulate growl and her hands came up, grasped Sarah's arms, and threw her away with astonishing strength.

Sarah cried out in pain from her injured arm. She

scrambled to her feet and, feeling dizzy and sick, approached Valerie again, but more cautiously this time.

It all happened very quickly after that.

As Sarah watched, wary of the knife Valerie still had, she saw Valerie go very still and stiff, and then her body shuddered, as if a current had passed through her. When it passed, Valerie rose from the floor and looked at Sarah, smiling.

The smile, broad and gloating and cruel, was not Valerie's smile.

Her eyes had a hard, yellow gleam which Sarah recognized and which chilled her. It wasn't Valerie looking out of those eyes any more.

As Sarah watched, waiting in agony for what would happen next, trying to plan her own escape, the yellow light flickered in Valerie's eyes and went out.

"No," said Valerie, her voice firm.

Sarah held her breath, hoping.

Valerie raised the hand that held the blood-stained knife. She was looking straight at Sarah. Very little space separated them; in a step Valerie could be upon her, slashing and stabbing. But Sarah did not move. She did not even breathe. She concentrated on Valerie, trying to read those flickering, changing eyes; trying to reach the Valerie who was fighting for existence. She did not dare move, afraid of tipping the balance the wrong way. She could only watch, and hope, and concentrate as hard as she could, hoping her thoughts had some power. *Valerie*, she thought. *Don't let him have you. Hang on. Kill that bastard!*

"Kill you," said Valerie.

And her arm came up and around in a gentle, perfect curve, and the knife bit deeply, surely, irrevocably into Valerie's own throat.

And as her life's blood spurted out, in the seconds before she died, Valerie, most improbably, smiled. It was her own smile.

Chapter Fifteen

Now, after more than a week away, she was home again.

Sarah sat in her car and stared at the house and wondered why she had come. Was it just stubbornness? After all that had happened, anyone else would have given up the house and moved elsewhere with a feeling of relief. What was she trying to prove, and to whom?

Part of the reason she had come back, Sarah knew, was that she didn't want to go on living with the Marchants. Beverly was her friend again—all problems had been buried when she saw that Sarah needed her—but Pete was not. Things were not the same among the three of them, and Sarah wondered if they would ever be. He kept his distance. No matter what they talked about, Pete was guarded, as if he could not trust her. And he looked at her with a coldness that made her want to cry.

There was an apartment in the Marchants' complex which was available. She could move there easily enough. Perhaps she would. It wasn't giving in, to move. It wasn't an admission of defeat. But that decision couldn't help her now. She might decide not to live here, but she had to go back inside, at least this once. If only to prove to herself that Jade was gone.

Courage is doing what you're afraid to do, because you have to, she told herself as she got out of the car and walked towards the house.

The last time she had seen it there had been an ambulance and two police cars behind the house, and she had been trying to give the police some sort of coherent story. She had telephoned for help within a minute of Valerie's cutting her own throat—telephoned, and then, still afraid Jade would have some last deadly trap waiting for her, had bolted out of the house, and waited on the street below as the sound of sirens came nearer.

The police had been suspicious, but not at all unkind. Sarah had been taken to the hospital, where her arm was stitched up, and she was kept there overnight. For observation, they said. Sarah reflected that it was better than a jail cell, but in fact she liked it. It was nice to be taken care of, to be obliged to do nothing but sleep. And while she slept, and ate the bland, pleasant food, and watched television shows she would never have looked at under other circumstances, the police were checking out her story. Sarah had kept close to the truth in what she told the police, only leaving out her own dealings with Jade, implying that Jade was an imaginary obsession of Valerie's. Valerie's lover testified that Valerie had attempted suicide at least once before—not in his presence, but he had seen the scar on her wrist—and that she believed herself to be in communication with some sort of demon or devil who told her what to do.

It wasn't long before the verdict was in: Valerie had committed suicide while the balance of her mind was disturbed, possibly under the influence of drugs, and Sarah was an innocent bystander lucky to have escaped with her own life.

Valerie is dead, and so is Jade, Sarah told herself now. Jade was dead, he had to be dead. But still she felt the niggling fear that Jade had somehow survived, that he had been able to abandon Valerie's dying body for some other, nearby, mortal shell—a bird on the roof, a cockroach in the walls.

Sarah looked around at the weedy lawn, at the dead brown leaves and bare branches against the grey sky, and wondered if somewhere a pair of eyes, yellow as fire, watched her. She let herself in by the back door.

The house was quiet. It was an old, empty house. Sarah paused and listened and all that she heard were noises from outside: a few, trilling bird cries, and the rushing sound of traffic, and the wind in the trees.

In the living room the broken wall still gaped, revealing the fireplace within, but the rubble had been swept away, cleaned up along with the blood. Sarah wondered if she had the police to thank for that.

She wondered where Jade had gone.

Had he evaporated, simply vanished like a drop of water on a hot stove, erased by the hammer blows and the final slice of the knife? Was there a hell somewhere that claimed his spirit?

Accept it, she told herself. Believe it. Jade is gone.

But she had no evidence. She wanted something more certain than a pile of green sand and the memory of Valerie's smile.

Sarah trailed around the house feeling at a loss, already bored. There was nothing for her here. The house was too big and empty. She had nothing to do here. No more demons to fight, no more mysteries to solve. The thought made her oddly sad. And then she knew she would not stay. Someone else could live here; someone who would be free of her memories and nightmares. She would see about that apartment the first thing in the morning. In a different place she would still be alone, but there would be other distractions, and fewer memories. It would be nice to live so close to Beverly without feeling she was intruding, and good to live on a shuttle bus route, to escape the problems of finding parking on campus every day.

Having made her decision, Sarah was suddenly restless, eager to get on with her life. Already her life in this house was fading into the past. But she would spend the night here —having made such a big deal about her ability to do so to Pete, she could hardly go back to their apartment now. She would need some things for breakfast—a trip to the store was an easy, immediate answer to her restlessness.

As she pushed her cart up and down the aisles of the Safeway, Sarah fell into a daydream about the apartment she would rent. She imagined it as being much like the Marchants', only smaller. Her elderly, mismatched furniture would make it look very different. She thought of the advantages of central heating and air conditioning.

She turned down the next aisle and there they were. Brian and his Melanie.

It was too late to back up. They had already seen her, and she would not be the one who retreated. She had nothing to be ashamed of; it was Brian who should blush and feel uncomfortable. She felt a cold, steely anger towards him. He had not called once in the past week, although he must have known. For all his professions of friendship he was a coward. He had not had the courage to call her at a time when all her friends were offering their sympathy and help. Her hurt had turned to anger, and that made it easier to face him now.

"Hi," she said when she drew near.

To her surprise Brian looked neither guilty nor embarrassed. Instead, his face lightened when she spoke, and a look of pleased relief spread across it with his smile. "Sarah! Good to see you! Of course, you must shop here now—I'd forgotten we were in your neighborhood. We came here because Melanie's got a card on file and we needed to cash a check. She used to live in an apartment just off Medical Parkway."

Sarah shrugged away his nervous babble. "I won't be living around here much longer," she said. She spoke to Brian, and concentrated on him, but bits of Melanie came through almost subliminally. Melanie was very pretty. She was blushing and her eyes were cast down and she leaned against Brian like a shy child. Against his bulk, she did look as small and vulnerable as a child.

"Really? You're moving? Why?"

She stared at him. Everyone else, after hearing of Valerie's death, had assumed that Sarah would want to move out, to leave that horrible experience physically behind. But Brian had obviously not thought that; his broad, handsome face was guilelessly puzzled and interested.

She shrugged, wondering if he would see her decision to move as cowardly. She still wanted him to think of her as brave. She could never lean and blush, like Melanie. "I just don't want to stay there," she said. "You know."

But it was obvious that he did not know. "What, is it too big for you, after all? Or too far out of the way? I guess it might be kind of tough for a woman alone, but you did seem to like it."

"I changed my mind." Was it possible? Could he really *not* know? She couldn't imagine why he should pretend ignorance—it wasn't like him. Brian often evaded difficulties, but he wasn't a liar. She knew that he often managed to live in his own private world, undisturbed by outside realities. But even though he often went for weeks without glancing at a newspaper or watching the news, surely her name, or the address of the house, would have caught his attention? Surely someone, some mutual friend, would have commented on it. Valerie's suicide had been very much in the news for two days.

"You found a new place yet?" he asked.

Sarah shrugged. "A possibility. Nothing definite."

Brian hugged Melanie closer to him. "It's an interesting coincidence," he said. "Mel and I have been talking about getting a bigger place. A place where we could have a dog, maybe. The place we're in now—well, you know it's kind of crowded for two."

Sarah nodded, her gaze flickering across Melanie and back again to Brian, thinking, *Crowded, yes, but I thought you liked that. That suffocating warmth and closeness. Symbiosis.* She remembered Brian's words the day he had told her about Melanie—words that still hurt. *She needs me. She needs me to take care of her. She needs me in a way you don't.*

You're right, Sarah thought now. She needs you and I don't—at least, I don't need you in the way you need to be needed.

But there was no triumph in the thought. She might not need him, but she still wanted him—she still felt his absence like a painful emptiness inside her. Even her anger at him, even the desire to hurt him, didn't change that.

"So maybe we could work something out," Brian went on in his most persuasive voice. "You're looking for something smaller and closer in, and we're looking for something bigger. Why don't we trade?"

Sarah stared at him, scarcely able to believe what he had said. His suggestion went beyond insensitivity—it was obscene. She couldn't answer him.

"Sarah? What do you think?"

"No. Hell, no." Her hands gripped the metal and plastic handle of the grocery cart and she leaned into it. "How can you even ask? What do you think, Brian? You think I miss you so much I want to move into your old apartment and make it a shrine to you? To help me remember you better?"

She knew that look on his face well. He was trying to avoid a fight. He thought she was being unreasonable, and he was trying to find words that would soothe her rather than stir her to greater rage, and knew already from past experience that he hadn't a chance.

She shook her head and backed away before he could speak.

"Sarah, look, don't go. Don't get upset. What are you getting so upset for? It was just a suggestion. If you're not interested—"

"Damn right I'm not interested." She turned the cart around and continued to walk away from them.

"All right, you're not interested in my place. But we still like yours. It would be perfect for us, all that space. Could you mention us to your landlord?"

He had been raising his voice steadily as she walked away from him. As she turned the corner, Sarah looked back over her shoulder and said, "Forget it. Just forget it."

But of course he didn't.

The telephone rang a couple of hours later, while she was watching television. Repressing a quick, nervous tremor, she walked back to the kitchen to answer it. It was Brian.

"Look, Sarah, I'm sorry if I upset you at the store," he said, speaking quickly as if afraid she would hang up on him. "I just wasn't thinking—I mean, I meant it as a purely practical suggestion. I wasn't thinking of the emotional aspects. I didn't realize how it would sound to you."

Sarah grimaced. No, of course he hadn't. If he had meant to hurt her it might have been easier to bear. She detected the hand of Melanie in this call: on his own, it would not have occurred to Brian that he owed her an apology.

"All right," she said. "I overreacted. Apology accepted."

"Great." She could almost see his smile. "So you don't mind us moving into your house?"

She stiffened. "Yes, I would mind."

"So you *are* carrying a grudge."

"It's not that."

"Then what is it? Sarah, you've only been there a few weeks and you want to move out. How much sentiment can you feel for it? Why should it make any difference to you if total strangers move in or if we do?"

Sarah sighed. "Brian, believe me, there is a reason. Don't you wonder why I'm moving out of this great house?"

"Well . . . like you said. It's awfully big for one person, and it's kind of out of the way."

She closed her eyes. "No, Brian. I didn't say that. *You* said that." But she hesitated. If he really didn't know—

"So what is it? Bad plumbing?"

"The girl who lived here before I did. She was crazy. And she killed herself."

Interest sharpened his voice. "It's haunted?"

"No!" Too vehement. Sarah bit her lip. "No, Brian. She killed herself just last week. While I was living here. She came over here with a big knife in her purse and she cut her throat right in front of me."

"My God," Brian said, sounding awed. "She probably meant to kill *you*."

Sarah said nothing.

"Oh, wow," he said softly. "I see . . . I understand. I'm sorry, Sarah. It must have been awful for you."

Sarah shrugged and said nothing.

"But, Sarah, there's no reason for us not to move in. I mean, horrible as it was for you . . . the house isn't going to stand empty. Somebody is going to move in. I'm sure there are apartments and houses all over town where people have died and other people go on living there. The idea doesn't disturb me at all."

"What about Melanie?"

"Huh?"

"She might not like the idea."

"I'm sure she'll agree with me. She'll like the house once she sees it."

Of course, thought Sarah. Melanie would go to hell on vacation if you asked her to. And agree with you that it was a great resort, if a trifle too hot. She felt tired of the argument, and tired of Brian.

"Look," she said. "Just forget it, please. There are plenty of houses in Austin. I'm sure you and Melanie can find one you'll like a lot better than mine."

"It's not like you to be so selfish, Sarah," he said angrily. "I'm not asking you to make some huge sacrifice. All I want to know is the name of your landlord. You don't even have to recommend us."

"I haven't even told her I'm moving out," Sarah said. "When I do . . . I'll give her your name."

"You mean it?"

"Yes, I mean it. Her name is Mrs. Owens. She's probably out of the hospital by now—she had a stroke. She'd probably be grateful to me for finding a new tenant, to save her the trouble." As she spoke, Sarah could see Valerie's thin face and sly smile as she told her the same thing.

"That's great of you, Sarah," Brian said, making his voice humble. "I knew you'd understand."

Sarah made a face and saw it reflected, distorted, in the glass in the kitchen door.

"When were you going to move out?"

"I don't know. As soon as I can. Maybe within a week. Just as soon as I've got a place to move to."

"That's great," Brian said again, meaninglessly. "I'll talk to you about it some more later, okay? I really appreciate this, you know. We both do."

The "both" stung, but she tried not to mind it. As she hung up, Sarah had a sudden, vivid image of Melanie —fragile, childlike Melanie—standing in the middle of the kitchen floor, body twisted and tormented, her face a mask of pain and fear. She saw a bloody knife; saw a line of scarlet blossom at her throat.

Hatred, a feeling as hot and sweet as pleasure, rushed through her. How she would love to see that, to see Melanie in agony, destroyed. As quickly as the desire had come it was gone, and Sarah felt weak with shame. It was natural to resent Melanie, natural to want revenge, but she couldn't let herself think about that—she didn't *really* want that—not for Melanie or anyone.

The unexpected violence of her emotion left her feeling shaky, and she looked around uneasily, wondering if she had been wrong to give in to Brian. But Jade was gone, she told herself. He was dead. The house was empty, empty and safe. Brian and Melanie would be perfectly safe here; just as safe as anyone else who lived here. She would be safe herself, but she did not choose to stay.

Sarah had a hard time falling asleep that night. She lay awake a long time in the dark, empty bedroom, tossing on the new bed. She tensed at every sound, afraid that something was wrong. It was hard to accept that the battle was over and she had won, that she could sleep safely now. When she didn't think of Jade, her thoughts turned relentlessly to Brian. Her earlier annoyance with him had faded, leaving behind the old, familiar ache. How long, she wondered, before she stopped missing him, stopped wanting him back?

I need to find someone else, she thought. It was time to get out, to meet new people, to go to parties again. It was possible in Austin to find some sort of party every weekend. It was time to stop mourning and get back into the swing of things. With someone new to think about and hold, she would not miss Brian so much.

That settled, Sarah snuggled deeper into the bed, pulling the blankets closer around her. The sound of the insects outside lulled her. It would be like the old days, she thought, when she and Beverly had found dates for each other.

She was half-asleep now, remembering the past and drifting into dreams. She rolled over in the soft, yielding bed and pressed herself against the comfort of Brian's warm, naked body. Vague, sexual thoughts stirred within her, and she pressed her breasts against his back. Was he awake? She slipped her arms around him and trailed her fingers teasingly down his chest, his stomach, lower still . . .

He caught her hands gently and folded them around his penis, which was already half erect. She felt it swell within her hands and she sighed, pleased. He moved, turning within her arms to face her.

Moving to accommodate him, Sarah opened her eyes and was alone. Her arms, reaching out to embrace a phantom, were empty.

She shuddered, and tears rose in her eyes. A dream. Just a dream. Moonlight spilled coldly through the window, illuminating nothing but the emptiness around her. She didn't belong here, alone in this big, empty house. She had no home.

Chapter Sixteen

Sarah hurried across the West Mall, her arms full of books and her mind full of lists. The day was unseasonably warm and sunny, and someone had strung garish red and silver Christmas decorations on all the pathetic boxed trees that broke up the monotony of the paved mall, but Sarah scarcely registered any of it. It was the last week of school before Christmas, and she had far too many things to do before she could leave town. She planned to hole up in the library for as long as possible to avoid the temptations of phone calls, visits, parties, and the accusing list of presents still unbought.

"Sarah, for heaven's sake, are you deaf?"

Beverly blocked her way.

Sarah smiled and shifted her books against her chest. "Sorry. I was just plotting the impossible course of my life the next few days."

"I need to talk to you for a minute, okay?"

Sarah raised an eyebrow at the mystery in her friend's voice and followed her to a bench in the nearby Union patio.

"Look, I don't want to stir anything up, or make you unhappy," Beverly said. "I've been put in the middle of this, though, and you should know about it. Brian called me this morning. He wanted your address. He said he knew you'd moved into our complex, but he didn't know the apartment number. I told him he could call you, and that he could get your new phone number from information, because *I* wasn't going to tell him."

Sarah laughed affectionately, although she felt a pang. "My duenna," she said. "Protecting my virtue." She gave Beverly a quick hug. "Believe it or not, Brian thinks we are still friends. He probably wants to send me a Christmas card. He's very big on that sort of thing. It'll be signed by both of them—as if Melanie would want to send me a Christmas card, or I'd want to get one from her!"

"That's not very likely," Beverly said soberly. "The word is that Melanie has split."

Sarah stared. "Brian told you that?"

Beverly shook her head. "You know that undergraduate course in Folklore I've been auditing? I just came from there. Melanie's best friend is in that course, and I overheard her gossiping with her little clique about Melanie. It put a whole new light on Brian's call, I'll tell you.

"It seems that Melanie has left him and gone running back to her parents. She won't tell her friends why, and they were clucking like a bunch of hens over that defection, saying how much she had *changed*, wondering whatever had happened to their sweet little Melanie, to make her change so."

To make her change so.

The words caught Sarah like a lump of ice forced down her throat.

Beverly leaned forward and pressed her hand. "So you see why I'm worried. If he and Melanie have split, he's probably feeling sorry for himself. And he may want to come crawling back to you for comfort. If he does, Sarah —kick him in the teeth. You don't need that. Not after what he did to you. Don't let him take advantage of you."

Sarah nodded and managed a smile. "Don't worry about me, Bev. I can take care of myself. I always could." She rose. "I've got to run."

She walked to the library out of habit, scarcely aware of where she was going or why. But it wasn't Brian who occupied her mind. He faded away to insignificance compared to her sudden fear: that Jade had survived, after all, and had managed to possess Melanie.

Not my fault, she told herself, head down, walking rapidly. I did everything I could. I thought I'd won. No one could have done more.

In any case, she was overreacting, fixing on a piece of overheard gossip which could mean anything or nothing. Perhaps Melanie had simply gone home early for Christmas. What did it mean that some dim-witted sorority girls said she had "changed"? There was nothing sinister at all in the idea that Brian and Melanie had broken up. Perhaps the passion which had flared up so suddenly between them had been extinguished with equal suddenness. Perhaps Melanie had discovered she "needed" someone else, and left Brian for him.

She would call Brian, she decided, and ask him what had happened. Beverly would not approve, but Sarah didn't believe her suspicions that Brian meant to plead with her to take him back. At most, he might want a shoulder to cry on —perhaps even advice on how to win Melanie back.

That thought made Sarah smile. How wounded he would be when she refused. How completely uncomprehending. But aren't we *friends*—?

She had no intention of being hurt by him again. She would keep her distance.

In the library, Sarah was able to put it out of her mind and concentrate on her work. There were a few distracting moments, when vivid and unsettling images appeared. Valerie, her face contorted in madness, the shining knife slashing across her throat; meek little Melanie, her eyes blazing golden, possessed and transfigured. But the moments passed, the thoughts faded, and Sarah was able to lose herself in reading.

It was late when she left the library, and full dark when she finally reached her apartment.

Brian was waiting for her.

Because she had left in the morning, she had not thought to turn on the porch light. Brian was standing in the well of darkness before her door, his features obscured, but she

would have recognized him anywhere, in any light or
darkness, merely by the way he stood.

Despite her intentions, her heart began to race at the sight
of him. She felt foolishly glad to see him.

Watch out, she told herself. Remember what Bev said.
Kick him in the teeth. Don't let him hurt you again. It's his
turn to suffer. But, oh, what if he really missed her? What if
he really wanted her back? How could she refuse him what
she most wanted herself? She felt herself becoming warm
and soft, ready to melt at the least encouragement from
him.

"Hello, Sarah," he said.

She had always loved his voice. It was soft and warm,
the light coating of a latterly acquired Texas drawl taking
off the harsher edges of a Boston childhood. Early in their
courtship he would call her in the evenings and woo her
over the phone while she lay in bed. She loved, especially,
to hear him say her name.

"Hello, Brian," she said. It didn't come out briskly, as
she had intended. It didn't sound challenging at all. "I heard
you were hassling Bev for my address."

"I was afraid that if I called, you might hang up on me.
And I really need to talk to you, Sarah. I wouldn't blame
you if you sent me away, but I hope you'll listen to me."

"So you can whine about how much you miss Melanie?"
She shifted her books from hand to hand and dug into her
jeans for the apartment key.

"Melanie was a mistake from start to finish," he said. "I
realized finally that it wasn't working out and I asked her to
leave."

Ridiculously, shamefully, her heart leapt. She kept her
face down, hidden, in case Brian could see better in the dark
than she could. She didn't want to give anything away just
yet.

"I should never have broken up with you," he said. "I
was an idiot to let you go. I think I was scared, and looking
for something less demanding, simpler. I didn't realize that
what you and I had was the real thing." He drew a deep
breath. "I want to talk to you, Sarah. Really talk. Can we go
inside? I still love you. I'm asking for a second chance."

His words were balm. She had been starving for months

and he was feeding her again. She remembered her plans to hurt him, but she couldn't do it. She would hurt herself twice as badly as she would hurt him. She couldn't send him away. She couldn't say no to the man she wanted.

"You may as well come in," she said.

She had to move very close to him to put the key in the door. She could feel the warmth of him, and it was all she could do to hold on, to keep herself from falling against him. Her hand shook as she turned the key. She wondered if she was affecting him in the same way, and prayed it was true. It wasn't fair, it wasn't right that he should move her so profoundly and remain unmoved himself.

"Sarah," he said, when they were both inside and the door was closed. "Sarah, I've waited so long for this . . ."

His strong, familiar, capable hands had her by the arms, and Sarah no longer wanted to resist. She could no longer resist. She turned and half fell into his embrace, praying that this was not another dream she would wake from alone.

After a moment she pulled away slightly, raising her face, wanting to see him. The room was largely in darkness, but there was light spilling in from the kitchen.

He crushed her to him again and kissed her searchingly. Her eyes closed, but not before she had seen something different about him. Something wrong.

She pulled away again, opening her eyes.

His eyes. It was his eyes that were different.

They weren't dark brown any more. They were yellow, almost golden. And something about them—some power —made them seem to glow as if they reflected flames.

As he looked back at her, calm and smiling, his eyes burned into hers and she felt their searing heat.

Then his mouth came down hard on hers, swallowing her scream. Eyes opened, mouths together, they stared at each other, closer than they had ever been before, closer even than when he had been inside her mind.

And suddenly she was no longer afraid.

Sarah felt desire moving through her, stronger than any she had ever known before, more potent and all-encompassing than mere sexual passion. And she knew that she was feeling not only her own desire, but his as well. They were like twins, in a way—evenly matched, equally strong. She knew what she wanted and she knew what he wanted, and it was one and the same thing. She felt drunk, giddy, powerful. With his kiss he seemed to suck the very soul out of her and send it back, recharged.

When at last they broke apart, she was laughing. A moment later, an echo, he was laughing, too.

"Ah, my darling," one of them said. "I've got you at last."